UNDER

THE

BROCCOLI

CANOPY

BARBARA PETERSON

This is a book of fiction. Names, characters, places, and events are either the product of the author's imagination or are used fictitiously. Any resemblance to actual persons, living or dead, is entirely coincidental.

Written for ages ten and up.

It contains no offensive language or violence.

DEDICATION AND THANKS

As always, this book is dedicated to Clay, Brook, Bowie, Phillip, and Lindsay. Your help, love, support, and encouragement are appreciated beyond words.

I also wish to thank Rob Bignell from Inventing Reality and Lorna Reid from Reedsy for editorial and formatting help, my online family for help and advice, and my early readers for their constructive story feedback.

PREFACE

WHAT YOU ARE ABOUT TO READ started as something quite small and unassuming. Over the span of a decade of off-and-on writing, whimsical verses tiptoed into existence and gradually formed a collection. In 2019, I bundled those rhymes into an unpublished book called *From the Forest* and gifted it to my family. Never once did I imagine that those simple rhymes would one day grow into the full novel you are now holding.

Those early rhymes were tiny tales of the forest, snippets of stories about imaginary plants and animals strewn together with my memories of visiting property we owned in central Wisconsin. My hope was that each rhyme could be enjoyed on its own, while also hinting at something larger beneath the surface. I wanted readers to wonder, just a little, if the tale could be real, and let that wonder linger long after the final page.

By 2025, that original project had transformed. The verses expanded into reshaped little stories with the goal of completing a full adventure for young readers. The title evolved and the early collection became the foundation for this new fictional world, *Under the Broccoli Canopy*.

Now, I am inviting you into the world beneath the broccoli canopy and inviting new readers to come along with me.

The book takes you into a fantastical world born from my imagination. It is a world that captures the struggles and triumphs of forest life and follows plants and animals through their hardships and joys.

This book became more than a collection of story vignettes; it grew into something I treasured. You'll also notice that the story is told through many pairs of eyes. Though the narrative stays in a steady past tense, third person voice, each subchapter gently shifts your reading to a new inhabitant of the forest. At moments, the narration steps back with a broader perspective—just enough to let the woodland breathe and shine as a connected community. This felt like the most natural way to tell a story that truly belonged to a community of plants, animals, and the quiet forces guiding it.

Thank you for stepping beneath the broccoli canopy with me for this first adventure. I hope your journey here brings you the same sense of magic and meaning it brought me while writing it.

And I hope you'll return for more books in the *Under the Broccoli Canopy* series, where new plants and animals wait to meet you. They'll be rustling their leaves, straightening their feathers, and filling their cheeks in anticipation of your visit.

Wishing you many beautiful sunsets,

Barbara Peterson

June, 2026

PROLOGUE

BEFORE HUMAN FOOTPRINTS WERE pressed into the moss, before the wind carried secrets, there was a world beneath the broccoli canopy. It was a world where every creature, every root, and every whisper mattered.

From above, the forest looked flawless, a patchwork of green brought together by sunlight and time. But beneath those rounded crowns, where the light barely touched the ground, life was a delicate dance of hope and hunger, dreams, and survival.

And yet, even in those earlier days, something began to stir. Now, change was coming. The forest could feel it, and it was afraid. By each tremor in the soil, hush in the air, there was a sense that the old ways would soon be tested. It felt something unseen and ever-present that watched, waited, and ready to intervene if the balance tipped too far.

On the eve of transformation, every life, no matter how small, would matter. Every secret, every sacrifice, would shape the story of a forest on the brink of something new.

TABLE OF CONTENTS

PART
ONE

Before the Footprints:
The Primal Canopy

CHAPTER ONE
Voices Beneath the Canopy

Summer,
Return to the Green Canopy

LOOKING DOWN THROUGH CLOUDLESS skies, she watched the world glide beneath her. Alone in her spherical, wind-driven vessel, she vanished from sight and traveled wherever she fancied. The 360-degree viewing window revealed every detail, and the sphere darted and pivoted effortlessly to make sharp turns and quick stops.

For this world-famous globetrotter, it was just another day at the office—if your office happened to float above the treetops.

Mother Nature was heading north to survey several forests, to inspect their health and track the effects of weather over time. To get to the forests, she flew over the Great Lakes of the region. This was always interesting, as it enabled her to study the deeper center areas of the lakes in dark blue and the shallower areas in a lighter blue.

She was close enough to see fishing boats as they jumped the waves. The hungry seagulls were overhead and looked for discarded fish. Nothing could see her, but she waved downward anyway. She needed no coaxing to admire the natural beauty of the waters and forests.

The water was left behind as she soared, and vast forested areas loomed before her. From this height, the region looked flawless and radiant, as if it had escaped the weather's ravages. The view had captivated her, as always, but she knew it would be a dereliction of duty not to steer closer and focus on a single forest. Every forest mattered, and even the smallest demanded her attention.

From her vantage point, the trees clustered in rounded, lush masses, resembling the crowns of dense broccoli ready for harvest. The many shades of green, from fern and moss to forest, honeydew, and evergreen, dazzled her eyes with their breathtaking beauty.

A playful idea came to mind and a mischievous grin spread across her face. She pictured herself with outstretched arms, letting the wind take her playfully over the trees. She would bounce from broccoli top to broccoli top, landing with glee on the greenest crown. She smiled thinking about it.

For just a moment, Mother Nature was tempted to forget her duties and have a little fun. But then she remembered all the forests she had to visit today and the thoughts of playing hooky disappeared. She was under a time crunch, and all this nonsense must wait for another day. But the image still brought a smile.

On her last visit, she had discovered a small forest in this region that teetered on the brink of disaster, which compelled her to return today. Although the forest was small compared to the sprawling woodlands with thousands of acres, she valued it just as highly. This forest destination loomed on the horizon.

From above, this looked like a beautiful, verdant forest, but she wanted to get closer. The health of the forest floor worried her because she knew that the real story lay under the canopy.

This broccoli forest had been on her radar since her last inspection. She couldn't see through the canopy and envisioned darkness and gloom looming below it. On her last visit, dark conditions had already started on the forest floor, and she'd assumed it would only be a matter of time before it needed help. This forest had been put on her 'to do' list.

She flew closer and slipped through an opening in the canopy and immediately detected stark contrasts from her last visit. The young trees drooped, undernourished and forlorn. She saw stretched, spindly trunks leaning forward, while weak-looking branches clawed desperately for distant light. They bore sparse foliage and had pale green or yellow leaves, while sunlight barely pierced the canopy above.

By mid-morning, animals that should have been foraging for food either weren't or they wandered sluggishly, drained of energy. She detected a pervasive sadness due to hunger and resignation, as if the entire forest pleaded for her intervention. It clamored for her attention, and she resolved to make it a priority.

This broccoli-top forest quickly climbed on her list of places that most needed help.

The Following Spring,
Let's Meet Max

Max thought the ants were odd little creatures. He lay on his stomach, as his chin rested comfortably on his front paws. His eyes followed their every move, as he tried to ascertain the reason for their hurried, erratic behavior. Max wondered if his life was so boring that he got entertainment from watching ants run around. Apparently, it was.

The ants paraded ridiculously in and out of that hole, seemingly under orders, but from whom? The bear wondered if they thought about the pointless lives they lived. Yet the bear couldn't take his eyes off them and that hole. He found himself questioning the purpose of their existence, as well as his own. *Was there something going on in that hole he should know about?* He wondered what they were even doing down there and why they never stopped moving. *Don't they ever sleep?*

As Max watched the ants, he compared his life to theirs, wondering if others saw his life as pathetic and pointless.

He just existed in these woods—roamed, ate, and slept. When he wasn't doing that he hibernated. His main purpose was to look out for number one. When he looked around, he saw animals with their young, watching with pride in their children's growth and achievements. Those animals had a purpose in life. But what was his? He had a tinge of jealousy and knew that because of the nature of his species, he would never have what they had. It had been drilled into him that male black bears should think only about themselves. He concerned himself only with eating and sleeping, the occasional dates with female bears, and the occasional rumbles with other male bears who tried to steal their food or mates.

When he was bored he had weird thoughts. He questioned his existence and wondered if there was more to life than what he had. He had never been involved with the raising of offspring; in fact, he had no idea where, or who they were. The mates handled all of that, but sometimes he wished it could have been different. He wouldn't have minded having what the other animals there had. They had a purpose in life, pride in raising children, and most importantly, someone to spend their lives with. It would be nice if he had someone to sleep next to him.

What was his reason for being here? If there was an answer, he hoped it would become known soon because perhaps his life could be different. But for now, it remained the same tiresome, monotonous routine.

Like every day, he just wanted to be left alone. He had no use whatsoever for the outside world; to him, it was just noise, a distraction he didn't care to participate in. He reasoned that if he were social, he would only be contributing to the noise that other recluses like himself detested. So, he stayed put and only concerned himself with eating enough to keep himself alive.

He felt that eating and sleeping all day were a privilege that came with age, whether he had earned it or not. If his body didn't want to make the effort to get up, he would stay in bed all day. If he wanted to just stare at ants for hours, he would.

That day his mind drifted to a different time, back to his early years when he was a bear to be reckoned with. He considered how long ago that had been. It seemed like ten, but maybe it was fifteen years ago.

He'd been a big, handsome brute, and the ladies loved him. The other guys knew he was bigger and more powerful, and they had always backed down to his dominance. He had his pick of the female bears back then because none of them could resist the allure of his shiny black coat. As he thought about the female bears now, he paused. He had known many in his lifetime and assumed that he had fathered many offspring.

But those days were gone. He was older and had come to terms with the fact that, because he was such a brute then, it had resulted in him being alone. Nobody loved a brute and, unfortunately, he found that out the hard way because he had no friends or a mate. He still remembered the strength and power he once wielded—that was then, but not today.

Some days he was forced to make an appearance whether he wanted to or not. When he heard his stomach rumbling, he listened. It would make the most horrid sounds all day unless he satisfied it with food. Sometimes his stomach made noises that scared off the crows, and it took a lot to scare them. He prolonged getting up and going out as long as he could, until his mind started playing tricks on him and his gut started revolting from the inside. He reckoned he wasn't quite ready for the proverbial permanent fast.

Despite being very hungry that day, Max considered holding off until tomorrow. Part of his reluctance was knowing he hadn't taken care of himself again this past week. If he went out looking like a slob and smelling worse than an angry skunk, the neighborhood birds would notice. They relished snubbing their noses and hurling insults. Because of that, he didn't feel like doing anything about his smell today.

With all these arrogant and judgmental birds, he questioned why he even lived there. He could have had his pick of any neighborhood in any forest and probably be happier.

Max thought about his next move. *Should he brush off the forest's rude whispers and stares and let it track and scrutinize his steps? Should he just ignore his unkempt appearance?* He thought that was *their* problem, not his. He just needed to eat.

Going out was the sensible thing to do, but that day he didn't feel sensible. Thinking about the impending judgment, he'd lost his resolve, and the laziness, lethargy, and hostility returned. He didn't care if he died that day from starvation; he wasn't going to put on a show for anyone. Hunger lost out that day as he pushed aside the pain and remained flat on his stomach.

Max's attention returned to the ants who were only a foot away. He was so engrossed that he worried he might go cross-eyed if he watched too closely. They either didn't see him or didn't care about any danger he might pose.

He could eat the ants, but they were too busy to notice him watching. He decided to leave the ants alone since they entertained him that day. Strange little buggers.

The Next Day

Mary was one of the black-capped chickadees in the area. She flew over and sat next to Frederica, the female cardinal, on her branch. Both had been busy flying back and forth building their nests, to have them ready for their spring egg laying. They stopped building only to have occasional words with their mates or nearby friends.

"Well, look who finally got out of bed!" Frederica said loudly, as she watched the bear finally stand up. With no reaction from him, she shouted louder, "I wish I could sleep all day like that bear does!"

Frederica knew the bear had heard but ignored her.

Mary had an idea and whispered to her friend, "Girl, what do you say we follow him and see where he goes today? Maybe he'll lead us to some food. Sometimes that lazy old bear can be useful."

Frederica liked her idea because she was sick of working on her nest. She whispered back, "Okay, let's do it." They waited for the bear to move.

Hungry Max

The sun was almost directly overhead, and Max realized he'd slept longer than he should have. He squinted at the sun and noticed how warm his fur felt and how thirsty he was.

As usual, Max's insides told him that he had to find something to eat and quickly. He stood with wobbly legs and steadied himself. He needed water because his mouth was parched. If he found any food, he worried he might not have enough fluid to swallow it.

Looking around, he opened his mouth and yawned. As usual, the gossipy chickadee and cardinal were sitting on the branch above watching him. *Here we go again... no peace again today.*

He tested his legs, not sure if he could walk. Maybe it hadn't been such a good idea to lie around all day yesterday. He walked forward a few feet, and they didn't buckle on him. *So far so good.*

Finding food that day was going to be hard. He had come out from his long sleep only two weeks earlier, and the woods were still bare. The trees were just starting to bud, and plants that had survived the winter stood like spindly sticks.

He needed to be creative to find food. Not far from the birches there was an incline. If he climbed surefootedly, there was a flat area that held sun-warmed rocks. In past years, he had always managed to find ants sleeping underneath them.

Max trudged slowly to the base of the hill, which was usually an easy climb when the ground was dry. Today the soil was wet and slippery, making any careless step a chance to slip, splay his legs, and fall flat. With every step, his claws dug in for a firm grip on the wet ground and pushed his body up toward a leveler area where he could rest.

The rocks he remembered were in this level area. If he reached them, he would be home free. He walked past the dried sumac bushes, which he wouldn't eat anymore. Just seeing them reminded him of the time he had stupidly eaten white sumac berries instead of the red ones and had gotten horribly sick. After that one dreadful experience, he just stayed away from both.

The larger warmed rocks came into view, and he sniffed at their bases. His snout picked up the scent of ants that slept underneath. He pawed to overturn them, but without success. Giving up on the big rocks, Max reluctantly let those ants live to sleep another day.

Instead, he concentrated his attention on the nearby smaller rocks. With some effort, he was finally able to flip over several rocks and found the ants. Feeling clever to find these little buggers still asleep, he proceeded to eat them without guilt. His tongue moved over them so fast that they wouldn't know what hit them. Flipping more rocks, he slurped up all the sleeping ants. Under other rocks, he found sleeping bees, termites, and other bugs to eat. It wasn't much, but it was something to put in his stomach.

Moving away from the rocks, he noticed the two birds who had followed him had flown down looking for bugs he might have missed. He noticed the nosy trees were also watching him. At least they could only follow him with their eyes.

He found an area with more sun and ate the emerging grass shoots. He also found new buds on plants, and a few dried apples still on the ground under that old apple tree. He knew that the apple tree was old and hoped it produced apples for a few more years, at least while he was alive. It was one of the few dependable food sources this forest gave him. After foraging for several hours, he was exhausted and decided to go back home and rest.

Once back to his bed under the birches, Max flopped back down. He was still thirsty, but water had to wait for later. He could handle only one pressing task at a time. He hoped rain would fall during the night, leaving puddles in the morning to drink from. Rain made his life so much easier. Just as he was about to close his eyes again, he heard the cardinal's voice.

"Hey, bear—over here!"

Don't open your eyes, don't open your eyes. Pretend you're sleeping.

Louder he heard, "I see you sitting down there. Oh, you smell bad! You're stinking up the whole area!"

Ignore, ignore.

"Don't pretend to sleep when I'm talking to you!"

Without moving his head, Max partially opened an eye and looked up. The annoying cardinal sat alone on a branch ten feet overhead and looked down at him.

May lightning strike and kill me right now. He opened the other eye and glared at the bird.

"Don't glare at me! Listen up, big lug. I just want to tell you that I'm going to be laying eggs in this nest any day now. I will be singing over you every morning and flying in and out. Leave me alone and I'll leave you alone."

Not responding, he closed his eyes again. What she said was all fine with him; he wanted absolutely nothing to do with her.

"If you hear me crying, don't pay any attention. It's none of your business."

All right, already—just shut up!

"Hopefully, in a few weeks, my eggs will hatch. Then I'll be busy." Max ignored her and slept.

Max and the Cardinal

That female cardinal had been a thorn in his side for the past two weeks, ever since her big egg-laying proclamation. She had been a source of constant irritation, flying back and forth, talking to her mate, and never shutting up. Her mate also flew in, bringing in hair and fuzz and all kinds of garbage to pack in their nest.

The two disrupted his sleep with their chatter and nest building. In their haste to get their nest finished for the eggs, they dropped nest materials which landed on his fur, and they didn't even apologize for doing so. He was irritated to wake up and find his home strewn with bird debris and wondered if it was being done intentionally to irk him.

This part of the forest had been his home for over sixteen years. He remembered the year he became the dominant bear and laid claim to this territory and all the female bears. He'd pushed his way through the brush to make his home and worked hard to mat it down and keep it tidy. The trees were closely spaced and gave perfect shade, and the branches that cascaded in the wind kept him cool. After being content here all these years, he felt his privacy had been invaded.

He didn't like the cardinals, especially the female, and wanted his solitude back. He hated her expectations and her air of superiority. She called for her mate early every morning and expected him to be at her beck and call. The calling happened when Max tried to sleep, and she expected him to put up with her demands without complaint. Yet, if she heard him snoring, she complained the next morning. If she smelled him, she complained. If he got up and made noise, she complained. It infuriated him. He didn't want to move from there and tried his best to tune out and ignore her.

He went about his life, business as usual. He decided to put up with her incessant complaints, knowing soon those eggs would hatch, they'd leave the nest, and, hopefully, she'd be out of his life. Life would return to the way it was before the cardinals; he had to be patient for a while longer. Despite her constant yakking, he hadn't responded to anything she said. As far as he was concerned, she wasted her breath and talked to the trees.

Max's Spring Trip

Max was restless and in need of a break in his normal routine. The temperature was warm, and the skies were clear, the perfect day to get ready for his trip. Before he headed out, he wanted to clean up, because his fur was crusty and dirty. He would spiff himself up for another long trek in search of female bear companionship.

The bear considered being away for a week, maybe more, and wanted to look presentable for a lady. He didn't know his destination but hoped his instincts would guide him. He wanted to find a certain female bear he had met once before but hadn't encountered in five seasons.

He'd rubbed against trees, brushed off the bugs, dust, and twigs to make his fur appear cleaner. After he thought he had reclaimed some of his coat's former luster, he decided it was the best he could do.

As he got older, his coat wasn't as spectacular as it used to be. When he was a bear in his prime, the sun's rays would dance on his fur because it was as shiny as a raven's wing reflecting on a calm pond. It was as black as pitch black, making any animal who encountered him stop in their tracks. This spring, his fur is black, but a thin, dingy black, probably due to his months of neglect. In the summer, if he lets the sunlight beat down on the thin areas, it burns his skin, which can also make his life miserable.

He sat on his haunches and picked sticks, small stones, and accumulated junk from between his claws and paws. This was a task he hated doing and usually pushed it off until his feet hurt and couldn't walk. He knew he had a long walk ahead of him and doing it then would make his walking easier.

He stretched his head in every direction and licked his fur to clean it, all to appear presentable for a female bear. If he didn't look presentable enough, she might not let him get near her.

When he departed first thing in the morning, he hoped to find enough food along the way to sustain his energy.

He hadn't eaten much this past week because his appetite had diminished and replaced with longing for the companionship of a female bear. This longing hadn't happened in a few years, but for some reason, it had this year. He hoped he might run into the cinnamon-colored female he'd met before. He wanted to find her scent again, be a courteous gent, and try not to scare or intimidate her.

In his younger years, that always worked for him; he hoped he hadn't lost his touch.

The next morning, Max started out on his trek. He walked through thick woods every day, sniffing the air constantly. There was no sign of any other bears in the area.

After he had roamed for a week without seeing or smelling any females, he finally decided to call it a day to find a place to rest and sleep for the night. He was saddened because he'd tried and failed but this excursion had dwindled his energy. The next day he planned to head home.

Since it was midday, Max should have been hungry, but he wasn't. He was more tired than anything else. He saw thick brush, pushed in, and trampled it down for a secluded place to rest. Just before he settled in, he lifted his nose and checked again for a scent. It surprised him when a faint breeze brought the unmistakable scent of a female bear. He checked again and, yes, her scent was still in the air. Having found no trace of females for a week, he needed to act on this before she walked out of range.

Rest could wait, because now there was a scent trail to follow. Max followed it but couldn't tell whether he was alone, or if another male also trailed her. He had to be careful because running into another male following a female could trigger a fight. Years ago, he would never back down and never lost a fight. He knew he had to be careful and not rush his approach.

After all the walking today, he was exhausted. Max breathed heavily and needed to rest. He knew she was aware of him following her. He watched her sit down in an area of emerging sedge grass, eyes glued on his approach. Finally, her ear twitch was his signal he was welcome to come closer. Max walked in, stood fifteen feet away, and noticed she wasn't afraid. Since she didn't bolt, Max knew he was safe. He walked even closer and touched his nose to hers. She reacted with surprise, but the nose bump didn't upset her. He backed up and sat down a few feet away.

Both bears were cautious, their noses constantly checking the area for trouble. He checked the air for the scent of any approaching male bears, and she may have been doing the same. They moved their heads back and forth, discreetly scanning the area. The bears were safe, and after a few more minutes, they both relaxed and lowered their heads. They sat and rested together and slept in the sedge grass until almost dawn.

The next day, Max approached and nuzzled her and found out that her name was Belle. They stood and ate the surrounding grass. After eating the grass, they enjoyed the sweet stems of other young plants and purposely rubbed against one another to express their desire to mate. They both knew what the other wanted; they acted casually about it, but then finally acted on their mutual need.

All day Max and Belle walked and foraged together, relishing their new friendship. Even though they had mated, he knew that day would be their last together, and in the morning, they would separate. Max would go back to his forest, and she would leave for hers, knowing they would probably never see the other again. But because the run-in had been enjoyable, he hoped they might.

Frederica Helps Max

After a week and a half away, Max was tired, hungry, and cranky. Cranky, because the summer food he craved wasn't growing yet. He would have given anything to spot young grass sprouting still with its morning dew, all springy and cushiony under his feet. He knew grass loved the sun and the warm grass was where they sat when he met Belle. If he stumbled upon a patch of clover or dandelions, he would have feasted all day and afterward enjoyed a long, satisfying nap. But there was neither sun nor any tasty grass in this forest and dreaming of it was pointless.

His fur was full of twigs, and the gnats were trying to bite through his fur. He didn't care and would deal with his discomfort later; he just wanted to lie down on his bed and sleep.

The entire time he was away, deer flies had circled and buzzed his head, taunting him to swipe at them. If they considered it fun making a bear go insane, he wanted nothing to do with their idea of play. If he had a magic wand and one wish to grant himself, it would be to wish these hateful flies to leave him alone forever. He brushed the flies from his snout and attempted to rest again.

Max couldn't fall asleep because one of his eyes throbbed. When he tried to open it, he couldn't, because the lids were sticking together. When it finally opened, it hurt worse, and he immediately closed it again. Keeping it closed and squinting through the other eye, his eyesight became fuzzy. He thought he must have picked up dirt or maybe a dead bug was lodged in the corner. He needed to get it out. He pawed furiously at it, hoping to dislodge it, but couldn't, and the throbbing continued. Disgusted, he gave up and decided to deal with it later. Thinking he would suffer through it, he spread himself out to sleep.

That annoying, tiresome, maddening bird voice—the one he had loved not hearing for over a week—was heard again. On top of having an eye he wanted to rip out, that bird was back to making his life miserable again.

"Stay right where you are," he heard. "I'm coming down to take a look at that eye."

Oh, for the love of peace and quiet.

He wished she would leave him alone—if he keeled over dead right now, she would be the reason. He thought his head would explode if she spoke one more word.

But she flew down anyway. He took a deep breath, exhaled in frustration, and sighed. There was no way he wanted aid from a bird nurse.

"Bear, I've looked at your incessant blinking and squinting for too long and it has given me a headache. Let me see what you've got going on here."

Saying that, she hopped over and looked him straight in the eye. A few moments later, she announced she needed to relieve pressure from that big red spot by his eye. It was the cause of his pain.

That was the last straw. If she thought she was going to fix his pain, she would have to think again. On second thought, he figured he didn't have anything to lose, except maybe his eyesight.

Max hollered, "Bird, if you do *anything* to me and I go blind, they'll find your body parts scattered all over this forest. If you spit on me, you're going to taste so good!" His head hurt so badly that he figured help from this bird was better than no help at all. He lay back, resigned to having her try anything.

Frederica looked shocked at the sound of his voice and his angry words. "Oh, wow, he speaks. Will wonders never cease? You just lie right where you are. Don't worry, I'll be careful. Just trust me."

Through his squinting good eye, he watched her go about sharpening her beak by rubbing it against her wings. Without giving him *any* notice, she quickly bent her head backward, thrust it forward fast, and her beak went hard into his sore spot.

Wham! His head flew back. Stunned, he let out a loud, "OW!" Max was astounded by the amount of force that bird mustered and used on him. *What just happened?* He was astonished at her audacity to forcefully put her beak right where it hurt the most. That beak of hers felt like a needle piercing his eyeball, not that he had any knowledge of how that felt, and he thought that was the worst pain he'd ever felt in his life. He could feel something moist draining toward his snout. *Is my eyeball leaking? Oh, that hurt! I'll deal with that bird later. I'm so tired.* His head dropped, and he was soon out to the world.

He slept for several hours but could have slept longer if those annoying crows hadn't flown over and made noise. He was confused because his eye wasn't throbbing; in fact, there was no pain whatsoever and could see clearly out of that eye. When that bird jabbed her sharpened beak into him, it must have done the trick. He sat up and looked at her facing away on her branch. He needed to get her attention and thank her. But he still detested her.

CHAPTER TWO
Spoiled Plan

Noisy Crows

THE SAME THREE CROWS CAME back to this forest every year. He could hear their incessant screeching from two forests away. If they weren't so noisy he could almost tolerate them, but they were never quiet. They flew over at least once a day, either looking for food or pestering to make their presence known. The crows were considered a nuisance and irritated everyone there.

"Caw! Caw! Guess what we saw? The big gray owl had a mouse in his claw."

Oh, shut up! Nobody cares! Every day they flew over and shouted their stupid announcements downward. All they knew how to do was flap those wings and yap their big mouths. And they were always looking to get into trouble.

"Caw! Caw! Of none, we fear! Just for laughs, we spooked the deer!"

When Max was younger, he would climb a tree, reach out, and swoop at crows with his paw, trying to knock them out of the sky. Back then, all they did was laugh at him. But these new crows, if anyone here dared to speak sideways to them, they got testy and dive-bombed. Of all the birds there, they were the fastest and the meanest, and there was nothing anybody could do to stop them. It was at the point now that everybody feared them. Nobody knew when they would become the butt of one of their pranks.

"Caw! Caw! We saw some moles. It was fun chasing them down their holes!"

Occasionally, the crows were afraid of something they saw and would fly over to warn the forest. They didn't feel it was a duty to warn; they only did it to feel important. If they spouted something important, the forest would take notice. Most of the time, however, it wasn't important, and the forest couldn't care less about the crows. It tried to sound them out.

"Caw! Caw! The sky is getting darker. A storm is coming. Everybody take shelter!"

Stolen Eggs

Frederica dug up a worm for breakfast and returned to her nest. She planned to spend the next few hours lying on her three eggs and keeping them safe and warm.

This was Frederica's fifth batch of eggs since she had been Tate's mate, usually laying two batches a year. She was happy to be his mate, and they were devoted to each other. She and Tate were the only cardinals in this part of the forest, as he had claimed the area as his and shared it with her.

He was tall, and she thought him very handsome with his bright red feathers, black mask, and the tall red crest on top of his head. When they first met, she hadn't been able to resist his advances. She always knew their male offspring would be the reddest and most handsome cardinals in the whole area, that is, if they ever hatched any eggs. In the last two years, she had not successfully hatched a single egg.

She had been away for less than a minute. Then she flew back and found her three eggs missing. *What? Not again!* She let out a loud agonizing scream. "Help me! Help me!"

She knew the plants and animals in the immediate area had heard her scream. Hers was a familiar scream; one she knew they had heard many times over the years.

Frederica knew exactly what happened and who had done it. This happened every single time she laid eggs. If she left her nest unattended for even a moment to find food, she came back to an eggless nest. Frederica knew that if she tried to accuse the thieves, they would make her life miserable.

Having heard her cries, a pair of chickadees flew over. Her friend, Mary, asked, "What's wrong, Frederica?" She bent down and investigated the empty nest. "Oh dear, I see now. I'm so sorry."

Frederica said, "I left my nest for just one minute with all my darling eggs still in it. I know those bad crows saw them and flew in and took them. I was too late again. It was the end."

Frederica sat and sobbed into her wing and waited for Tate to fly back. *Where is he anyway?* The chickadees flew down to the ground to look for evidence of broken shells or perhaps the missing eggs but found nothing. They looked up and saw Frederica still sobbing. *Why always me? Why just me?* Finding no evidence of eggs, the chickadees flew back to their tree, knowing there was nothing more they could do to help Frederica.

Frederica sat and thought about her life and how much she wanted revenge on the crows. She sat and hung her head. *My heart is broken in six places. My whole life has been a waste. Two years in this forest, and not a single baby bird to show for it. I just want to be a mother. Is that too much to ask? I want to feed and nourish my babies and watch them grow. I'll never see motherhood because of those vile crows. I want my eggs back. I want revenge!*

She sat on the limb next to their empty nest. She was all worked up and needed to calm down. Staring out, she considered herself a failure as a mother. Tate finally arrived after hearing her calls. He sat close by and consoled her.

Frederica noticed the bear on the ground and realized he'd been watching as she and Tate inspected their nest. The bear had probably heard their exchange of curse words, seen their frustration, and witnessed Tate comforting her. She sensed he understood what had happened and felt a tinge of compassion for them.

Bad Crows

Stu, the largest of the three crows, sat with his brothers in their secret tree hideaway. He was the most unscrupulous, devious crow of the three, who convinced his brothers to make the theft with him. Noticing the guilt the other two felt for stealing the eggs, he reassured them they did the right thing.

"We *couldn't* help it; there was nothing else to eat this morning. We *had* to go in and snatch them."

They had been waiting for the cardinal to leave the nest. When she did, Stu had flown in first and carried away an egg and his brothers followed suit. With eggs in their claws, they managed to carry them back to their hole in the tree to eat.

Stu made excuses for their bad behavior. "In our defense, that bird left her nest unattended again. Not our fault! We had no choice *but* to fly in and take them. Us crows love eggs! We couldn't help what we did. Too tempting, we couldn't control ourselves! If the birds didn't want us to take the eggs, they wouldn't have left them in plain view."

None of the three had ever been a parent; hence, they didn't know the sadness that birds go through when their nests are tampered with.

Stu continued to belittle the birds to convince himself and his brothers that they shouldn't feel guilty. "All right, if you insist." Stu bent his wings and flaunted his pleasure after he and his brothers performed this dastardly deed.

He strutted in their hideaway and joked about their actions. "Eggs are a very delectable meal before they're hatched. That mother bird, every year she offers us another dinner. Sometimes, twice a year. The way I see it, we did her a favor. She should be happy because now she has no work to do. She can sleep all day and not worry about feeding those babies."

With their crops full, they flew out. They flew fast in case those cardinals saw them and opted for revenge.

"Come on, brothers, let's go find more food. Let's head back to the field and look for mice."

Making Introductions

He thought about their situation here. That bird obviously had no intention of leaving and neither did he. Max considered if he wanted to get involved with the cardinal. It would be so out of character for him if he did. *All right, he would do it.* He would put aside his bad feelings toward her, considering her helpfulness with his eye problem, and now the loss of her eggs.

Max settled into the bird's morning rituals. Her singing and flying back and forth didn't bother him anymore, and he slept right through it. He thought he could tolerate the bird and be nicer. It was time to set aside bad feelings and initiate a conversation with the bird.

Out of the blue one morning he said hello to get her attention. Her head jerked when she heard his voice and turned and looked down at him. He looked up and called out, "Could we talk for a minute?"

"Humph," she muttered, curious when she heard words coming from the bear. As she came down, she muttered under her breath, "Well, he *finally* speaks again."

There it was again, that condescending attitude, but he let it go because he didn't care if she wanted to keep up that charade.

After all these years of not engaging with the forest animals, it was hard for him to change. But he began talking in his most friendly tone, "I'm sorry about my temper earlier. My name is Max. I'm just old and I get cranky when I'm tired and don't get enough sleep. I just wanted to thank you for what you did earlier; my eye is feeling much better. What can I do to repay you?"

Frederica moved closer, first she checked on his eye, and then they sat and conversed.

"Hello, Max, my name is Frederica. I'm happy to finally meet you and I'm sorry if I was rough on you. Your eye looks much better; I'm glad I didn't make it worse. That's nice of you to offer, but you don't owe me a thing."

He sensed the trees had listened to them and took notes. The bird told him about their past attempts to start a family, which explained why she hated those crows. He understood how she felt about the crows. She told him about how she and Tate decided to stay through the winter, but she almost froze to death. "Never again," she had vowed.

Since it was going well, Max decided to open about himself a little. He confessed it had been difficult for him to make friends and didn't have any here. He preferred being alone, but sometimes he missed the companionship the other animals seemed to have. That was why he took off to find another bear.

"I have an idea of how I might be able to repay you. Would you like to hear it?"

Later That Summer

Stu's brothers' names were Jack and Bobber. They had hatched two days after Stu, technically making them his younger brothers. Since he was older and the bigger bird, they respected him, and the brothers generally agreed to whatever Stu suggested.

"I'm starving," grumbled Stu one afternoon. "I see the mother cardinal has laid three eggs again. Let's cruise on over and see if she's in her nest. If she isn't, we'll snag 'em. I get to have two and you guys can share one."

Max also knew Frederica had laid another batch of eggs. He wanted to help her. He said if she let him know whenever she wanted to go for food, he would babysit her eggs. He promised to protect them from being accosted by the crows. She yelled down to him quite often, and Max wasn't getting much sleep, but he didn't mind because he promised her his help.

He saw the crows circling one morning with their eyes on the nest. He knew they saw him and were wary when he stood and glared at them.

Stu saw the bear and was fearful. "All right, guys, there's no way we can get them now with that old bear guarding the nest. Let's come back later."

Max kept constant patrol for the crows whenever Frederica was absent. Every time the crows flew over to check her nest, Max was ready to confront them. Whenever they flew in the vicinity of her nest, he stood, glared at them, and growled loudly. The crows weren't sure what the bear was capable of, and not taking any chances with their lives, flew off. But they kept on trying, and each time Max scared them away. One time, they got bolder and swooped down at the nest to antagonize and test his energy. This riled the bear, and he stood on his hind legs, pawed at the air, and growled even louder until they realized he meant business.

Stu finally said, "I'm sick of this. Forget her and forget those eggs. That bear friend of hers is just too powerful; we'll never be able to get them. Come on, we can do better than those eggs anyway."

Stu and his brothers flew off and never bothered Frederica's nest again.

After not seeing the crows for several days, Max said to Frederica, "If they hadn't gone away, I would have climbed up this tree to guard them. Good thing I didn't have to, because in my old age, I might have lost my footing, slipped and fallen on my butt, and broken something." He and Frederica had a good laugh.

Eggs Hatching

Frederica could not have been happier. After almost two weeks of sitting on her eggs, she woke and felt movement beneath her. She sprang to her feet and was overjoyed at the sight of three newly hatched chicks.

"Tate! Tate! Get over here!" She screamed excitedly to get her mate over to the nest.

A minute later, Tate arrived with a worm and handed it over to Frederica to eat.

"Look... look," said Frederica, pointing to the hatched eggs.

He stared at the nest, not believing what he saw. She watched Tate gazing into the nest and saw his wings fluttering in excitement at seeing the hatched eggs.

Then he yelled out for all to hear, "We did it, finally! We have a family!"

Tears welled up in Frederica's eyes. She was so happy seeing that her mate shared her exuberance at seeing the new hatchlings.

Frederica saw Max watching them fussing over the nest. She sensed he knew it was good news. Because of all the commotion, she assumed the forest held its breath, wondering if their eggs were stolen again or if they had hatched. It was the latter; she knew the forest would be relieved. Their three eggs hatched without a scratch or bruise, and she knew Max was pleased with himself, knowing his help had made all the difference.

Frederica said, "Tate, you stay here. I must go to make birth announcements. I'll bring back some food." With that, she flew off, to leave Tate in charge of the nest.

Back in the distance, she heard Max call up to Tate, "Congratulations, Tate."

Tate looked down and replied, "We wouldn't have hatched our eggs if it wasn't for you. Thank you, Max, for saving them from being snatched and eaten."

Max's humble reply was heard, "Oh, it was nothing. I'll keep an eye out for thieves though, can't take any chances."

She assumed everyone within earshot of the birds had heard the news. Frederica told the squirrels, who danced in happiness for her. She also knew the trees listened and took note of the new births to send down to their roots to record. A doe and her fawn were unexpectedly walking through and Frederica surprised them. As she flew down, and landed on the doe's back, she announced her news.

The deer replied, "That's nice, my dear, now your work starts."

"I know! I can't wait!" Frederica replied and headed back to the nest.

Frederica had eaten several insects while she was away. She instinctively knew she should regurgitate them and give the babies their first meals. She forced the insects up, and the babies held their heads up to receive food. A few moments later, they were hungry again for more.

"Your turn," she yelled at Tate, "Go on, bring more food." She felt good to be back giving orders.

Frederica sat on the nest and grew impatient as she waited for Tate. He took so long to come back with food. He finally returned as they passed food to the babies. She occasionally looked down and saw Max on his back watching them as they took turns coughing up food. She knew their new parent antics probably gave him an entertaining show. Finally, there was no sound and the babies were asleep. Frederica stayed on the nest while Tate sat alongside her. She let her eyes close while Tate stationed himself over her and the nest.

Learning to Fly

The three baby birds were eleven days old and had insatiable appetites. Besides being constantly hungry, they poked, pushed, and prodded each other because the nest was cramped. One of the young birds was named Peeps. That day he decided he was going to change the overcrowding situation.

Peeps pushed his way to the edge of the nest and gazed out. He saw the open space out there, felt the shifting air movements, and pondered how it would feel to sit on a sunny branch instead of in their shaded nest.

All the birds made flying look effortless as they steered through trees, starting, stopping, and turning. It didn't look hard at all; in fact, it looked very easy. He was sure he was old enough, his hearing was excellent, and his sight was top notch—he wanted to be the first baby cardinal in his family to fly.

He wondered why he even stayed in their crowded nest. Other birds of his size glided through the air. If they could do it, so could he.

He needed to exercise to build up his wing muscles before he could do this. He did what he could in the space he had by doing little laps in the nest, stepping over the other birds, and flapping his wings. His brother and sister must have figured out his plan because they looked at him with concern. Every time he rose off the nest, his wings flapped faster and harder. *Yes, he was ready!*

When he settled back down in the nest to rest, he wondered if he was truly ready and started questioning his choice. He considered that his siblings weren't in any hurry, so why should he be? Maybe he should wait another day or two to be sure. What if he failed? What if he jumped, started flapping, and fell right to the ground, broke a wing, or, worse, land on a snake who would grab and swallow him up?

If he survived a fall to the ground, there would be the embarrassment factor to deal with. The other birds would see his attempt to fly and his failure and laugh at him. He didn't want to be laughed at or if injured, be pitied by anyone. He then had second thoughts about the whole idea.

Besides, there was something else to consider. Every night their mother stayed in the nest with them for protection, but during the day either she or their father usually sat watching the nest. Sometimes the sound of passing crows scared them but one parent always arrived to sit next to the nest to protect them. A big fear was being by himself. He would not have protection from the hawks and crows if he left the security of the nest.

Peeps saw his mother sitting on a nearby branch watching the nest. She had a worm dangling in her beak. He wondered if she was tempting him to fly over. Her coaxing him with the worm was all it took. All right, that did it, he was going to do it.

He walked to the edge of the nest again and with every ounce of strength, flapped his wings. Then he stopped to rest. He knew his mother could see him and was waiting to give him the big worm. He was hungry and didn't want her to eat the worm herself or give it to one of the others. He would be the first baby cardinal to fly. That would be *his* prize!

As he looked out of the nest again, he glanced over at the next branch. His mother still sat there, dangling the worm and watching his indecision. He yelled over to her, "Mama, look at me!" He jumped up on the edge of the nest again.

He saw her place the unmoving worm on the branch and then shouted, "Watch what you're doing! Go slow or you'll go right to the ground. Stay steady—don't quiver—this isn't the time to fool around."

He looked down. It was a long way down. Then he heard another voice that wasn't his mother's. The voice seemed to be coming from the branch their nest was sitting on. Hmm, this was a first, he never knew he was able to hear trees.

"Fly over to your mother's branch, little birdie," the tree coaxed, "Hang on tight. Don't be afraid—you can do this."

Flapping his wings with all his strength, he pushed off the nest. He flapped his wings with as much force as he could muster to fly towards his mother. He felt strong but still worried he might not make it.

His mother shouted, "Almost here, almost here." Peeps saw one of his mother's wings twitching back and forth to cheer him on as she waved him in.

Then the tree's voice was heard again, "You made it, little birdie. I've been watching you. I wasn't sure you were going to do it, but you did. Yay, look what you just did, you flew! You should be proud of yourself. Look at your mother sitting there, she is just beaming with pride."

His mother quickly gathered him in and placed the worm in his mouth. It had all been worth it.

Peeps had pushed himself and faced his fears. He was pleased with his flight and got the prize from his mother. The best part was pleasing his mother and making his brother and sister jealous of him. He stepped up and down on the hard branch, gripping it tightly with his feet to get the feel of the new surface.

"Good job," said his mother, "Now fly down to the ground with me and I'll show you how to find your own worms."

CHAPTER THREE
Life Under the Trees

Late Summer,
Roots of the Past

FOR MILLIONS OF YEARS, trees were the caretakers of the forest. They watched and listened to the activity in their viewing proximity. From the year they first sprouted, they stood in their birthplace and steadfastly monitored the forest.

Trees were always in constant motion. Their branches swayed up and down and side to side with the wind to catch forest events. A deer and her fawn walked through, a mouse scampered for cover, or a plant died. Each event, no matter how miniscule, was confided to other trees through their root systems.

The trees knew everything that happened, no matter how seemingly insignificant. They noticed when new plants sprouted and old ones died. They knew the age of every species of plant around them and the reason why a plant cried.

Every bit of news was sent underground to the roots. Their ingenious root systems delivered news to other roots who then passed it on again to other roots. With so many plants, much of the news might have been duplicate alerts. However, to parent trees, even duplicate news about their offspring was welcome news. The roots of millions of different plants mingled and spread underground. Some were large roots, some were tiny baby roots, but all shared the underground. Were it possible to see through the surface, it would appear to be mess and mayhem, but to the trees, it was all perfect order.

The roots lived harmoniously together and coexisted peacefully. Each root knew its own structure, its function, and its lineage. This knowledge was sent down to them from the parent tree above. Each plant strived to preserve its own heritage.

An apple tree named Pippen lived in the forest. When he turned six years old, his age and growth were announced far and wide. His friends watched his laughter and smiles and sent the news underground to the roots. His birthday and happiness were all recorded in the forest's historical accounts.

Forest Festival

The forest floor bustled with activity. All the above-ground plants and animals were excited, as were the underground inhabitants. The bugs and bees flew in circles as they tried to get everyone's attention. "Wake up, wake up! It's our day!"

The roots were invigorated from the previous night's rain and were ready to party. They stretched and talked to their friends and reminded them what day it was. In their tunnels, the little wiggle worms had not slept at all. They jumped up and down in anticipation of the festivities that were due to start soon.

This was the forest's annual celebration of life and the start of summer. They had survived another year and summer was here, which alone was enough reason for a party. Creatures from all over came to cheer and shout and let loose pent-up energy. Animals who rarely attended emerged to join the festivities. With everyone here, the party was about to commence.

In past years, the ants could never participate and always felt left out. They were so tiny and were always afraid of bigger creatures stepping on them. To give them enjoyment, a special area was cordoned off around Pippen, the little apple tree, for the amusement of the ants. The previous day, with Pippen's permission, the ants removed dirt from around several of his plant roots and formed slip 'n slides for their fun that day. They took turns and slid down his roots, hit their butts on the ground, and scurried back to the surface to go again. All the animals were asked to stay away from under the apple tree.

The birds all flew in, settled on branches, and tapped their feet in unison. Their tapping, along with their cheerful singing, created a lively beat in the forest. When the animals heard the music, they began to dance slowly, but as the tempo quickened, their feet did also. When the birds paused for a break, the animals collapsed onto the ground overcome with laughter. When the birds resumed their music, the animals sprang up and danced again with a lively rhythm.

Underground, the roots were having their own celebration. They heard the music coming from above, joined their root tips together, and swayed back and forth.

Above and below ground, everyone was having fun in their own way.

The roots became frightened because, suddenly, the lighthearted sound they heard coming from above turned to a loud rumbling. The sudden change sounded like a thunderstorm was coming and they were afraid. News reached the underground that Max, the black bear, heard the merriment and rambled over, astonishing everyone. It seemed he liked the beat, sat in the middle of the activity, and stomped his feet in time with the music. He couldn't dance but wanted to attend the festivities and be friendly.

The bear's presence shocked everyone. In all the years living with them, he had never participated in their festival. He had always slept through it or walked out of the area. That year, Max's change of heart surprised everyone, including himself. He wanted to try to socialize with the animals. They were not prepared for this new Max because he was usually so aloof. When he opened his front paw and a baby bunny hopped up and sat down, they knew he meant no harm. The underground adjusted to his heavier foot tapping and welcomed this new Max.

The music stopped when crows appeared overhead. Evidently, they had also heard the music and flew over to investigate. Surprisingly, the crows brought good manners and greeted the other birds. When the crows took to the ground, the animals scattered in fear. The crows started having a good time, strutting, and prancing to the beat, and being congenial. The little animals hesitantly came back out and rejoined without fear.

The tiny daisy roots took turns as they slipped and slid down the larger roots. With every slide, they landed on their bottoms, giggled, and ran up for another turn. The deer, foxes, raccoons, squirrels, and rabbits all walked over.

After their initial wariness, they stood together and watched the smaller animals have fun. Every forest creature had something to celebrate, as they had all lived to see another year. Any hostility or thoughts of devouring each other were set aside for another day. Festival day was considered their 'safe' day.

The party broke up after an hour. The birds fell silent and quickly flew back to their trees. The ants went back to their holes in the ground and went back to work. The bear was exhausted and slept face down in the middle of the forest floor. The animals looked at him sleeping, curiously studying his disheveled appearance, frowned, and shook their heads. They had never known Max to be so friendly and outgoing before.

Everyone anticipated the festival being repeated the following year. The forest lost some participants as plants and animals passed away, but they were assured that new participants joined to take their places. Mother Nature always saw to that. They spent the whole year anticipating this day again, counting down the months for the first days of summer. Because of everything plants and animals had to endure to survive, this fun was due them.

Night Feeding

On a crisp evening, the sky was clear, and the moon, like a silver lantern, cast its light. The time was close, but not quite right, for the deer to come out. They had gathered just inside the trees on the edge of the field and waited for the cue. Every night they listened for unusual, unnatural sounds or movement off to the side that might have signaled danger. The natural sounds a forest made—the quiet sounds of the raccoon family chattering, the bear snoring, crickets, or hooting of an owl—they paid no attention to. It was the unnatural sounds that startled them: Clicking, a rubbing, knocking, coughing, or anything out of the ordinary. These had scared them into running.

They had been taught to be skittish around possible danger. Being attuned to threats was what had saved their lives. Deer were large animals, but they knew other animals, if given the opportunity, would have loved to gnaw on them to satisfy their hunger. They didn't want to be put in that position.

Silence was their illusion of safety, and that night the air was quiet. A doe stepped out of the trees, stood up straight, and looked for movement. She also listened for any unnatural sounds and smelled the evening air. Since it was already twilight, she hesitated to wait any longer. Her head moved from side to side, checking for any unusual movement. There was nothing to fear; she lowered her head and signaled the 'all clear.' The others had been waiting for this cue. The hidden deer walked out and started feeding in the moonlight.

With the moon's soft glow, the deer leisurely moved about and ate. Their shadows gave the illusion of a greater number, which relaxed and put them in a peaceful state. Even with the illusion of safety, their senses were always attuned to danger.

They heard the hoot of an owl, which came from the trees behind them. They turned their heads in unison, but they did not fear owls and resumed feeding. They knew the owls were only searching for tiny animals to catch and feed to their young. But off in the distance they heard a howl of a coyote or was it a wolf? Either could possibly have been headed their way. They feared their howls as they might have alerted other predators that it was time to feed, and they could be headed to their field.

They would not take any chances, especially those having their young along. It was time to move back into the woods and conceal themselves. They all separated and walked into different parts of the forest. Each found food and once satisfied, bedded down for the night. In the morning, they would gather again in the constant search for food.

The Brothers Three

The crows flew over the forest in the early morning on their daily food quest. That day, their eyes swept the forest and looked for animal remains to eat. Their motto was: Self first, then friendship. They created hostility and ended friendships with other animals to satisfy their hunger.

There was nothing dead to scavenge that day, so they looked for unattended eggs. The other birds, however, were aware of their modus operandi—fly in casually and steal—and hadn't left their nests. This irritated the crows, and they decided to wait for an opportunity by perching in trees and hiding from view. But it was to no avail, as there was no opportunity to grab any eggs. They were frustrated and gave up.

They remembered having an easier time finding food the previous year. That day, it was hard and frustrating, and many days they went without eating anything. They walked on the ground searching for seeds and nuts, but it seemed that either the smaller birds had already cleaned them up or there weren't any. Even a few worms would have made a nice breakfast, but the roots had warned the worms of the crows' presence, and they'd all crawled deeper out of reach of their beaks.

Their constant food cravings never went away. All day they scavenged for food to eat. Their job of finding food got harder as food became scarcer.

The crows flew where Stu told them to fly. He had proclaimed himself the cleverest, wisest, and dominant crow. Jack and Bobber followed wherever he went and conceded to his rules.

His dominance started almost immediately after he was born. The three crows were born two springs ago to the same mother. While still in the nest, their mother favored Stu by putting food down his mouth first when she came in. By doing that, she created an offspring that craved attention, felt superior to his brothers, and became the crow family narcissist. He craved admiration and, if he didn't get it, he lashed out at anyone or anything around him.

His behavior had diminished his brothers' respect, and they complained about him behind his back. At the same time, he had the keenest eyes, and they depended on him to find food. This was why they let him rule over them.

Because of his personality disorder, Stu also needed his brothers. He required constant praise and respect and liked it when Jack and Bobber provided him with that. The two brothers cawed his name loudly through the trees whenever the three succeeded in a food quest. When Stu heard his brothers' shouts and his name echoed in the forest, that showed they admired how he'd led the operation. Because they stepped aside and let him have his way, it showed they respected him, even if most of it was phony respect.

The three needed each other for different reasons and became thick. They banded together like musketeers and lived by the motto *"all for one and one for all"* and flew in solidarity. All food found was shared and devoured. If their cravings were satisfied, they didn't care what or who they ate. After eating, they flew out again and looked for their next meal.

That day, they had found little food, only eating a few seeds and nuts and a few spiders that had walked unsuspectingly across leaves. Night was upon them, and they craved one good meal before they roosted. Since it was too dark to see anything, Stu called it a night and said, "Let's go, guys, and roost with the others."

Off they flew and left the forest behind. As they flew, they called and chased each other, which helped the crows unwind. Large birds had even larger bird predators and didn't take a chance sleeping alone. Just like all bird species, they felt safer in numbers and roosted together. The warmth they generated was shared among all the crows on chilly nights. That evening, they found their fellow crows in sheltering trees and perched with them to spend the night. Early the next morning, they would start their food search all over again.

Angry Crows

Faint light started to appear in the morning sky. The brothers were restless to feed but waited for the signal given to leave the roost from the older and wiser crows. Finally, one crow left the roost, then another, and another. Stu then decided, "Come on, brothers, let's go!"

They loved ogling their hoard of priceless treasures. Every morning before feeding, they flew up to Wazoo, the name given to their secret hideout. It was a hole high in the tallest tree in their forest. This was where they stashed their collection of shiny stuff, bones, odds and ends, and food. As two-year-old crows, they loved the shiny stuff and sat and admired it. The bones were their reminders of meals past, and the food was being saved for winter when meal pickings were slim.

Stu shouted, "Faster, faster!" Jack and Bobber sped up to meet him at their tree hole. Stu was especially keen to get there first because he liked catching a robbery in process. If any intruders were up there, he tore into them and made them feel sorry they were there. "Hurry," said Stu, "We can eat after we check the tree!"

Little Tree was the tallest tree in the forest, much higher than all the other trees. The forest respected his height, and many birds and small animals sought shelter in his branches. He'd only sprouted a short time ago, but over the span of those years, he had grown taller than all the others. The whole forest was amazed at his growth spurt. Everyone except his parents.

Earlier that spring, the crows decided to carve this cavity into Little Tree to stash their hoard. They thought the tree's height would hamper intruders, hoping it made the site secure from anything curious with legs. The crow's hole was carved very high in Little Tree's trunk, making it invisible from the ground.

Little Tree watched as the crows approached and looked forward to some early morning entertainment. He saw the intruder go up into the crows' hole but hadn't seen it come out. *This is going to be fun.*

The crows landed and stood on the branch leading to the hole. Before they entered, they took a cautious look inside. The three crows saw their prize pile strewn around the cavity but did not see any intruder inside.

"Wazoo is ours!" Stu shouted into the hole. "If you're there, show your face in daylight—don't be a coward!"

They waited, but no intruder showed his face. They assumed whoever had been here had already escaped, perhaps with their precious treasures.

"I'm starving, let's fly out for food. We first need to get our strength to find and fight this thief. We'll come back, take inventory, and see what's been stolen. Then we'll go after him."

Jack and Bobber agreed to Stu's plan. They took one final look inside before they flew off. Suddenly, Jack's sharp ears heard a sound coming from inside the hole.

"Quiet, you guys," Jack whispered, "I hear something." His brothers quieted as Jack turned an ear towards the hole. He listened, heard the sound again, but this time stood in fear. It was the sound most hated by crows, the hissing of a snake.

Crows Feasting

"I'm so out of here! I'm not fighting that thing!" Jack had no intention of sticking around and wrangling with a snake. He flew from the branch.

Stu jumped out to the end of the branch and yelled, "Get-your-lazy-fraidy-ass-back-here! I'll tell you when you can leave!"

Jack, afraid of Stu's wrath, flew back. He knew that Stu could and would—correction, *had*—clobbered him over the head when he was angry. He didn't want to be on the receiving end again of Stu's mean streak; last time his head had hurt for days.

Stu walked back and forth along the branch and said, "Guys, I'm so hungry, I can't even think straight. Let's go find some food first and then come back. We are *not* letting that snake claim our stuff. There isn't any way he's stronger than we are."

The two brothers conceded to his wishes. They had to; there was no way they were going in by themselves.

Stu went on to say, "Let's go eat, then we'll take care of this situation."

Stu was right. One snake against three crows—there was no way a snake had a chance. But one crow alone wouldn't have a chance trying to tangle with a snake.

The three flew off to address their hunger issue. The grasshoppers were out basking in the sun. When they took flight, the three easily picked them off with little effort. Spiders were crouched next to their webs waiting for bugs to relax on their silky mattress. The crows thought themselves especially clever when they snatched spiders waiting for insects to land on their webs. Those little meals temporarily satisfied the brothers' hunger, and they wasted no time going back to Wazoo to deal with that snake.

The three crows flew back and landed on the branch. They walked forward slowly, not sure of the whereabouts of the snake.

"Stu, you go inside first, since you're the closest," said Jack. Stu felt like he wanted to clobber Jack.

"Yeah, you're the oldest and the boss—that's what you've always told us," Bobber said, feeling no fear, only disgust for his domineering brother.

Stu sneered at his brothers for their sarcastic jabs, but he knew they were right on all accounts. He walked closer to the hole with his head darting around for any movement.

He walked through the opening and cautiously checked the inside. He wondered where a snake would hide.

"He's not in here!" Stu shouted. The three heaved a sigh of relief but were concerned about what contents might be missing.

Bobber, still outside, looked down to see how high they were from the ground. When he looked down, his keen eyes spotted movement. "Ah, guys, look down there." He stuck his beak downward and pointed to the snake meandering down the trunk. "Look who's trying to sneak away."

"Let's get him!" The three flew down, and each grabbed a part of the snake's body. Stu had his head in his sharp claws, Jack's claws were latched onto the snake's middle, and Bobber had his claws in his tail section. They lifted and flew with him over to the field, at which time they filled their bellies with fresh snake. They flew back to Wazoo and hoisted the snake's remains into the hole to devour for supper later. Three crows sat on the branch, exhausted from their run in, but their hunger was satisfied for now.

CHAPTER FOUR
Trials and Triumphs

Summer's End,
Mother's Disappearance

THE LITTLE BUNNY HUDDLED close to his brothers and sister in the nest. At three weeks old, all four baby rabbits had pressed close together. They were finding comfort in being together and sharing warmth.

He was the smallest, and even though he felt his family's fur when they were all together, his surroundings were black and confusing. Even though his eyes had opened, he could see only darkness. He relied on his nose to know when his mother was inside. When she appeared, he breathed her familiar scent and he felt safe.

The nest, built from grass, was lined with his mother's fur. The nest felt warm and snuggly, just like her. He smelled the dirt overhead and sensed the low roof that kept them hidden and safe together.

His mother always left early in the morning to go searching for food for herself. He missed her so much when she was gone, but she always came back, and he and his siblings would suckle her milk and snuggle close. They never wanted her to leave, but morning would come, and she would soon leave them alone in the burrow again until that evening. She was their world and their protector, and they depended on her for everything.

Then one morning, she didn't come back, and they were getting restless and hungry. As the hours passed, he was getting weaker and thirstier. He tried pushing in against the other kits, but they were all too tired to move or cry. All four were weak, dehydrated, and wanted their mother's milk. The littlest bunny wondered why their mother had not come back. *Did she not love them anymore? Had they done something wrong?*

Laying there, he felt something brushing the top of his head. He raised his head to sniff it. He liked the smell and texture and nibbled at it. It tasted strange, so different from his mother's milk, and it satisfied him a little. He wished he could see what it was, but he only ate as much as his head could reach. Whatever he had eaten was moist, and he wished he could see to find more.

The darkness seemed unending. His brothers and sister were no longer moving. Without their body warmth, the nest grew cold and silent, and he lay by himself. He was getting so sleepy and was losing hope of his mother ever hopping in.

Then, suddenly, something was different. With great effort, he raised his head and sniffed the air. A new scent hit him that was unfamiliar and sharp. He didn't know what was there, but he knew it wasn't his mother.

He feared the scent, but his body wanted him to go to sleep like the others. He fought his body to stay awake. Something told him that if he slept, he might never wake up again. Something was here, maybe watching him. He didn't know what it was, but the scent told him he was in danger.

Mr. Mole to the Rescue

Some animals liked to feast on little animals like moles and tried to dig them out of the ground. To outsmart them, moles made many exit holes—while something dug for them in one hole, they ran for safety out another. Sometimes it was just too easy.

A few days ago, Mr. Mole found the rabbit's nest when he burrowed to make another exit hole for his family. He'd accidentally busted through the wall of the rabbits' nest and felt awful. He immediately patched the wall damage over with dirt and dug in another direction for his exit. He hoped that the mother rabbit would not notice his quick and somewhat sloppy patch job.

Since finding the nest, he'd been curious to see how the babies were doing. He relaxed at the same entrance to his tunnel each night while his missus tended to their children underground. He liked to watch what was happening in their little neighborhood and could quickly run down his hole if he saw a crow or a hawk.

Every night he watched the nest and waited for the mother rabbit to return to feed her babies. When she did, she was always in a hurry and never stayed long. She was always back in the morning to feed them and stayed a bit longer before leaving again. When the babies were left alone, he would run over to make sure the four babies were still safe.

Mr. Mole noticed the mother rabbit hadn't returned to the nest for three nights. He saw that the babies were barely moving for lack of food and couldn't help but be concerned. There was nothing Mr. Mole could do that night, and he planned to check on them again in the morning.

On the fourth morning after finding the bunnies, Mr. Mole ran over and cautiously stood at the opening of the nest. He was shocked to see that three of the babies had not survived. They lay huddled together on one side of the nest. The fourth, much smaller than the rest, was still alive, though its breathing was weak.

Mr. Mole decided he had to do something to save the remaining rabbit. He dashed out and chewed off several blades of grass for the baby to eat. He ran back and dropped them next to the baby.

He waited and watched, but the baby didn't move. He walked right up to him and tapped him on the head—still no movement. Tapping again a little harder, the baby slowly opened his eyes. Mr. Mole stood just inches away, but the little guy stared blankly out, still not moving.

Since he didn't move to eat the grass, Mr. Mole picked up a blade of the fresh grass and tickled the bunny's nose with it. The bunny crinkled his nose at the unexpected touch. Seeing this movement, he put the end of a blade of grass in the bunny's mouth, and the bunny started chewing on it. He was happy that the baby chewed on it, but he also knew he needed water to survive. *What to do, what to do?*

He frantically dashed back to his hole where Mrs. Mole nursed their babies. She looked up and saw the concern in his eyes.

"What's wrong? You look like you've seen a hawk."

"Mother, those baby rabbits have all perished except for one. I *knew* this was going to happen if their mother didn't come back! I need to get water to that baby, but how?"

He detected the exasperation in his mate's tone when she said, "Oh, for goodness sakes, go break off a leaf with dew still on it and let it puddle in the middle. Drag the leaf over to the nest. And don't spill the water."

"Ah, good idea." He ran out of the hole, now knowing what to do. Minutes later, he dragged a leaf holding cool dew and placed it in front of the baby. This normally would have been enough water to last a bunny all day, but he lapped it all up in one sitting. *That kid was thirsty!*

Mrs. Mole came out and joined him at the nest. Together they watched the baby rabbit, who seemed unaware of their presence.

Mr. Mole saw his mate pressing her front paws together in worry and heard her whisper, "He should be afraid of us standing here, but he isn't. I don't think he can see us. Oh, dear, that poor thing. He's not going to make it unless he can see. Something will get him." She said the same thing he was thinking.

Mr. Mole continued feeding the baby bunny while his mate attended to their children. Every day, he picked greens and brought them over with water. The bunny grew accustomed to eating the greens and seemed to be getting stronger. Mr. Mole watched him walk to the edge of the nest, but he never ventured beyond it. The moles decided to keep bringing him food until he regained his strength. Then, when he was back on his feet, they wanted him to learn to forage and survive by himself in the forest.

Mr. Mole kept a watchful eye on the bunny since he saw him by the hole entrance. One day, after eating greens, he saw the bunny hop to the front of the hole. The bunny seemed curious about the warmth he felt coming from outside. He faced his head upward and basked in the warm, comforting sensation. Soon after, the bunny drifted off to sleep just outside the door.

Mr. Mole felt he had to intervene and approached the bunny. He gently tapped him on the head to wake him. The bunny timidly woke and looked confused.

"Who's there?"

"Just me, Mr. Mole. I'm your neighbor. Don't be afraid of me. You're sleeping in plain view of everything, which is not a wise thing to do. You're in danger if bigger animals see you out in the open."

"Do you know where my mommy is?" asked the bunny.

"I'm sorry, I do not," said Mr. Mole regretfully.

Mr. Mole watched as the bunny stumbled back inside his hole, crouched behind the wall, and hid. He was clearly frightened and feeling alone again.

Later that evening, he discussed the situation with Mrs. Mole.

She insisted, "Father, that baby should live here with us until he gets bigger. You should make our tunnels wider so that he can come down here with our family. He will be much safer."

"But that's so much digging. So much work."

With a scornful look, she replied, "I don't care, just do it! I don't want that little guy getting snatched by hungry hawks."

"Yes, dear." He knew this was going to be a lot of work, but he agreed.

He worked for two days, pushing out dirt to make their door entrance and tunnel walls wider. When the task was completed, he visited the baby rabbit in his nest.

"Mrs. Mole and I are inviting you to live with us. We will share our meals with you, and you are welcome to huddle with our family."

"I would love that," the bunny replied, "thank you."

Hearing that, Mr. Mole was relieved and said, "Grab hold of my tail, and I'll show you to our tunnel. It's not far, don't be afraid."

Walking slowly, mindful of every step, he led the bunny down his tunnel and into their living quarters. He knew the complete darkness wouldn't bother the rabbit since he was already accustomed to it. But he still wanted him to be safe.

The bunny was introduced to his mate and their five children. He saw how the children, curious and cautious, walked over and rubbed against the bunny. The children were shocked at his size, being almost four times larger than they were. But when they heard the bunny's laughter, they knew he was a kid at heart. It wasn't long before the youngsters were climbing up on his back, jumping back down, and having fun. Mr. Mole hadn't seen his children so happy and lively in days.

Troubling news came to him that a hawk from a neighboring forest flew in one day, saw the rabbit, and attacked her. Mr. Mole thought her death was unfortunate, knowing there were babies left without a mother.

He gathered his family and the bunny together to share the sad news. He took the opportunity to remind everyone, especially the bunny, what small animals had to fear. He warned that not everything that lived there was their friend. There was danger all around, and they always had to be alert and on the lookout for predators. If they were outside the hole and there was trouble, he said they had to move very fast and hide. He and his family were saddened, knowing the troubles that lay ahead for the bunny without sight.

One day, as he watched the bunny struggling, he had an idea that just could save the bunny's life, and he presented it to his mate. Mr. Mole was relieved that she was impressed and thought it could work if the other animals would cooperate. Maybe they could give the bunny a real chance at survival.

Mr. Mole Called a Meeting

The day arrived when he presented his idea to the forest animals—but only those he trusted not to hurt the orphan bunny. The little animals in their community had always pledged to be there for one another. He hoped they would understand why it mattered to him so much.

Besides other mole friends, Mr. and Mrs. Mole were friendly with most of the smaller birds, as well as the bees, mice, and squirrels. If any member of their group needed help, the others were at their beck and call to lend assistance. Everyone was comforted knowing they looked out for each other. *Will they be willing to help this time?*

He asked the animals to spread the news to their kind that there would be a meeting right after lunch. It would be held in the commons area to discuss an important matter that involved each of them. He said no food would be provided; they should bring their own snacks to eat. When asked what it was about, he only said it was about an orphan bunny. He reasoned, if he waited to tell them, they would listen with open hearts.

A few hours later, they were all gathered in the commons area for the meeting. Mr. Mole asked them to quiet down and began the meeting. *Here goes nothing.*

"As some of you already know, the missus and I have taken in an orphan bunny who was at death's door. A big hawk killed his mother and left four babies as orphans. The rest of the family died of starvation, but we were able to save the smallest one. We expanded our house to make room for him because he had nowhere else to go."

He heard whispering among the animals, but they soon resumed listening to him.

Mr. Mole pressed on, "The situation is dire because the little guy is blind—he never got a lick of eyesight. We've been feeding him, and he's getting bigger, but he's about to outgrow our space. We think he's old enough to live on his own and can survive, that is, *if* he has help. If he doesn't have help, I'm afraid he won't make it. He won't be able to see to find food or to run from predators."

He paused and saw the looks of concern and confusion in the group. Everyone started speaking at once to their neighbor, drowning out what he was saying.

"Friends! Please!" Everyone quieted, and he was able to resume the meeting.

First, Mr. Mole explained his plan and how they came into the picture: "Since we are a small community, we all know where each other lives. The bunny wants to go out and find his own food but can't. It's too dangerous. I can't be with him every minute of the day, and neither can Mrs. Mole. I thought that whenever any of us were outside and saw him, we could watch out for him. He would get to know us, and we could warn him when there was danger and tell him to get back home or hide. He's old enough to find his own food. He's got a good sniffer. He just needs warning if there's danger."

After a discussion, they all agreed to help. They would abide by an oath: *"When danger outside, we warn to hide."*

"Let the little guy come out, we'll take care of him," they chimed.

Mr. Mole was relieved to hear their decision. Before they went home, there was one other matter he wanted their help with. He said that the little bunny would now be part of their forest community. He wanted him to feel included and adopted by them, and that he needed a name. The animals were happy to be a part of this and began chattering about possible names. They settled on the name Benji for the bunny. They thought Benji was a friendly, approachable name, and easy to remember.

This made Mr. Mole very happy, and he thanked them for their help with the bunny's name and the promised help outside. The animals went home and relayed the request to others in their family.

Back in the tunnel, Mr. Mole told the bunny the name the community had given him. The bunny was overjoyed to have a name. It pleased Mr. Mole when he saw him wiggle his nose, perk up his ears, and walk in close to the others to show his affection. Mr. Mole could tell he was happy.

"Benji, I've talked to our neighbors, and they have agreed to warn of danger when you are outside. Since you cannot see, whoever is closest to you outside will warn you if they see predators. These warnings will ensure you can find your own food freely and survive on your own. Soon I will help you build your own place because you are getting too big for our home."

Benji was happy to hear of the help but was scared.

Mr. Mole continued, "Feel free to go out and forage, but don't walk too far. Remember which way you came so you can find your way back. There will be eyes on you, friendly eyes. One of us will warn you when there is danger. Try to make friends."

"But I'm scared," said Benji, "What if that hawk flies off with me?"

"He won't, we'll see to that."

"Will you stay with me the first time?"

"Of course. Just take tiny steps out at first, a few more each time until you feel sure of yourself."

"Okay."

"Let's go right now. I'll see who's outside and introduce you."

"Okay."

He and Benji walked to the front door. Mr. Mole watched Benji stop outside the door to feel the warmth of the sun. Benji moved in a circle to feel it on his entire body. He stood still and listened to the sounds of the birds, rustling leaves, and bees busily buzzing. The outside was enchanting, but he was apprehensive about going out further. Mr. Mole wanted to reassure the lad.

"Come down here, Davina," he said to a bee buzzing overhead. The buzzing got louder and then the sound stopped right next to them.

"Benji, this is Miss Davina. Miss Davina is a honeybee. She's very nice."

He then introduced Miss Davina to Benji. "Miss Davina, this is Benji, our young rabbit houseguest I was telling you all about."

"Hello, Benji, I'm happy to meet you. My, aren't you a handsome lad. And so big! You won't step on me when I land, will you?"

Benji giggled and shyly replied, "No, ma'am."

"I'll try to make myself known when I'm near the ground," she added. "If you can smell flowers, that's where we bees will be. We're over by them right here."

Mr. Mole watched Benji take a few unsure hops and stop. A few of the other honeybees flew over to watch him walk about. Tate and Frederica were sitting overhead and were watching his movements, along with several curious chickadees.

Mr. Mole said, "Come on, Benji, let's go back in." He led the bunny back to their hole. Just before they entered, Mr. Mole turned back and said to those watching, "Please remember your promises." He waved and went down.

After that, Mr. Mole noticed that Benji began coming out on his own several times a day. He saw how much Benji loved feeling the warm rays of the sun on his back, and how he enjoyed the breezes, the smell of flowers, and the sound of rustling leaves. The feeling of walking about freely had taken Benji some getting used to, but Mr. Mole could tell he felt safe.

Mr. Mole often saw Benji hesitate when he heard unknown sounds. He would ask his friends what the sounds were and they would do their best to answer. Whenever he heard a new bird call, he would ask Miss Davina what bird made the call and if it was a warning or just a song. If he heard new insect or animal sounds, he asked about them. Benji became less anxious knowing he had help from the forest creatures watching over him.

Benji was learning where his favorite plants were for nibbling and where rainwater collected in a dip. The other moles often came over to play with him, and Mr. Mole noticed that Benji was recognizing the buzzing pattern of several of the honeybees in the area and even knew their names. Benji learned the friendly calls of the chickadees, cardinals, and robins, and knew what to do when he heard crows or hawks calling overhead.

Mr. and Mrs. Mole were glad he was safe and guarded. To Mr. Mole, life seemed brighter for the little blind bunny.

On His Own

He lived with the moles for four weeks until he began knocking down too much dirt going in and out, which irritated Mrs. Mole. She complained constantly about having to clean up after him, but never to his face, only to her mate. Mr. Mole told Benji it was time for him to build his own place.

Benji wanted to dig his home close to his friends the moles and other animals he knew. He dug himself a shallow hole near thicker cover for safety, within running distance to visit the moles and some of the other friendly animals. Mr. Mole had found the dig spot for him, which was right next to the commons area, making it easy for Benji to attend meetings. He would also have access to his trusted friends, who watched out for his welfare. Benji spent two days digging his burrow under the watchful eyes of the bees working in the area and, of course, Mr. Mole.

At eight weeks old, Benji hopped around the perimeter of the commons area and became acquainted with many new scents. One day, he caught a whiff of an interesting new scent that smelled fruity. He was excited and followed his nose to an area of just-opened blossoms. But he wasn't alone. It seemed the bees were also interested in the new blossoms and were already foraging for nectar for an energy burst.

It turned out this was a patch of blooming wild strawberries, and there was a lot of interest in the flowers. He was told there used to be an abundance of strawberries in the forest, but they had all dried up and died. This small patch was all that remained, only because the plants had access to some sun.

Word spread, and many animals came to smell their aroma. Many had no interest in the flowers but had more interest in eating the actual berries. As for Benji, he would eat either and that day he nibbled on the tender strawberry leaves as he happily ate alongside the industrious bees.

One day, Benji was out and Miss Davina struck up a conversation with him.

"Hello, Benji, how's our boy today?" Miss Davina asked. "My word, smell that pollen. Let me in next to you."

Benji moved over, making room for his friend. He casually asked, "I'm doing well. How's the sky looking today?"

"It's a beautiful day, no clouds from what I can see, and there's no danger. It's probably best you don't stay out too long, though. I wanted to tell you that there are a couple of old apples still lying on the ground under that little apple tree. Go on, use your nose, and sniff them out before some other animal finds and eats them."

"I will, thanks! I have never tasted an apple." He hopped away from the strawberry plants and caught a different sweet scent. He thought these had to be the apples. *He could do this. He'd find them.*

The birds had looked at each other in amusement. Benji tried so hard to find the apples, but he walked in circles. They watched him get frustrated and sit on the ground to sulk. But he got up again, determined to find them. He finally homed in on the apples and sat on his haunches to eat while sniffing the air. He was happy there was still a little meat on the remains.

The day he moved out, Mr. Mole sat him down and taught him how to leave his scent. He said that since Benji couldn't see, he could mark areas with his scent to know where to come back later. At the time, Benji had thought it was a weird thing to do, but he decided to try it and left a few droplets by the apples. He hoped he would be able to smell his scent and come back to the apples later. Benji hopped home, hoping to finish eating later.

Just then, Miss Davina yelled from overhead, "Quick, take cover from the hawk!"

Benji wasn't the only animal afraid of hawks. All the small animals here were on their menu and all of them scattered for safety. Benji turned in the direction of the bushes and ran into them. He knew he was covered from view because the stems were picking at his fur, and leaves were brushing his head. To be sure, he sat and hunched down to look smaller, hoping his fur blended with the foliage and wasn't seen. He was taught to sit perfectly still and act like a rock, as any sudden movement would attract the prey's attention.

The large hawk flew overhead looking for a small animal to snatch. Other animals besides Benji heard the bee's warning and ran for cover. The warning worked because the hawk flew out of the area without spotting anything to eat.

"All clear!" yelled Miss Davina, and Benji relaxed. Bird singing resumed, bee buzzing returned, and the animals in hiding reappeared. Except for Benji, he didn't move. He was content, curled up in his little ball with a full belly, and preferred staying where he was since it was safe and quiet. He couldn't keep his eyes open any longer and soon dozed off, dreaming about strawberry leaves, the sweet taste of apples, and kicking out dirt.

Pippen and the Bunny

Pippen was a five-year-old apple tree, one of only two in this forest. Five years old is still young; some would say he was still a toddler tree. He knew he's had his share of help and luck to get as tall as he had because many young trees never make it to his age.

He survived because, back then, he was lucky to have sprouted in an open area with access to sufficient light. Pippen loved turning his leaves up to the light and feeling the warmth. He stored the warmth in his trunk and roots, and that helped him stay alive over the winter. That was something his father, Great Apple, had taught him to do.

These last two years had been easier because his trunk was much stronger, and it didn't bend as much. It was always a struggle, but he stood up against fierce storms and managed to keep standing.

When he was four, he had his first flowers and grew three apples—a whole three! But this spring, he'd had many more flowers, which turned into many more apples. He knew animals liked apples, and, just like his father, he helped feed them. Two of his apples had been left alone by the deer and miraculously clung to his branches. They recently fell to the ground and lay dried and misshapen.

Pippen saw a small bunny working his way over to his tree. He'd heard the scuttle about the forest adopting an orphan bunny and thought that was an awesome thing to do. But he had never seen the bunny until that day. *That had been that bunny.*

Pippen watched the bunny, and it amused him that the little guy was walking in circles. His little nose was going up and down and side to side as he sniffed for the apples but couldn't find them. He wondered why the bunny was having trouble but then remembered hearing that the bunny couldn't see. He wished he could help by placing them in front of him, but he couldn't. Pippen was pleased and relieved when the bunny finally found the apples and was taking small bites.

Pippen wished the bunny could have noticed him. If he had, he would have asked him to stick around and talk to him. He'd heard the bee's warning about the hawk. He saw the bunny run for cover. The tree thought someday he would get that bunny's attention; the bunny would look up at him, and they could get to know each other. Pippen liked that idea because sometimes he was lonely standing by himself.

Pippen's Problem

Pippen's branches were producing apples every year, and he was stoked about that. There were many apples on his branches that the deer could reach. That was okay if apples were all they ate. But, no, they wanted to eat his apples *and* his branches. Pippen wondered how he would ever grow taller *and* wider if those deer didn't leave his branches alone.

Desperate for the deer to stop, he shouted, "Please stop eating my branches! I need my branches to grow. Stop, you're hurting me! I'm giving you apples— just leave my branches alone."

He knew they could hear, but they chose to act like snots and ignored him. Pippen wondered what it would take to get them to stop. At least they were not eating his very top branches. Those branches helped to record his growth every year for whoever kept track.

He just wanted his lower branches to grow beyond reach of the deer. He did not mind the deer eating his apples because he liked supplying food. He even loved it when the birds and other animals like rabbits, squirrels, and raccoons, would come around to eat. Once, the bear walked over, but there were no apples for him that day.

Pippen needed to think of a way to redirect the deer's attention away from his branches. But how? He decided he'd speak to the plants, bugs, worms, and small animals. They had helped the blind bunny to be safe. Pippen thought they might also help him to grow taller.

The Forest's Plan

Mr. Mole was sitting outside the opening of his tunnel, watching his children play. Everyone in the immediate area was waiting for the start of the community meeting. He knew the subject would be Pippen and how to stop the deer from eating the tree's branches.

He felt there was a lack of decorum because nobody seemed to be in charge. The animals all talked at once, whispering to their neighbors about Pippen's problem. He looked over and saw Max sitting off to the side, looking uninterested in being there. Mr. Mole thought that if someone didn't start the meeting soon, Max might leave.

He had a feeling there was also chattering happening underground. Since small animals, like him, were closer to the ground, sometimes, but not always, root voices could be heard. Sure enough, Mr. Mole only had to lower his head, and he heard their voices from the surface. He heard, "Look at Pippen's little roots. They look sad and defeated." The roots seemed to know which were Pippen's.

Nearby, the mice, moles, and rabbits gathered in their own groups. He heard them say they wanted to help after hearing Pippen's problem. "Let's put our heads together and think of a way to help him out," one suggested.

Mr. Mole noticed the ants had scurried over and were sitting quietly in rows by themselves. None of the animals could detect their voices, but he was sure the ants listened at their meetings; they listened but couldn't contribute. He assumed they preferred to talk to each other anyway.

Looking up, he saw the blue jays, two cardinals, and the owl sitting in the trees. He knew that they knew that pouncing on food during meetings was forbidden. They obediently talked quietly among themselves. He overheard Frederica say, "He's such a friendly and likable tree. I hope he starts producing more apples—we all love them."

A chickadee agreed, "The least we can do is take his request seriously."

Mr. Mole was losing interest because no one was stepping up. He was normally hesitant to speak out unless he knew he was safe from being accosted. He sat back thinking, while everyone else was jabbering. However, because of the "no pouncing during meetings" rule, he felt brave enough to speak and start the meeting.

"Ahem, *AHEM!*" Mr. Mole saw all the heads turn to him, and he had their attention.

He started, "I have an idea that might work. I'm not sure, but maybe. I know those deer are hungry during the winter and..."

"Aren't we all, Mole! What's your point?" the blue jay rudely interrupted Mr. Mole mid-sentence.

With an exasperated look, Mr. Mole continued. "As I was saying, the deer are munching on him because they can't find anything here to eat. If we can offer the deer other choices they like, maybe they would stay away from the apple tree. If we work together to supply food, then they will forget about eating his branches."

Mr. Mole saw everyone considering his words and nodding their heads. It appeared the premise of his plan sounded reasonable.

"Come in closer, everyone, so you can hear me. I don't like having to shout."

The birds flew down, and the animals crept in closer. They circled around Mr. Mole, seemingly interested to hear what he had to say. He knew he was a tiny animal, but the others were treating him more respectfully because of what he'd done to help Benji.

He looked down and saw several curious worms on the surface. They knew they were safe above ground and wiggled up to catch the discussion. He knew they couldn't hear very well, wouldn't stay long, and their attention spans were short, but they were good about relaying what they heard to the other worms.

"Okay, everybody, settle down." Mr. Mole presented his idea and, surprisingly, everyone thought it was doable. When the idea was presented, everyone clapped and agreed they would do their part to help. The animals wanted to begin right away, but Mr. Mole curbed their enthusiasm. The plan was discussed and fine-tuned until it was workable, and the animals knew the part they would play.

Tate, the male cardinal, then spoke. "Mr. Mole, I think you're clever for coming up with this plan, but you know what this means, don't you?" Before the mole could answer, the cardinal continued. "It means our already stressful lives will become more stressed. We'll have less time to spend with our families and less time to prepare for the beast.

We'll also have less time to clean and maintain our homes and care for our sick and elderly. Because of all this extra work, I don't think we should be doing this, but, and I think I can speak for everyone here, let's do it anyway!"

"Yes," agreed Frederica, "we need to put aside our needs for Pippen's sake."

The animals that could jump, jumped up and down. The bees were buzzing, the worms were wiggling, the ants were anting. "We'll be known as the Acorn Patrol!" shouted Frederica.

"Acorn Patrol! Acorn Patrol! Acorn Patrol!" shouted the animals in unison.

"Shh, guys, not so loud!" whispered Mr. Mole, "We can't let the deer hear. Now, let's get a good night's sleep, and we'll begin first thing in the morning."

Fall and the Following Spring,
The Acorn Patrol

With the title of Unofficial Official, Mr. Mole now had the responsibility of heading up the work. It was agreed that the animals would supply the deer with a replenished food supply every day, hoping that it would keep deer from raiding Pippen's branches. The plan was to gather acorns from under the white oak trees and place them in piles around the forest. The deer would find the piles and eat the acorns instead of Pippen's branches.

Mr. Mole whistled shrilly between two blades of grass to call the animals to attention. He shouted for everyone to work for two hours until they heard the same sound of dismissal.

Mr. Mole had noticed that Max had been more cordial lately, but he still seemed unsure about working with others. That morning, he knew Max must be hungry because normally he would be out looking for his breakfast. Mr. Mole was shocked because, just like the others, Max had reported for duty before eating. He was happy that Max joined and wanted to work for Pippen's sake. He saw Max pushing brush around searching for acorns.

"Max, go over by the oak trees, that's where they're at," Mr. Mole directed, making sure the animals knew where to go. Max dutifully followed the others to the oaks, being careful not to step on any ants. As the animals foraged under the trees, Mr. Mole reminded them, "We only want the whole ones. Don't pick up anything rotten or broken."

The owl had been sitting in the tree watching the animals gather. Mr. Mole knew that owls didn't like acorns and wondered if he was there to help or hinder. Then he heard the owl grumble, "Yuck, I don't know why deer eat those awful things." Then the owl flew down to help.

Mr. Mole and the rest of the acorn patrol gathered under the oaks and went to work. They found good acorns, picked them up in their mouths, and dropped them in designated piles. When the wind blew, they saw and heard acorns dropping to the ground and everyone rushed over to add them to the growing mounds.

The ants were amazing workers. Mr. Mole watched as groups of six ants worked together to hoist a single acorn onto their backs and carry it to the pile. It took them an hour to contribute one acorn to the pile, but when they succeeded, they cheered and congratulated themselves before running back for another.

The wiggle worms showed the same dedication. Two or three worms worked their way aboveground at a time. They worked in shifts to find an acorn and pushed it forward with their front ends. If it took them a week, they vowed to get it to a pile. Some birds eyed them as food, but everyone followed the rule set for work—no preying on each other during work hours.

After two hours, Mr. Mole blew the whistle again. The ants shuddered because the sound hurt their ears; dropped their nuts and, poof, disappeared. Everyone else dropped what they were doing and disappeared into the forest.

After a week of making acorn hills, the deer became curious. One day, as they walked toward the apple tree to nibble, they were distracted by a new scent. They walked past the tree and followed the scent.

The deer discovered the acorns and couldn't believe their good luck. Acorns were already piled and ready to eat. Word spread, and more deer gathered to see the fresh, neatly-piled acorns. Nervously, they walked to the mounds, and each took a turn eating. Mothers walked in with their young, cautious bucks stood guard, and eventually all the deer joined in.

Mr. Mole and some of the patrol animals stayed hidden and watched the deer eat. Mr. Mole found it comical to see them taking turns and displaying such good manners. They took their time and didn't gobble—no burping, belching, or squabbling.

Day by day, the animals continued their task. All summer and fall, they worked their two-hours shifts gathering acorns for the deer. But during the very cold months, a crew was impossible to assemble. The animals either went into hibernation or hunkered down in tunnels to keep warm. Birds had flown south or were busy just trying to survive.

Mr. Mole noticed how, before the birds flew south, they gathered acorns and dropped them into the crevices of downed tree trunks. He admired their dedication as they continued this as long as possible before their migration.

The birds who stayed for the winter promised to stockpile acorns. The cardinals, blue jays, woodpeckers, and chickadees kept the acorns supplied before the snow covered the ground. It was a lot of work, but they continued doing it as long as they could because they believed in the cause.

Word eventually reached the deer that the animals and birds were behind the acorn piles. Once they discovered the reason, they vowed to keep their tongues away from Pippen's branches. Mr. Mole watched as the deer ate sparingly to make the acorns last the whole winter.

When spring arrived and Pippen's branches began to flower, Mr. Mole called a community meeting under the apple tree to share important news.

Mr. Mole said, "I think you all know Hollyhock here. I'm going to turn this meeting over to her to make an announcement."

He watched as Hollyhock, a full-grown deer who had lived in this part of the forest for several years, stepped forward shyly. Public speaking made her uncomfortable, except among other deer. She agreed to speak because Mr. Mole was her friend and talked her into it.

"Thank you, Mr. Mole. My name is Hollyhock, and... I am an apple tree nibbler," she said, her head bowed in embarrassment.

"*Former* apple tree nibbler," someone called out.

Mr. Mole saw Hollyhock raise her head with a small smile.

"Thank you, yes, *former* nibbler. Mr. Mole asked me to come and help congratulate Pippen on his new growth. Watch me as I walk under his branches."

Mr. Mole watched with pride as Hollyhock walked under Pippen's branches, stretching her head up as high as she could.

"I cannot reach his branches. It appears Pippen has grown six inches in less than a year. My fellow deer and I would like to tell Pippen we are sorry for what we did to hamper his growth. We also want to thank you all for your kindness in supplying us with food. We know from now on we're on our own."

As Pippen lifted his branches toward the sun, Mr. Mole's heart swelled with pride. He saw the other animals watching as they shared in the moment. When his branches lowered again, Pippen thanked all present for what they did for him and that he was grateful to know his growth was now assured. He said that someday he hoped for offspring to grow nearby, so that he could pass on the story of how his friends had stepped up to help him out.

CHAPTER FIVE
Seasons of Growth

Year Two, Spring,
Pippen's Birthday

PIPPEN DID NOT LIKE GETTING up early. He had a habit of staying up late at night to watch the stars appear in the sky. His trunk stood and pondered things such as why stars seemed to move in the sky each night, what the moon was running from when it changed locations, or what could have taken a bite out of it.

He also liked to watch the different animals that walked the forest at night. He saw the raccoons, foxes, and skunk families all foraging. Because of his late nights, he usually slept in, unless he had a reason to wake early.

Two black-capped chickadees flew in and landed on a branch to see if he was awake. Pippen didn't wake, unaware that this was a special day.

Two yellow canaries joined the chickadees and the four decided he needed to wake up. "Rise and shine, rise and shine! Wake up, wake up, it's your birthday!"

Birds were making noise on his branches, and he wished they would go away. *What are they saying?* Then he remembered what day it was and woke up. It was his birthday!

Stretching his lower branches to get his sap flowing, he knew that the forest always had a birthday surprise for him.

They sang in a chorus, "The forest has a gift for thee, silly little sleepy tree. It's from every one of us, even the buggy bugs make a fuss."

The birds flew down to the ground to strut and join chipmunks, squirrels, and an assortment of bugs in a birthday dance. Then the young moles, Benji, and the mice joined in and paraded around him and decreed, "Pippen, we want this to be a special day for you. Congratulations, you turned six! Happy birthday little tree! This is our forest-wide decree."

He thought it was a very short party, but he was still happy to be remembered on his birthday.

The Star

Faraway star, I see each night,
High in the distant sky.
I spread my branches on the chance,
You'd spot me from on high.

Some nights you are my only friend,
When darkness overtakes these woods.
With willows weeping and valley sleeping,
I'd touch you if I could.

Each night, I stand here steadfastly,
Branches spread in stately array.
Your starlight fills this wooded realm,
Casting shadows as I pray.

When sleep finally overtakes me,
And my limbs succumb to rest.
Your vision fades and darkness pervades,
Sleep is a welcome guest.

I will dream of stars and fairytales,
Of mighty trees and kings.
I wish for golden wings to fly,
Pleasant dreams for this sleepy sapling.

On the Forest Floor

Every living thing in the forest—plants, animals, birds, bees, ants, even microorganisms—was given their time under the sun. While a master creator created the sun, moon, and all life, another unseen entity was created and tasked with overseeing and nurturing life. That entity was Mother Nature. She helped and monitored nature to ensure living things fulfilled their purpose of keeping Earth alive.

But the master creator also created another entity to assist Mother Nature in her role. This other entity was Time.

Time and Mother Nature worked hand in hand in their roles. The role of Time was to give each lifeform their "moment" of time under the sun to do their assigned tasks and reproduce their species. While some moments lasted only minutes, others lasted centuries. Mother Nature helped and nurtured life during the moments assigned to assist with their tasks.

Time and Mother Nature have worked together for millions of years and, hopefully, will continue for millions more. There had been some hiccups along the way, but Time helped resolve the hiccups. Generally, it had been a smooth partnership.

Although their collaboration worked quietly in the background, the forest had no reason to believe it was being observed or guided. As far as forest life knew, its only purpose was to survive.

In the forest, unbeknownst to them, roots played an important role in helping Mother Nature do her job. Besides stabilizing themselves and the forest floor, roots were tasked as Mother Nature's historians. Plants watched and passed down important information to roots to have a record of every plant and animal's existence on Earth. This monitoring and recording by roots had become part of their normal daily existence.

Animal and plant life, including human life, survived as a species and reproduced. Reproduction of the species was necessary for Mother Nature and Time to meet their objective of keeping the Earth alive. Microorganisms broke down dead matter and recycled them back into the environment to help species on Earth survive. By all working together, life was extended and Earth survived.

Baby Cubs

Her growing hunger and a whiff of spring were all it took for her to leave her winter enclosure. Belle would stroll away from the den once the cubs were settled and safe inside. She never ventured far and always returned after a needed short excursion.

The cubs were a month old, and their eyes were open and curious. They moved awkwardly in the darkness, and Belle knew that once their legs strengthened and the air warmed, they'd be ready to join her outside.

After nursing, the cubs slept in a tangled pile. Looking at them, Belle watched them jerk and twitch. She wondered why they slept so fitfully at this young age. *What could they possibly be dreaming about to make them twitch? Did they jerk because I ran out of milk while suckling? Was I not keeping them warm enough? Did they think I didn't love them enough?* She would never know.

That morning, they looked so small and helpless lying there. In a few short years, they would become confident and dominant black bears in their own corners of the woods. For now, much work was ahead to raise them.

It rained during the night because she smelled the dampness in the air. Dampness and warm air were a good combination because they helped plants to grow. Drawn by the warm air, she eased away from the huddled cubs. They watched as she pushed herself forward on her belly to the front of the den. Once again, the warm air coaxed her out completely. Turning and looking back, she saw the cubs looking at her, curious about her actions. Without saying a word, her eyes told them, "Stay right here." The cubs knew that look and settled back down.

Before stepping out fully, Belle checked ahead for any sign of danger. Her nose detected no unusual scents, only wet soil, and decaying leaves. Nothing was out of the ordinary and it was safe to go out. Looking back once more, the cubs were still in their pile. She crawled out and rose to her feet.

A long stretch loosened her muscles as she did a slow circle of the immediate area. Before crawling back inside again, she glanced through the trees for anything different. The cubs cried again for food, and she settled once more beside the cubs as they eagerly pushed in to nurse.

These three cubs were her second litter in five years. The two cubs in her first litter had grown and gone off on their own, giving her a six-month rest before she met Max last summer. These three cubs were born in the den this winter, and Max was the father. He would never see them and raising them would be her only job for the next two summers.

For now, she was living off her fat reserves, but soon she needed to start foraging for food. Before long, she and the cubs would leave this shelter and live out in the wild. Keeping them safe and looking for food would occupy all her time.

Cubs Meet World

The snow had melted, the air was warm, and the breezes swayed the trees back and forth. Green grass was trying to entice the cubs to come out and step on it.

Belle sat outside in full view of the cubs, who huddled inside the den. That day, she decided they were ready to come out and meet the world. Besides, her body was weak and needed food. She would introduce the cubs to the wild and how to safely follow her, enabling her to forage for food.

"Come out, children, don't be afraid." Belle saw the fear on their faces.

One cub cried out, "Momma, we're scared, we just want to stay inside and play with the roots."

Belle knew the nearby trees quietly listened and watched. Just like her, they had been curious to see how things would play out. She sensed that they enjoyed watching her cubs walking about in the spring. Their little stumbles, their attempts at running, and their playful movements, seemed to delight the trees as much as they delighted Belle herself.

The bears lined up sitting at the door of the den and looked at her. Belle walked forward and brushed each of them with her nose, backed up again, and sat on the grass ten feet away. Belle looked at the cubs individually, giving each a knowing head lowering to come forward. Seeing that, they stood, stretched out their necks, and looked around. They hesitated; Belle was being patient and waited.

She glanced at the nearby trees and, sure enough, she could hear their whispers. They sounded amused as they watched the cubs apprehensively sniff the air. *Would, or wouldn't they, walk out to their mother?* That seemed to be the big question.

The firstborn of Belle's cubs was Sharon. She took three steps over the threshold and stopped, then tiptoed over to Belle. Sharon sat next to her as they both looked at Bruce and Lloyd, who still hesitated.

The boys stood, tapped the grass, and watched it spring back up. The grass felt soft, the air was calm and the outside smelled inviting, she could tell that they were curious. Each took one step forward and was surprised as a breeze brushed their faces. This startled them and they ran ahead to their mother. She guided them into her, and mother and cubs sat close together. Belle stifled their fear and said, "Don't be afraid. If there is danger, I will protect you."

Just like with her first cubs, she knew the time would come to say goodbye. They would grow tall and strong and become confident bears, as their species was known. They would grow up knowing their mother had given them the best care she could.

The day was warm with sun on their backs, as they lay on their mother and nursed. Out in the open with nothing to fear, she felt happy and blessed to be the mother of these cubs.

Happy and content again, they slept next to her. She decided that when they woke, she was going to take them on their first stroll and introduce them to their new forest home.

The Threat

Many months later, Belle walked a new part of the forest with her three cubs. As she looked for food, the cubs followed her, not hesitating to jump and play whenever they were in the mood for fun, which happened often. She walked and foraged, nursed, and rested, then started all over again. This had become their daily routine. The cubs became quite fearless and adventurous and often lagged to investigate smells while Belle stopped and ate. She would let them have a small degree of freedom if the area was safe.

These cubs were the second family Belle had raised in five years. Her first family of two, Harry and Stanley, grew up quickly and left her to be on their own. She did think about them but couldn't miss them; there was no time to dwell on the past with these new cubs to raise.

Sharon, Bruce, and Lloyd obediently followed her everywhere but goofed off and hid whenever she wasn't looking. They didn't know she was aware of their shenanigans and always knew where they were. Her eyes constantly scanned the area for danger and, if angered, she was ready to fight off anything to protect her cubs.

She turned and saw the cubs clumsily balancing across a downed branch. The woods were their playground and classroom all in one. Bruce found edible plants on his own and did not share with his brother and sister. Meanwhile, Lloyd ate ants from an overturned log and kept an eye on his siblings, who wanted to help eat his find.

The area felt safe, and Belle sat and rested. She watched the cubs wrestle on the ground and pretended not to see them. Sharon nipped Bruce's ear, and he let out a sharp squeal. He swiped back at his sister for revenge just as Lloyd came running and jumped on top of the others. Lying on their bellies, they were all played out. She would give them more time to catch their breath before calling them back to join her walking again.

Belle was happy they were growing fast. Every day she taught the cubs new skills. The cubs obediently followed her everywhere. The importance of always looking for danger had been drilled into their heads early on. Even when they were playing, they stopped and looked around. They would be with her for two more winters, and then they would be ready to head out on their own.

What was that? She caught the whiff of another bear. Belle didn't fear for herself; she was a fully grown bear and could protect herself, but the cubs were less than a year old and could be attacked by a hungry bear. She didn't have to warn them; they had already caught the scent and climbed up a tree. She stayed where she was to stand up to the bear. She watched the black bear come forward. The cubs were high in the tree, claws clinging to the trunk and looking down.

Belle was angry. *How dare this male bear come in so close! He would regret it if he tried anything!*

Twenty feet away, the bear stopped and looked at her. Taking an angry stance and looking the bear straight in the eyes, she growled as a warning not to come closer. She gave him a piercing stare, and he stared back. Suddenly, recognition hit, this bear was familiar, but she continued giving him her piercing look, which told him to stay away or else. The big bear backed away, knowing getting closer would not be the smartest thing to do.

The cubs were relieved to see the big bear retreat. "Come on down, it's safe again," Belle shouted.

"Did you see those ferocious eyes?" asked Sharon.

"Mother, you were so brave, he was twice your size!" Bruce added excitedly.

Lloyd, standing tall on his back legs, watched as the bear disappeared into the trees. "I guess we showed him!"

The cubs stood beside her, as she also watched the bear disappear into the woods. She knew this encounter was another lesson they wouldn't soon forget.

Belle watched Max retreat and knew he meant no harm to her or the cubs. She had put up her brave stand for the benefit of the cubs. They had to learn of the danger from older bears.

She watched as they tumbled on the ground, already over this experience. They rolled around, stood and got dizzy, and stumbled backward. The cubs playfully jumped on her, but she knew they had their mother figured out. They knew from experience that she would grumble, but if they nuzzled her sweetly, she got over it.

Max Returned Home

Max spotted the moss and decided to rest. He dug his claws into the moss and yanked out bunches to put in a pile to cushion his bed. He dropped, liking the feel of his spongy, cool bed. He'd rather be home in his own forest, in his own bed, but this would have to do.

Max had been in more of a hurry to find Belle than he was to return home. He had thought about this trip for weeks, and two days ago, he just woke up and decided to take off. As he lay with his chin on the ground, he thought of Belle, who he had found today.

He yearned for her companionship, but after today, he knew he might never have it again. She was still with cubs, which was good and bad news. Good, because they were probably his, but bad because he wouldn't be able to approach her for at least another year. He didn't know if he could wait that long. He understood the warning look she gave him but also knew she recognized him.

He would never know for sure if he was the father of those cubs. Other bears out there could be their father. Once a male bear mated, they never saw the female bear again, most of the time, that is. Once juvenile bears left their mother, they never saw her again or knew who their father was. When he was on his walks, he ran into juveniles. The thought occurred to him that they might be his offspring, but he had no way of knowing and didn't dwell on it.

Belle was doing a fantastic job. He saw the cubs up a tree and knew she had taught them well.

He had to rest before he could feed again. Max planned to get up early to head home. If he pushed it, he might be able to sleep in his own bed the next day. Just before he closed his eyes, he saw Belle again, with that angry look on her face. He knew again that today might be the last time he would see her.

The next morning, his body hurt with every step he took. The forest was talking, but he could hardly hear it. He thought it was rough getting old.

The Wiggle Worm Adventure

Chester and Bud were brother worms who lived together in their underground tunnel. They were two-year-old, fully grown worms with a sense of adventure. That adventurous spirit would get them into trouble whenever they decided that the dark, damp soil of the underground was too boring.

That morning, the brothers felt great as their long bodies drank in the moisture from the surrounding soil. It rained during the night, which moistened the soil, but not overly. Like all earthworms, these two brothers took in oxygen through their skin. When the skin was wet and slimy, breathing and living underground was easier.

Sometimes, if their skin became too dry, the worms would crawl down deeper to reach the moist soil needed to survive. Too much water drowned worms; too little forced them downward, making life unpredictable.

These two were adventurous and social worms, unlike some older worms who were content to eat and sleep all day. They loved stretching their bodies in accordion-like fashion to visit their root and worm friends. They rarely came up to the surface.

Earthworms didn't have eyes, ears, or noses, but they did have a mouth and they loved to eat. Without noses, they relied on receptors on their body to smell food and danger.

Chester and Bud were not ones for lying around on nice days. With their bellies full and skin damp, they wanted to move and explore.

Chester had an idea, "Let's go visit the ferns' roots and see what they're up to. If their roots are slippery, maybe they'd let us slide up and down them."

"Okay, I'll race you there!" Bud was already arching his body to get a start..

"You're on!" Chester sped ahead of his brother. The other worms sensed the movement and assumed it was Chester and Bud being their adventurous selves again. They wondered who they were pestering today.

They quickly found the ferns' roots, but the roots didn't seem to want visitors, saying it wasn't a good time. They asked them to come back on a different day. The worms thought that sounded rude, but they said goodbye and turned around to tunnel away.

"What should we do now?" asked Bud, but then he thought of something. "Hey, we haven't been by Digger and Phil's place for quite a while. Let's check on the old worms to see if they're still alive. You just never know."

Chester replied, "I'm sure they're fine. They might be old, but they still move fast. They're still the fastest and smartest worms down here. I heard they can escape from anything. But that's a good idea; let's go pay them a visit."

Digger and Phil were also brothers who had stayed together all their lives. They had lived almost seven years and led interesting lives. The younger worms loved listening to the older worms tell of their adventures and never tired of hearing stories of escaping death from hungry birds and animals.

After tunneling a short distance, they were already tired, and their bodies ached. "We must be a little out of shape," said Chester. "I wish there was a faster way to get there."

"If we were on the surface, crawling would be easier and faster. We'd be there in no time," said Bud. "But we're not supposed to go up there, remember?"

"Hmm... yeah," considered Chester, "but we could be over and down a tunnel before anything up there saw us. We're fast; we should do it."

Bud was hesitant about going up. "I don't know about this. Everyone tells us not to."

"Oh, come on, don't worry, it'll be fine. Let's ask a root if we can climb up."

Chester tapped on a nearby root and asked if they might attach to climb to the surface. The root gave permission and up they went.

Near the surface, their receptors detected the change in temperature, going from cool to warm. If they went above and their skin dried out, they might die. This was risky, and they were hesitant to come all the way up. They crawled up farther and their bodies sensed the dry air which wasn't good. But since there was no wind, they figured they wouldn't dry out so fast. The worms calculated the distance to the other worms' tunnel and decided to go for it. If they wiggled fast, they would be there before the heat overtook them. They decided there was no going back now.

"Come on, let's just go. We'll crawl together, side by side," Chester said, suddenly making the decision.

They crawled out completely but then hesitated. There was no way of knowing if a bird had already spotted them. They moved as fast as possible and crawled a few inches. *So far, so good.*

Suddenly, there was a drop in temperature and the air speed picked up. They resisted, but the wind was trying to push them backwards. Making matters worse, raindrops started falling. At first, the water didn't bother them, and it felt good, but then it started accumulating on the ground. They knew now they were easy meals for birds. "We gotta get out of here!" shouted Bud.

The walls of a puddle burst and a river of water had formed from a puddle. They saw a torrent of water higher than their bodies rushing toward them from behind. The approaching water sounded menacing, and they trembled, knowing it could wash them away if it reached them.

In a matter of seconds, the rushing water reached them. They were tossed up and down, back and forth, sideways, and spinning. Their moist bodies reached for air whenever they could. Their bodies were stretched long beyond their control, as the deluge swept them onward. They wondered if their quiet adventure could go any worse.

Finally, the shower stopped and the current slowed. It brought them to a stop as the water seeped into the ground. Water flowed down surface wormholes and disappeared.

They took advantage of the opportunity and exited down the closest hole. Before going deeper, they paused to check on each other.

"Are you okay?" asked Chester.

"I am, but what a ride!" Bud replied, gulping in oxygen.

"Whew, if that rain hadn't stopped, we might have been seriously killed." Chester was spitting out water as he talked. "We better get moving before it starts again."

Bud noticed the tunnels were cleared of water and his front end pointed to a nearby tunnel. "Look how wide this tunnel is. This has got to be one of Digger's tunnels. Let's see where it goes."

Digger was a fat worm, and when he made tunnels, they were wide. But his tunnels were short because he tired easily and had to rest.

Bud went first, and Chester followed. Going just a few inches, they could make out the voices of Digger and Phil up ahead.

"It's us, Chester and Bud. Can we come over?" Bud shouted in the direction of the voices.

"Sure, but hurry before the rain starts again!" The boys were happy to hear Digger's voice.

Once settled in their friends' cavity, Chester told the story of what happened and how they got there. Their friends were appalled and shook their heads in disapproval of the risk taken. The two younger worms knew a scolding was coming.

"Don't ever, *EVER* do that again! Stupid, stupid, stupid!" said Digger. "You're lucky to be alive. You could have been easy pickings for Mother Robin or Mother Mole to feed to their children. Worse yet, you could have been swept down a gopher hole!"

Phil, who had been sitting back and listening, added to the scolding. "Guys, don't take chances going aboveground. You might think that because the birds act friendly, they're our friends, but believe me, they are not. Friendliness has one purpose for birds: One day they like you, the next they eat you. If you want a long life, you must stay underground where it's safe."

"All right, all right," sighed Chester. Both worms knew the older worms were right and now regretted taking the risk.

Chester and Bud moved in closer to Digger and Phil. The four worms huddled together, enjoying all the warmth radiating from four bodies. In this comfortable cavity, the visitors didn't want to go home.

"Are you boys hungry?" asked Digger. "Why don't you eat with us tonight and stay over? We have a lot of leaves, twigs, and dried grass, and more than enough space for two more worms to stretch out. You can tell us what's been happening in your ground."

"That sounds great, thank you, we will," said Chester.

They spent the night and slept well. When they judged it morning, the worms yawned and stretched their bodies. They knew it was time to say goodbye and head home.

Worms generally don't like to share tunnels with other worms, as every worm claims the tunnels they build. The visitors were shocked when the elder worms offered them use of their tunnels.

"Boys, we insist you use our tunnels. You'll slide easily through them and be home in no time."

"Hey, thanks. We appreciate that," Bud replied.

In their friends' cavernous tunnels, their voices echoed when they spoke as they zipped along toward home. Their own intersecting tunnels came up ahead, and they switched to them for the last leg home.

But just then, their receptors caught a whiff of impending danger. Both worms stopped in their tracks, and their bodies went stiff with fear. Their mother had taught them that when they smelled this, they should immediately tunnel down deeper. She'd say, "Don't hesitate, just go!"

They recognized the smell of a skunk. It meant one was walking aboveground and making a nuisance of itself looking for food. Skunks would eat just about anything, but they especially loved worms. The worms knew they were in danger and needed to tunnel deeper or the skunk would dig them out. As they dug downward, they could feel the vibrations of other worms doing the same thing.

Wiggle Worms in Danger

Chester and Bud crawled to their escape tunnel. Every worm had a tunnel to disappear down to escape danger. They traveled down a foot and stopped, thinking about their next move. They could feel the ground vibrating and knew the skunk was still in the area.

"We need to go down a few more inches. I'll do the digging, you just follow," offered Bud.

"All right, I'm ready," agreed Chester.

When they'd left home, their mother drilled these words into them to keep them safe: "When you're in danger, go deeper, deeper underground. Travel as fast as you can and be quiet. Stay down until the roots tell you the threat has passed." The brothers had always remembered her warning.

All the worms were waiting for word from the roots. The scent of the skunk lingered; it might last for several days. A root then tapped Chester's and Bud's bodies twice with a message, "The skunk is gone; he didn't get any worms. He found a mouse and went back to his own woods." These were the words the two worms had waited to hear.

"It's cold here, let's go home!" They turned at an angle, circled around, and crawled back up through their escape tunnel. Happy to be home on warm ground, they filled their insides with food. They desperately wanted to crash and let their food digest but could not. After getting back from the skunk fiasco, the roots announced to the worms a developing news situation.

"Oh, what now?" Chester was irritated but lazily rolled on his side to hear what was happening.

"Listen up, worms! It's been reported that several baby worms are missing after the rain last night. They won't be kissing their mother goodnight tonight unless we find them. We're asking all worms to search your immediate areas." The roots seemed to have this announcement on repeat because it was blasted continuously.

Chester and Bud had the same thing happen to them as little worms. They were following their mother one evening when she stopped to feed. She expected them to wait behind her, but being inquisitive worms, they did not. Chester remembered bumping into another entrance tunnel and went in. They were afraid after a few inches and wanted to go back but could not find their way to Mother. They were lost and kept crawling farther into the unfamiliar tunnel. When they couldn't crawl any further, they sat together and cried and wished their mother would reappear. But she didn't, and they spent the whole night cold and alone, clinging to each other to keep warm. With no survival skills, they could have been eaten by night feeders, but they survived the night. The search crew found them early the next morning and took them home.

That felt like yesterday, and the fear was vivid. Yes, they *had* to help find the baby worms.

Then they heard the frantic words from mother worm: "Help me! My babies vanished when it rained. I'm so worried. I won't be able to sleep knowing they're alone. Please do everything you can to find them."

A search party was already forming.

Earthworms looked out for other earthworms. They didn't need to be coerced, as they relied on each other every day for survival. The worms all spread out into different tunnels looking for the babies. After several hours of searching, they were finally notified to stop because the babies had been found and were on their way home.

The mother worm was caressing her children and spoke. "Thank you, worms, for going over and beyond to get them back to me unhurt. Since we've all had a hard couple of days, let's get a good night's sleep and rest all day tomorrow." Everyone agreed that it was an excellent idea.

Finally settling in for the night, Chester and Bud reflected on their last two days away from home. What was supposed to be a friendly visit to the roots, turned into their tempting fate by going above ground, and ended when they helped find the lost worms. They slept well that night and ate and rested all the next day.

On the second morning, feeling refreshed, Bud excitedly said, "I know what we can do today. You and I should go sneak up on those crabby ferns again and knock on their roots. We'll run off and hide. When they turn and see nobody again, they'll holler out like they always do. It's fun to hear them cuss when they don't know who was there."

"What a bad worm you are!" The brothers laughed.

Then Chester offered another idea, "Or we could just stay here and throw each other around. You ride piggyback on me, and I'll carry you until I throw you off and dirt buries you. When you dig out, I'll ride on you, and you can watch me squirm to dig out."

"Hmmm," said Bud, "the problem with that is that we'll be wrecking our tunnel and burying our food—more work for us later."

"Yeah, you're right, not a good idea," said Chester.

In the end, they just rested. The sound of a lonely whip-poor-will was heard underground. For the moment, they were content listening and thinking about what their next adventure would be.

PART
TWO

Whispers of Change:
The Waiting Game

CHAPTER SIX
The Turning Leaves

Year Two, Late Summer,
New Bonds

LITTLE TREE WAS THE TALLEST tree in the forest, but despite his height, he was still a young tree at heart. His roots had made friends with every plant within his reach. That day, one of his longer roots stretched to the daisy field and made a friend over there.

His parent trees stood a short distance from him. They were in constant contact with Little Tree even though he wasn't so little anymore. They were proud of Little Tree's height and, even though he did not know it yet, he had an important future role in the forest.

His roots excitedly traveled over to his parents and told them about a new friend he'd made that day.

"Guess what? One of my roots went exploring, and it swung by the daisy area that I hadn't visited in a while. The roots there were always busy talking to each other, and whenever I came by, they never wanted to talk. They looked at me, seemed afraid because of my size, and backtracked."

His mother and father listened, exchanged knowing glances, and envisioned this happening.

"But today one of the little roots approached and touched me. She was tiny and giggled when she saw me. She wasn't even afraid. She said she was feeling refreshed after the rain last night. The little root's name is Mazy and she's one of the daisies in the big open area. I can see them from my high branches, but you should also be able to see them. Mazy said the daisies liked to play tag with the wiggle worms. They ran and hid from them and make sharp turns to lose them.

"Mazy and I explored new ground together. Her roots are not very long, and what seemed like a long distance for her was very short for me. But we had fun tapping and scaring other daisy roots and running away. Oh, and it was funny—one time we were traveling so fast that we ran smack into a rock. That hurt, but we got up, took off, and I followed her again.

"After that, Mazy wanted to rest, and we just talked. She talked about the life of daisies, and I talked about the life of trees. She was shocked to hear I was the tall tree that the daisies feared. I told her I was just a regular tree, and my roots liked to have fun too. Mazy said she had to get back, but she wanted to play with me again. I told her I'd like that and asked if we could be friends. She laughed and said, 'of course.' Then she was gone."

His father cautioned, "You just be careful around those little daisy roots; you wouldn't want them to get hurt."

"I am, and don't worry." Saying that, Little Tree said goodbye to his parents and rejoined his other tree roots.

"That tree, I tell you, he's going to get himself in trouble with all that speeding around. One of these days one of his roots will hurt another root."

"Oh, Father, don't worry about him. He's a kid yet, let him have his fun."

"I suppose you're right. Someday soon I'll need to have that talk with him. He needs to know what is happening to him."

Little Tree's Growth

Each day, Mother Nature took time out of her day to help selected trees from each forest become the tallest tree. In each forest, she selected several trees at birth to have this honor. Over the years, she helped each of these trees to grow to an astounding height. One of these trees in each forest is destined to take over at being the tallest tree to preside over their forest until death. This tree would take over when the current tallest tree passed away.

It was Little Tree's turn, although he didn't know it yet or why it was happening to him. He and about a thousand other trees today in this region would go through the same growth simultaneously.

Mother Nature knew Little Tree had no idea what was happening to him. His mother and father knew, and someday she knew that his father would explain the honor Mother Nature had bestowed on him.

Being Watched

Little Tree was uneasy that day. He had a feeling that an unseen presence was watching him. Some days, he brushed it off as absurd and forgot it, but on other days, the feeling was stronger, and it irritated him.

Most days, he spent his time racing with other tree roots until they were all exhausted. Racing was fun, but he knew his father didn't like him doing it because of the danger posed from the size of his roots. Still, he didn't care. He and his friends liked to stretch their roots out to the big rocks, tap them, and then race to see who would get back to the starting point first.

He'd heard their complaints about his larger size and his roots having an advantage.

He would hear, "It's not fair! You're so much bigger than we are and have longer roots."

Little Tree knew that was true, but he couldn't help it. He pacified the other roots by sitting out a few races and instead cheered them on.

He sat and watched the roots racing when the uncomfortable pulling sensation started up again. When his body wanted to rest and slow down, he couldn't, because his life energy flowed faster and harder than ever. Once the painful pulling sensation started, it wouldn't quit for several hours. If he could have jumped out of his trunk, he would have.

That day, his root didn't want to stick around. Little Tree said, "Guys, I'm going back. I'll catch up with you later."

His friends were surprised by his sudden exit and watched him backtrack in the direction of his trunk. Little Tree knew what was happening, and he didn't want his friends to witness it.

He was in excruciating pain. It felt as if this presence, or whatever it was, was trying to rip his trunk apart. It tugged and pulled, trying to stretch his main root against his will. The force was more powerful than he was, and he felt powerless to fight it. He felt violated. He didn't ask to be stretched, and the force never asked permission.

The terrible pain continued as his main root stood helplessly upright. A few hours later, the jerking, creaking, and moaning sounds let up and his longest main root elongated another fifteen feet. This meant that his tree's height above ground would also be considerably taller. He knew he swayed even higher over the entire forest.

Why am I growing so tall? Why just me? Why can't I be normal like other trees? Little Tree was hoping that someone, anyone, would give him the answers. He grew up hearing the stories of Mother Nature, supposedly the forest's supreme caretaker. If she was real, he was desperate for her to hear him and tell him why this was happening to him.

Words of Wisdom

Little Tree was anxious, as his next growth spurt could come at any time. It always seemed to happen around the seventh or eighth rising of the sun. Seven risings had passed since his last episode, and Little Tree was a bundle of nerves. He wondered if this would continue his entire life. The unpleasant presence came when he least expected it. While he waited, his main root traveled to his father tree.

"Father, I'm so bored waiting for that thing to happen again. There is nothing for me to do except stand around, watch branches move, and leaves fall. It seems all we trees do our whole lives is stand here. Why did Mother Nature put us here anyway?"

Little Tree could feel his father studying him, knowing he was thinking about what to say while being questioned. He hadn't planned for his words of exasperation to come out, but he'd been holding it in these past years, and it just burst out.

At last, he heard his father's voice pass to his roots.

"Son," he began, "when I was your age, my father explained to me the same things that his father explained to him. Every generation passes these truths from father to child. It is now time that I pass them to you."

His father paused. Little Tree knew something pivotal was coming, and his anticipation grew.

"Trees have been here for millions of years. We were one of the first plants on this land and were put here to do important work for Mother Nature. We are tasked to provide homes for many different species of birds and animals. They depend on us for shelter when it gets too hot, cold, wet, or dry. Our branches provide shade and cover for deer, bear, and other animals—even the tiny creatures we can't see. Every living thing in this forest depends on trees for shelter for their survival.

"There is a thing in the air called oxygen that every living thing needs to live. We trees are one of the main sources of oxygen. We don't even realize it, but we make oxygen every day and release it into the air for plants and animals to survive. Roots need oxygen, which is taken in through air pockets in the soil."

Little Tree thought about what his father had said so far. He'd said things he had never known before, and thought their job sounded very important.

His father continued, "Tree roots go deep and extend in every direction to protect us from falling over during storms. Our roots only go as deep as we can find oxygen.

"During heavy rains, trees absorb water to help reduce the risk of flooding. Our roots spread out and keep the ground stable for plants to survive."

Before continuing, his father asked, "Do you understand everything I've said so far?"

Little Tree thought for a minute before answering. If what his father said was true, this was huge. His trunk surged with pride as he considered these responsibilities. *Trees weren't just killing time here; they were the foundation of the forest while we live. Wow. Just wow.*

He finally answered, "Yes, I do."

"Good, because there is more. We are considered the guardians of nature, which is the one big job entrusted to trees for millions of years. It is an honor to be selected by Mother Nature for this job, and we must always remember that. All plants have jobs, but because we are the biggest and strongest, we have the most important ones. We must stand tall and be proud of the trust she has placed in us."

Little Tree had no idea of any of this and found it all very interesting, but he still had unanswered questions about himself and his role there.

His father continued, "There's one more thing I want to talk to you about because you're old enough to understand. Son, listen closely.

"Every generation of a forest has one tree that is much taller than all the others. In my generation, it is our friend, Oakren. The tallest tree is given the task of being the protector; the tree that plants and animals depend on for warnings, guidance, and protection. Because of its height, it sees things first, like approaching storms, fires, or beasts. Oakren always warned the forest of those things, but he is old and is near death. Mother Nature has selected you, Little Tree, from all the other trees to be his replacement when he passes."

Okay, this was all making sense now.

"You should consider this a very high honor. Your mother and I know she selected you and it makes us very proud. Mother Nature has been helping you grow to become the tallest tree, and she is behind your rapid growth spurts and the pain you've experienced. Your growth is almost complete, and your painful episodes will stop soon.

"Do you understand everything I've said to you?" his father asked again.

"Yes, I do, thank you for telling me," Little Tree answered, thinking about what he'd heard.

"I'm sorry, but there is something else. There is one more job you will have as the tallest tree. Your job will be to stand high above the forest and be the beacon for our beautiful butterfly fairies when they arrive each spring. Each fairy flutter is guided to their assigned forest by seeing the tallest tree. That will be you. They will have come a great distance and will be happy to see you, and, as you know, we are always happy to see the fairies each spring.

"I believe that your growth will stop soon. You should be ready to take over for Oakren at any time now."

Overwhelmed with all this information, Little Tree spoke, "I can't believe I was selected, and I'm happy and proud to do it. I want to make you and Mother proud of me. I promise I won't complain anymore. I'll do my job and stand tall and proud for as long as I live."

Little Tree was already thinking of the future, when he would be a father and be able to enlighten his children about the role of trees in the forest.

Autumn,
Watching the Fall Frenzy

Every creature in the forest noticed the musky, almost sweet aroma that permeated the entire forest. There was no escaping it because it stayed with the animals wherever they walked. They didn't hate it because it was familiar to them, like walking over damp earth and decaying leaves or the pleasant smell of wet grass. The cooler, dryer air that accompanied the scent reminded them that, in the next weeks and months, they needed to start preparing for the beast.

Fall was in the air, and the forest knew it. Mother Nature provided this scent as a prelude to the change of seasons. The animals noticed the shift, and each reacted differently. With the leaves turning colors and the days and nights growing cooler, each animal had preparations on its mind.

Max also started his feeding frenzy to prepare for hibernation. His days were almost entirely spent grazing until nightfall, when he rested to sleep off the food. Every day he gorged on anything he could find. He ate roots, insects, plants, even dead animals he came across. All was done to bulk up and build the fat reserves he needed to survive the winter.

The deer sensed the change coming, and their bodies started growing thicker fur. They surveyed the woods to find shelter from the expected wind and snow. When the time came, they wanted to have the best places picked out to hunker down in groups. They also sought out which plant stems might still be standing and edible during the winter.

Last winter had been nice because deer were fed acorns by the animals, but they wouldn't have that luxury this year. That was a thing of the past because Pippen had grown tall enough that they could no longer reach his branches.

The mice, moles, chipmunks, and squirrels were dashing through the woods looking for acorns and seeds to stock in their homes for the cold months. Animal parents brought in dried grasses and twigs to make their shelters warmer for their children.

The animals were annoyed by the actions of other animals. Why were some running in circles? Why were others hanging upside down from branches? Why were deer letting their antlers drop on the ground? Every animal thought their own actions were perfectly normal, and the actions of others made no sense at all.

Most of the birds couldn't, or wouldn't, risk the cold winters and flew south to warmer climates. They also needed to build up their body fat for the very long trip. All the birds, especially those flying south, were busy stocking up and eating dried berries, seeds, nuts, and fruit. Their food frenzy began in earnest.

The trees always found it entertaining to watch the birds' strange antics during their fall frenzy. Every year the birds unintentionally put on a comedy show for the trees. It wasn't planned; they just got crazy when they met up with their bird friends.

The trees thought it amusing and couldn't figure out why groups of birds started eating berries at one tree, flew to another tree, then another, and then came back to the original tree to eat berries again. The trees judged they either couldn't make up their minds which tree had the tastiest berries, the berry overload caused memory lapses, or they'd just gone temporarily bonkers. The birds' strange antics were impromptu performances for the trees, whether the birds intended them or not.

That day, Little Tree and his parents were watching the birds lose their minds again.

"What are those birds up to now? Look at them, they're acting like crazy clowns. Somebody call the bird doctor!

They're having bird breakdowns!" Mother Tree laughed, making her branches shake.

The trees watched a group of cardinals fly in, to feed on the red currant berries. They spent time perched on the currant bushes, ate a few, then flew to eat the black cherries from the forest's only remaining black cherry tree. There, they jumped branch to branch, cherry to cherry, eating until they were full. They were overloaded on sugar, and they appeared tipsy, weaving and struggling to stand.

The cardinals, who were usually cordial birds, flew into each other, shoving others away from berries. Their calls were obnoxiously loud, much like the crows. The younger cardinals thought it was a game and laughed as they dangled upside down from the branches.

Different bird species took turns feeding. Father Tree pointed to the flock of robins flying in. When the robins approached the cherry tree, the cardinals flew off.

Mother Tree laughed and said, "Just look at those protruding chests already stuffed full of cherries, yet they want more. Look out, trees, they're ready to explode!"

Father Tree laughed and joined her watch. "They're drunk, I say—plastered! They can't stand up anymore, let alone fly. You watch; somebody is going to get hurt."

They watched the show for a few more minutes, and then Mother Tree said, "I'm glad we trees don't act so foolish. My only pet peeve is losing my leaves. I fret each time my leaves fall because I lose my warm coat. But I feel better knowing my leaves nourish the soil and feed the wiggle worms."

Father Tree heard her mention staying warm. "Mother, did you say something about getting cold?"

Mother Tree looked at him strangely because she knew what was coming.

"I know how to warm you up. Let's let our roots entwine, get tangled, twist together, cuddle, and..."

She interrupted and teased, "You mean, *in-ter-weave?*"

"Yup, that," he answered.

"I *am* getting tired of watching these drunken birds. Okay, I guess it's time for my nap. If you want to mosey your way over, you can join me."

"Woohoo, on my way!"

Little Tree had listened to his parents' conversation and wondered who the adults were and who were the children.

Riley's Excitement

Riley, the young maple tree, excitedly called out to get the nearby trees' attention. "My colors are coming! My colors are coming!"

The trees looked at the little maple and, sure enough, his leaves *were* turning red. They chimed, "Way to go, Riley!"

The old maple heard his outburst and said, "Keep it down, will ya, we can see you've turned red."

When Riley shouted, he'd woken the old maple, who was not happy with the young tree's outburst.

"Sorry, sir."

Riley was one of many maples growing in this forest. He was just six years old and couldn't contain his excitement at this time of year.

He loved all the different fall color changes. His trees, the maples, turned bright red and orange. He thought their colors were the brightest and prettiest. The oak trees were just okay, but he thought still pretty. Some oaks turned red, but most turned dull brown. But the poplars, aspens, and birches all had gorgeous yellow leaves; that was his next favorite color.

He loved looking at the colors when they all blended into one stream of color. The reds, yellows, oranges, browns, even some purple leaves, were candy for the senses. Later, their spectacular colors would fade, and the leaves would start dropping to the ground. That's when he liked to see the animals come out and play or dig under the leaves as they looked for food. When the animals walked about, it gave the trees something new to look at.

Riley wanted to visit his friend Pippen to tell him about his colors. "Mother, may I go and play with Pippen?"

"All right, but don't stay long. I want you home before that rain comes in."

"Don't worry, I will be."

Riley's roots were digging very fast to find Pippen's. The two trees were the same age, but their roots were shaped differently. Riley's roots were thinner and traveled faster, while Pippen's apple roots were thicker and very strong. Their different roots always made for interesting play sessions.

Just as his root was about to reach Pippen's tree, he saw movement. He looked away for *just* a second when, SMACK! He crashed into another root head-on with such force that both roots saw stars and sat disoriented.

After a moment, Riley heard laughter. He looked up, and there was Pippen—he had crashed head-on into his best friend. They were both rubbing their eyes and looking at each other's bruises from the crash. Riley looked up and saw water dripping through the dirt. He put his tip up to the water and drank. "Oh, that tastes so good."

Pippen did the same but also let the water drip on his bruise, which helped sooth the pain.

"I was coming to find you." said Riley. "Did you notice that my leaves are *finally* turning? I thought they never would!"

"It's about time," said Pippen, "What took ya so long?"

Not waiting for an answer, Pippen raced off ahead leaving Riley to follow. After going several yards, they slowed to sit and rest. They were breathing heavily and stopped to get their energy back.

Laughter was heard coming from behind. Riley turned and looked back and saw two daisy roots coming up fast on them. Pippen and Riley sped off again, trying their best to keep ahead of the daisies' laughter. When they couldn't hear the giggles, the roots stopped for another break.

Just then, the two daisy roots whizzed past them. One daisy shouted as they went by, "Sorry boys, you may be bigger, but we're faster!" Girl daisy roots disappeared into the underground.

The Renewal Plan

Mother Nature always liked to be present the day the process started in a forest. Earlier that morning, she had found a comfortable place to sit in their tallest tree. Sitting unseen, she looked down and watched as it began.

This was another forest of the north that was being given the regeneration treatment to become healthy and robust again. Mother Nature traveled all over the world to attend hundreds of thousands of these treatments every year to view the "before," and then returned five years later to view the "after." She always found the results interesting and satisfying.

With each forest, it took a great deal of time to reach this day. First, the forest was identified, and for several years it was monitored to assess its decline. She had visited this forest over several seasons to check on the available food supply for the animals, the health of the plants, and, if its health was endangered, before she made the final determination.

The process began three years earlier, when the landowners recognized their forest needed restoration. This came after she had subtly prompted their awareness. Unbeknownst to them, that had started her plan in motion, and the owners carried it forward. She did not like to step in with the work after that point; her main job was to put the well-being of plants and animals, before and after the process, above all else.

Once the owners realized the urgency, they finalized and scheduled the date to begin, and she took over again.

It had been a long process over several years to watch and recruit her animal helpers. She had met with them to explain what was going to happen, describing things they had never known existed. Humans and machines would be coming, and the forest inhabitants had to prepare for changes beyond their control.

These ambassadors then met with the forest to convey what they had learned. They made sure that every plant and animal was aware of what would be happening at some future date and why. Like all the other forests undergoing this process, her job was to see that no forest was ever left unaware.

After watching the work underway for a short time, she determined everything was going according to plan, and she did not need to step in. She knew the landowners would also be monitoring the work.

In five years, she would come back, and, hopefully, see this forest on its way to greatness again. The job of watching a forest nursed back to health never grew old, and she loved it.

With nine more forests scheduled to visit that morning, it was time for her to enter her spherical transport and move on to her next destination.

The Forest Shook

The daisy roots tunneled back to the tree roots and immediately noticed the bruising on them. Miley studied Pippen's bruise from all angles and asked, "Did you guys get in a fight? Are you hurt?"

Still not wanting to talk to them, Pippen shrugged off any notion of pain. Trees were tough; they could take it. Even if their bruises did hurt, he certainly wasn't going to admit it to daisies.

"If you guys look this bad, how do the other guys look?" asked Miley, snickering.

Hearing that, Pippen couldn't hold back his laughter any longer. The picture of him and Riley punching out other roots was laughable.

Pippen was about to respond when all the roots heard a dull humming sound vibrating through the soil. The group sat and listened as it grew louder by the minute. Then the ground started shaking, and all four roots were afraid. They had never heard such a horrid noise in their forest, nor had the ground ever shaken this hard. The small daisy roots clung to the tree roots until the sound finally subsided. They sat and listened, waiting to see if the event had passed.

Two minutes later, the rumbling sound started low again and reached the same deafening level as before. The roots wanted to go back home but dared not move. They were forced to sit planted in place to wait it out. The roots were consumed with fear again as the earth roared and spewed angrily. They watched with horror as the tunnels all around caved in and disappeared under crumbled earth. All four roots found themselves buried and separated from their friends, but still alive.

The pressure was intense as the horror continued unfolding. Besides being worried about each other, Pippen and Riley were concerned about the tiny daisy roots, who were buried and afraid somewhere in the area.

The sound stopped again, but they couldn't see anything. Pippen dug around and found Riley, and together they dug until they found the daisy roots. Coughing and shivering, the daisies clung to the tree roots.

"Hitch a ride, girls," said Pippen, "We'll take you back home."

Side by side, Pippen and Riley inched through the hard ground and found their way back to the daisy patch. Jumping down and trembling, the daisies thanked the tree roots before going back to their parent plants. Riley and Pippen's roots both worked their way back to their trees to wait for news about what happened.

Then, for the third time, the ground suddenly moaned, shook, and vibrated. Pippen heard crying and screaming coming from somewhere above the ground. He could feel the vibrations of things crashing, trees uprooting, and roofs collapsing. Finally, the deafening sound let up. The roots sat quietly again and waited.

Pippen judged the horror must be over. He guessed that by now the animals and birds aboveground must be venturing out from their hiding places, but he could not know for sure. He waited for news to begin trickling down through the root network. It came down through the soil that it was worse than expected. Roots conveyed that fallen limbs and brush were strewn everywhere, much worse than the usual storm damage. Several trees were uprooted and lay on their sides. He heard many bird nests were smashed and strewn haphazardly on the ground.

The roots felt helpless hearing the animals running helplessly back and forth to check on one another. Tree roots were doing the same, trying to get news of fellow trees. Through the soil, Pippen heard the distress of Mr. and Mrs. Mole crying because their roof had caved in, and three of their children perished under the rubble. Many families still desperately looked for family members missing after their homes collapsed. He felt sympathetic to all the pain he was hearing coming from the surface.

Pippen's trunk lost one of his weaker small branches but still stood. He was relieved to receive word from his own roots confirming they were intact and uninjured.

Pippen was worried about his father, Great Apple, who lived on the far side of the meadow. His father was very old, close to seventy years, but he still produced apples. If something had happened to him, Pippen would be the only apple tree growing in this forest.

Pippen sent a message down through his main root, asking it to check on his father. He instructed his longest root to travel as far as it could and then rely on the surrounding root systems to continue the message train. Nearly two hours later, he finally received news back that his father was shaken, but alive. Great Apple was happy to hear the same about Pippen.

Later that day, Pippen received news from Riley that his own roots and tree were fine, only shaken up. Riley also said that one of their old maples uprooted and now lay on its side. Nobody knew if the tree was going to make it.

Over the weeks that followed, the deafening sound and trembling returned every day. Pippen sensed the forest was growing more confused after each passing tremor. After two weeks of enduring this, the sound finally subsided. Forest life was saddened and confused, not knowing the reason for this unwanted intrusion. They wondered if it was finally over, or if it would return at some unexpected time. They wanted answers.

There were so many possible theories, but none were feasible. There was only one unseen entity who could provide the reason and the answers.

For generations, the forest had told stories of Mother Nature's existence. She was said to be the powerful caretaker of all living things on this Earth. It was said she was all-knowing, sympathetic, and kind. She was constantly on the move, hovering and watching, looking for ways to help life continue. Even though she had never shown herself, the forest believed she existed. Just believing she was watching over the forest, gave Pippen comfort in these troubling days.

The Forest Voted

The sun rose and slept for three days in a row. Animal families tended to their injured and mourned the deaths of loved ones. Cleanup commenced, and everyone did what they could to make their homes livable again. Denser parts of the forest bore the most damage. Some older trees could not withstand the constant vibrations. This caused their already brittle trunks to crack and split, bringing limbs and trunks crashing to the ground. As new information arrived, roots quickly recorded each unfortunate event.

There had never been a reason to question *why* things happened in the forest. Forests grew accustomed to change if they were forced to deal with it repeatedly. For example, the seasons—they had dealt with seasonal changes for millions of years; they knew what to expect and had adapted to them. If plants or animals needed to question the reason for something, they asked their elders, who gave answers that had been passed down to them.

Throughout time, this forest had never been in enough peril or had an urgent enough reason to approach her highness, Mother Nature. But these recent weeks of disturbances had left even the elders perplexed about how to answer questions from the young. To the young and old, the disturbance had been a complete mystery.

After several weeks without disturbances, the forest called a community meeting to address questions and concerns. Animals converged from all corners of the forest, and trees were asked to pay attention and take notes. The matter of whether they would ask Mother Nature about these disturbances was going to be discussed and put to a vote. If it passed, the next issue would be how to initiate and carry out the contact.

The animals had an opportunity to tell of the hardships they experienced after the anomaly. This was a long and painstaking process, but it had to be done to get the bigger picture of the urgency. The stories would help determine the level of damage and fear and, sadly, the number of casualties.

Mr. and Mrs. Mole were both still visibly shaken. They told of how the vibrations loosened the soil over their house, making the earth collapse, which resulted in the death of three of their five children.

Frederica, looking quite pale, said the noise had caused her to have a hormonal imbalance, and she was unsure whether she would ever be able to lay eggs again. Tate looked at her with sorrowful eyes and showed support for his mate. The other birds didn't know what she was talking about but still nodded their heads because it sounded plausible. Some birds said the vibrations forced them to hold on to branches for dear life. Others said their young who could fly took to the air in fear. They hadn't seen them since.

The deer said the endless loud noise and rumbling had left them feeling defenseless. "Our ears are still ringing, and our eyesight has worsened since the trembling. There was no place to go to escape it. We thought for sure it was the end for us."

Benji said that when the rumbling started, he would run to his big rock, hide behind it, and squat down. He tried to be invisible and hoped the noise wouldn't harm him. Twice he dug a new burrow but was afraid to live in it. He had been living by the rock, where he felt safer. "Everyone had their own problems," he said, "I didn't want to ask for help."

"That trembling was so loud that I lost my appetite," Max said. The animals looked questioningly at each other. Was it even possible for him NOT to be hungry? He then added, "I'm so weak, I used most of my energy just to get here."

The crickets, ants, and other bugs stood and shouted to be heard. "The vibrations kept wiping out our homes. We rebuilt, and they went down again. We can't survive out in the open!"

The daisies confessed their roots were so frightened that many of them were unable to retain water and couldn't grow. "Many of our flowers broke off and fell to the ground. With the flowers gone, we could not produce nectar for the bees and hummingbirds."

Old Oakren, the tallest tree who normally presided over important meetings, took a beating from the disturbance, and asked Little Tree to handle the meeting that day. Oakren knew that Little Tree was taking over for him soon and he wanted him to learn to handle meetings confidently.

After much discussion, Little Tree asked if anyone else had something to add. No one spoke up, and it was time for the vote.

"All right, we're taking a vote on the question of whether we should find a way to contact Mother Nature about the source and reason of those disturbances. Just remember that your vote is never the wrong vote. Everyone's vote matters."

Little Tree asked, "Everyone in favor of doing this, say 'yay.'"

"Yay!" said the forest.

Little Tree, along with the forest, heard the forcefulness of the yay votes.

"Those not in favor, say 'nay.'"

The remainder of the participants said, "Nay." A smaller number of nays were heard.

The voting was over, and the yes votes outweighed the no votes. It was decided they would find a way to approach Mother Nature to get answers to their questions. The elders voted against this action. Many felt it was an unnecessary intrusion on Mother Nature's time. Others felt attempting to do this was unnecessary and might upset the natural order she maintained.

CHAPTER SEVEN
The Passing and the Peril

Year Two, Fall,
Old Oakren

OAKREN WAS A VERY OLD and revered red oak tree. Root records indicated that Oakren had lived almost 200 years in this forest. One hundred and fifty years ago, his father told him the reason for his astonishing height of 200 feet. Mother Nature had chosen him to be the new tallest tree and helped him to grow to his great height. For 150 years, he held the job of presiding over everything in this forest.

He loved his job and, besides being the forest's warning voice for storms and other dangers, he enjoyed guiding the butterfly fairies every spring. In his years on the job, he had made wonderful friends, met his love Victoria, and fathered hundreds of offspring. He had lived a good life without any regrets.

Oakren still stood but was weary of life. His bark had crumbled off, and many of his branches had either broken, fallen off, or were dying. Woodpeckers found his dead branches desirable and made holes to find bugs. Worms had invaded his trunk and left him with thousands of tiny holes. Any bark that remained had turned silver-gray, not the handsome reddish brown of his youth.

He had known for some time that his end of life was nearing. He'd also noticed the rapid growth of Little Tree and assumed the young tree was to be his replacement. He'd heard from his roots that Little Tree's father had already passed the news of the honor to his son. Oakren saw Little Tree as an excellent choice because of his sturdy frame and great height. On top of that, he had the friendship and trust of the forest.

Oakren thought about all the years he'd stood in the forest—most were good, some bad. He had such fond memories of life with Victoria, the tree next door. In his younger years, he loved growing up next to Victoria. As young trees, their roots played together as they got to know each other. As they got older, their roots preferred to talk quietly about life in the forest. They fell in love and committed their lives to each other.

He'd been utterly beguiled by Victoria and stared at her for hours. She was a beauty with her lovely branches and stately stance. She had captured his heart. Through all their years together, he had been the happiest tree in the forest.

One evening, Oakren saw dark clouds approaching their forest. He immediately sent down a storm warning to the roots, who would notify all underground inhabitants of the impending threat. Warnings also circulated aboveground, and every creature was told to find shelter immediately and to expect a long night of wind and rain.

The storm lasted a long time, with pelting rain and gusting winds. In the morning, the forest was in shambles.

The ground was deluged with water and the winds that traveled through were vicious and merciless to everything. Many trees were uprooted with no mercy shown to the young or old.

This was the storm that took his dear Victoria. A bolt of lightning came out of nowhere, struck her, and seared her trunk down to her core. As he watched her fall, his roots rushed immediately to hers. He held her until her roots became limp. Life was leaving her as he pleaded with her, "Come back to me, please, my dear, this can't be the end."

He prayed for a miracle, and for a moment there was one. A slight movement indicated her heartwood heard him and awakened long enough for him to hear, "I love you, Oakren." And then, nothing.

Throughout the night, he held her and thought of their lives together and all the children they had raised to see adulthood. He would remember and love her for the rest of his days. Finally, after a tearful goodbye, he released her roots so she could rest in peace.

His Last Breath

Many years later, he looked down at his trunk. His branches were bare, no longer healthy enough to grow leaves. The last time his leaves had fallen, they had never grown back. Now burrowing bugs tormented him because his bark had crumbled off and left him vulnerable to pests.

Oakren was mystified as to why he had lived this long. He'd lived longer than all the other trees he had known growing up. His parents were gone, his Victoria was gone, and most of his children were gone. He felt alone and wanted to move on, but every day he kept on living. His body told him it was time to go but, in his heart, he did not want to give up his memories. Reminiscing about his life had kept him alive.

Since the day he had first sprouted, he had loved this forest. Pictures of his life flashed before him as memories came to mind. He remembered his seedling buddies who became his fast friends for life, his parents, and the love they shared, and the day his father explained his role in the forest's survival.

Oakren thought of his growing years, and all the lessons taught by his father, *"Stand tall, take turns, and always love your mother."* His mother had been so patient and the most loving tree. She had consoled him through his growing pains, taught him to be humble and kind, and to be compassionate toward the less fortunate. She always praised him and showed pride in his reliable weather predictions.

He remembered Victoria and all those years by her side. They had always watched the beautiful sunsets together. They had loved looking at the fall colors, and every year they had watched the fall frenzy together. And, of course, he had never forgotten the storm and how he had wept the night she died. He believed it was her memory that helped him sustain life all these years. Her voice was what he still heard, and it calmed his fears.

The time had come, and he was ready. He stretched his roots out for the last time. With great effort, he said goodbye to the nearby trees, flowers, and grass. With a heavy heart, he bid all he saw a good life. His death was imminent, and he asked them not to cry but to remember him fondly. He knew his life had been grand as he let his spirit return to the earth.

A doe and her fawn lingered by his trunk. They seemed to know that Oakren had left them. They continued walking to tell the forest the news.

Oakren's Passing

Every tree, shrub, berry bush, and blade of grass received word of the old tree's passing. The plants all remembered Oakren as already being the tallest tree when they had first sprouted and had lived knowing no other tree. They had grown to rely on Oakren and his wisdom and knew he would be greatly missed.

The forest knew that death was a fact of life. Everything was on Mother Nature's clock and expected to perish at some time. Plant and animal remains diminished, but their names and life details had been recorded in root records. Every plant and animal left behind someone who remembered their existence. Stories were passed to new generations of plants about their ancestors, and those stories would continue to get passed down to future generations.

Trees passed on stories of enduring terrible droughts and how they had suffered without rain for many weeks. The ground had been parched, worms had barely hung on, and the roots had lain lazy and wilted. They had waited for rain but had not complained because there was nothing to gain by it. Instead, the elders had taught their children to restrict their movements to conserve energy, which would decrease their need for water.

Young plants heard the story of the year when a terrible storm had come through and downed many trees. Several beloved trees had been struck by lightning and killed. They were told of how old Oakren had lost his partner in that lightning storm and how, many years later, he had died of old age and a broken heart.

The forest mourned, but it carried on. On the day Oakren died, Little Tree immediately took over as the new tallest tree and assumed all the responsibilities the honor entailed. The news was sent underground, and the animals spread the word aboveground.

Life was hard in the forest, but they were forced to return to their daily routines. With the beast fast approaching, they had to begin preparing for their own survival.

Late Fall,
When Danger Lurks

The animals were tense and on alert. They were uneasy because they knew the beast was getting nearer. They had encountered the beast before and knew nothing could stop its entrance.

The beast was huge and would easily overpower anything in its path. Just knowing it was hungry and approaching their forest put everyone on edge. As they waited, they felt they were being manipulated by a more powerful force.

The winds warned daily of the proximity of the encroaching menace. Animals huddled with their kind, the birds had stopped singing, and the forest was in a state of dread.

The forest elders told stories of how the beast hid for weeks and then unexpectedly pounced. The elders were truthful when asked because the young needed to know what to expect and that their lives were in danger. They said when it pounced, it would try to overtake them, but they should stay strong to outsmart it.

Many birds would not risk falling prey and retreated from the forest until they knew the beast had gone back into hiding. Some birds, having dealt with it before, stayed and were prepared to fight.

The forest didn't know when the beast would pounce. Most of the time, it came at night when they woke up to its presence. Other times, it boldly showed its face in broad daylight. Every year it stayed hidden until the air was chilled, then made a surprise appearance. It was not invited or welcomed, but it arrived anyway. The forest hated its bullish behavior and obscene appearance but bore its presence in silence. It tormented the forest for months on end, took many lives, and would go back into hiding for another year.

Readying for Battle

The animals noticed the shortened daylight hours. The dropping temperatures prodded their bodies to grow thicker fur, and they began storing food in caches for the winter. The deer knew what was coming and became less active to conserve energy and add fat reserves.

The birds that didn't want to stick around rallied in groups. For the past weeks, they had been upping their food intake to build body weight and gain more energy. They then flew away in flocks to a warmer climate to escape from the threat. They planned to retrace their route back when the threat disappeared.

Stu, Jack, and Bobber were among the birds who didn't risk their lives by staying and flew south with some of the other crows. The other birds—the brave ones—did the same preparation work as those that fled but stayed to confront the beast. These birds were strong and courageous and deserved a medal for their bravery.

Max never wanted to test fate. He, like many of the animals, ate more and put on a lot of weight. He knew he needed the extra bulk for his body to live off during hibernation. Max usually waited until the beast was right on their doorstep; then he went into his den for his deep sleep.

Besides Max, the squirrels, chipmunks, and groundhogs all fattened their bodies to increase their fat reserves. With their shelters in place, they waited for Max to make the first move. When he went down, they all did.

Benji and the other rabbits in the area reinforced their walls and added more dried grass and leaves to their homes to be warm and safe from the beast. They stockpiled food in their shelters to be eaten only in dire emergencies. They hoped to be able to crawl out occasionally to look for food when the beast wasn't watching.

With preparations in place for the beast's arrival, the forest planned to outwit the threat with its common sense and will to live.

It Arrived

Temperatures dropped, and the forest was uneasy, not knowing the whereabouts of the beast. Creatures were exhausted from preparations and wanted the ordeal of the visit to be over. The eerie sound of bare branches rubbing against bare branches sent shivers through the forest as it envisioned the beast crashing through at any moment. But the noises were only a warning that it lurked and could pounce at any moment.

The next morning, the forest woke up to an icy white blanket. The menace had arrived during the night without giving notice and bearing a grudge. Frosty hatred was spewed as it looked for a fight. It got its fight because the forest was willful and ready to withstand its mean impulses.

The arrival was always accompanied by snow and cold temperatures. Many inches of snow buried the forest, and it had been bitterly cold. Day and night, the plants and animals stood up to the beast. They struggled but vowed to keep standing and not be toppled. For three months, the unwanted guest resided in their presence. With it came icy, blustery winds that made their lives miserable. Many of the young, less resilient plants succumbed to its wrath and lay bent over and lifeless. The hungry small animals, who dared to venture out for food, were caught unaware when cold winds paralyzed them, and they perished.

There was nothing more the animals could do except conserve their energy inside their shelters. They sat and prayed for the day the beast would go away, and warmer temperatures would come back.

Seven days passed, and the vile menace appeared to be sleeping. There had been no sight of it, and everyone hoped its days were numbered.

Mr. Mole took this opportunity to check in on Benji. When he entered Benji's hole, he found him sleeping and tapped his head to wake him. Benji rubbed his eyes and heard Mr. Mole's voice.

"Benji, how are you doing? It's a nice day and I thought I'd come over and check on you."

"Oh, hello, Mr. Mole," replied Benji, "Is that thing gone?"

"We don't know yet—it's too early to tell. But it might be. Some of us are venturing out to check on other families."

"Thanks for coming by. I'm okay, I've still got food. Will you let me know for sure when it's gone so I can go out too?"

"You bet I will. You take it easy and don't go out until I come back and say it's safe. I'm heading over to check on my cousin and his family now."

"I'm going back to sleep then. See ya later." He yawned and closed his eyes again.

"Bye, Benji."

As Mr. Mole headed to his cousin's house, he noticed the snow was covered with many other animal tracks. He was happy seeing he wasn't alone in taking advantage of this warmer day to go out and about.

Traces of the beast's presence would occasionally surprise the animals when they woke in the morning. However, by midday it had slithered away. With these brief returns and exits, the animals ventured out more confidently each day.

The elders cautioned, "It comes back when you least expect it. Be careful." Senses were on high alert in case the beast returned.

But the forest's prayers were answered. The threat grew bored and retreated to hunt new prey. They knew it had left the forest because the air smelled fresh and clean again. The stench, to which they'd become accustomed, had disappeared. It wouldn't be long now before their beautiful fairies arrived with their healing mists. The arrival of the fairies would be the sign needed to finally put their fears to rest for another year.

CHAPTER EIGHT
Wings of Change

Year Three, Spring,
The Mission Began

ZELINA WAS NESTLED COMFORTABLY on her right side, sandwiched between two other butterfly fairies. Her assigned spot was space 107 in row fifteen of the fifty-row-high tower of Flitterdom Building Five. She was sleeping with her chin, chest, and legs tucked into the body of the fairy ahead of her in space 108, with the fairy in space 106 behind her, doing the same.

The open-air quarters let the cool evening breezes flow between the rows. The sweet scents of acacia, gardenia, and jasmine wafted while the night birds sang the fairies to sleep. The body heat generated from the mass of sleeping fairies kept their quarters warm and comfortable.

That night, Zelina was restless. She reclined, thinking about the mission that their colony had been assigned. They didn't know when they would leave, but they were expected to be ready on a moment's notice. Each morning, the colony noticed the weather, waiting for the perfect conditions that would allow ease of flying. When the conditions were perfect, Mother Nature gave the go-ahead order. They would obey and immediately depart.

In her fitful sleep, Zelina suddenly jerked awake. Squeezing out from between the two other butterfly fairies, she stretched her arms in the air and yawned. Before her mouth closed, her eyes widened as her body detected the change in the morning temperature. She knew the temperature spike was Mother Nature's way of telling the fairies that today they should be on their way.

Every day, there was a different leader of the colony. Whoever was the first to rise oversaw waking up the others as no oversleeping was allowed. Zelina looked around, and all the fairies were lined up and sleeping. There was no sound coming from above or below to indicate any other fairy was awake. Zelina thought, *Oh, my goodness, I'm the first one up. I'm in charge!*

Zelina had never been in charge, and she hesitated to leave her position. But she knew she must act because Mother Nature might be watching and grading her actions.

Mother Nature had already planned this departure date and made sure the weather conditions were right. Whoever was the first to rise would automatically know they had Mother Nature's approval to depart.

First, Zelina cleared her throat and timidly spoke, "All wake up, please." There was no reaction from the sleeping fairies. She mustered her wits and will and filled her lungs with air. With great force, Zelina belted out, "Wake up! The change has come. We must leave!"

The fairies heard her that time. Everyone rustled from their sleeping position with a look of confusion on their faces. The change had come. *What change? Go where?* In an instant, the fairies' excitement grew as they realized what their leader had just said. Her message was spread to all the lower and upper rows and soon every fairy in Building Five was alert and awake.

Building Five was one of the many fairy dwellings in Flitterdom. Each was an open-air tower with 50 stacked rows, and each was designed to house thousands of sleeping fairies. Even though it was called Building Five, there was no building. There were no walls, only level upon level of sleeping platforms that allowed wind, heat, and scent to circulate freely throughout the colony.

The multitude of fairies filled every available airspace in Building Five. Each fairy, with their distinctive wing shade, flew quickly to assemble on the grass outside the building. It was an amazing sight as fairies, from young to old, with wings of every color and hue, arrived to gather in the staging area to be counted. Each fairy was already aware of their new mission, and based on the sound their wings were making, there was a lot of excitement to get underway.

Zelina watched as each fairy stood on the ground ahead of her and folded back their wings. She shouted, "Number off for roll call!"

Every morning, the leader took roll call to determine if any of the fairies were missing. A missing fairy might indicate oversleeping, a sleepwalking fairy who had wandered off, an obstinate fairy refusing to take part, or, sadly, a fallen fairy taken by the cold.

Starting with the number one, each fairy shouted out its number as Zelina kept track of any missing numbers. In the blink of an eye, they accounted for every fairy of the 10,000 fairies in Flitterdom Building Five.

"Fairies, follow me, it is time to go!" Zelina walked to the lead, unfolded her wings, and looked back at the eager group. The fairies were waiting for her to lift off, which would be their cue to follow.

Zelina smiled at them, raised one wing as a cue, and—poof—disappeared into the air. Then, poof, all the other fairies disappeared behind her to catch up.

To be the leader on any morning was a high honor, but to be the leader on the morning of a mission departure was an extremely high honor. She had to remember to do everything she was trained to do and do it carefully, because there were thousands of fairy lives depending on her actions. She slowed down and waited for the fairies to catch up. They were in sight, and she knew they saw her. With the fairies in sight behind her, Zelina moderately increased her speed to fly comfortably as a group to their destination.

The warm spring breezes were exhilarating, and sometimes they didn't need to move their wings as the breezes pushed them along. They planned a seven-day trip, two days to fly there, three days with the animals, and two days flying back—with nightly rest stops each day. After five hours of flying, Zelina felt no exhaustion and was pleased with her progress on day one.

Butterfly Fairies

The butterfly fairies in Colony Five numbered 10,000. They were only one of thousands of colonies living in the warm, temperate climate of Flitterdom.

The fairies were the creation of Mother Nature. Millions of years ago, she had created them to be her special helpers. She wished she could be everywhere at once, but in the spring she could not and needed help. In addition to tending to the important tasks of providing oxygen, water, and food, she also monitored the health of forests and sustained life.

She found she needed help fostering goodwill and renewing life each spring. The plants and animals that survived their winters were weak and downtrodden. Many were starving, their spirits broken, with little will to go on. Each forest in the colder parts of the world had inhabitants suffering and in need of special attention.

That was where the fairies came in. She created them to have unstoppable spirits, high-energy bodies, and loving hearts. Wherever she sent them, they unquestionably obeyed, and wherever they went, they always fulfilled their missions and flew back home.

Butterfly fairy bodies measured only one-half inch in height and were one-quarter inch in width without their wings. They were tiny compared to other creatures, but size was not a measure of their intelligence. They were among the smartest creatures in the world, possessing the strength and wisdom of the ages.

Their wingspan on each side measured several inches which was wide in relation to their height. Mother created them with large wings to handle any type of wind and reach their destinations quickly. Even when traveling with their large wings, they were hardly noticeable, as their wings were translucent and blended with the environment. Only creatures with very keen eyes knew they existed and caught sight of them.

Every year she sent them north on their missions. The forest she planned for them to visit that year was badly hurting after the beast departed. She warmed the temperature for the fairies that morning to get them on their way more quickly.

The land of Flitterdom was mystical, full of history and lore. Nobody knew its location except Mother Nature and her fairies. Butterfly fairy populations were huge and increased every year, but fairies were so tiny they lived virtually concealed. They were created solely to help Mother Nature on Earth and to let woodlands know they were not alone.

The Fairy Arrival

Back in Flitterdom, the fairies flew from station to station daily and trained for their missions, but they didn't feel the exhilaration of flying high and getting pushed by the winds. They were jealous of Mother because she got to do this every day. That day, they felt the same exhilaration.

From behind, she heard the fairies giggling. Zelina concentrated on their flight path and hadn't noticed other colonies flying beside them. The fairies were making funny faces and waving to the others. Zelina did the same but also kept her eyes on the airspace ahead.

She looked down and spotted a place that looked suitable for their nightly layover. There was a stream where they could wash their faces and the accumulated dust from their wings. They had flown for ten hours; Mother didn't want them to fly more than that in a day.

Her speed slowed, indicating to the colony that they would be descending. The fairies followed their leader and, without touching the ground, gathered in a mossy area beside the stream. Dewdrops puddled in nearby leaves, and the fairies assembled in small groups to take sips. When each had finished, Zelina led them to the giant elephant-ear leaf, where a bountiful supper was prepared before them. Mother had magically set the food out while they were quenching their thirst. The fairies were hungry after their full day of flying and were happy to eat their favorite foods of fruits and nuts, dainty fairy-sized sandwiches, and delicious macaroons.

Before going to bed, faces were washed, fingers combed through hair, and wings inspected. If any wing was damaged and needed mending, this was done before bedtime, as there wouldn't be time in the morning.

After their nightly roll call and tasks were finished, the fairies lay on the moss under the giant elephant-ear leaves and huddled close together, just as they did in Flitterdom Building Five. Soon, the trickling sound of the stream, combined with the fairies' body warmth lulled them to sleep.

Zelina oversaw the mission from start to finish. In the morning, she woke the fairies with the piercing sound of air passing between two blades of grass. This startled them awake, and they gathered for breakfast and roll call. They soon followed their leader for another full day of flying.

On the second evening, Zelina announced their destination forest would come into view after two hours of flight the next morning. Most of the fairies had been on missions before and didn't need to hear instructions. For the benefit of those on their first mission, Zelina reminded them of their responsibilities to plants and animals. She also cautioned them to return to the designated meetup place before sunset; they all knew why.

The next morning, after they had flown for two hours, Zelina thought she saw the tallest tree in the distance. A few minutes later, she knew it was the tree Mother had told her to look for. It was monstrous, standing stately and regal above all the others. The tree saw the colony approaching, and its branches moved in a welcoming fashion. It was a welcome sight for the weary travelers after their long flight.

The Deer and the Butterfly Fairy

Hollyhock's legs were unsteady, and her body trembled. She thought this was the path she remembered from last fall but wasn't entirely sure. There was always some type of berry or wildflower to eat there, but that day she found nothing. She sniffed the snow and smelled acorns. Putting her nose in the snow again, she found only broken shells; other animals had found and eaten them before her.

She made her way to the blackberry patch she remembered and hoped a few dried berries remained that she could eat. She found the naked stems of last year's bushes and walked into their midst, but there was nothing on the vines except thorns. Rather than walk in further, she backed out and then noticed the thorns had punctured her hide and drawn blood.

Standing outside the old berry patch, she became disheartened and didn't know where to go next. She didn't recall the beast ever being this harsh. It had worn all the animals down to shells of their former selves. She wished for the taste of wildflowers, fruits, and nuts. But the new growth hadn't started, making her hungry and impatient.

She heard an unusual pulsing sound and abruptly turned her head. Her first thought was that it was a bee, but it was too early for bees, as there were no flowers yet. Hollyhock considered running for cover, but then she saw a creature so tiny, its body no larger than a bee, with beautiful large translucent wings. As it hovered by her head, she recognized it as one of those butterfly fairies that visited her in previous springs. She knew there was nothing to fear.

For a creature this tiny, she shouldn't have been able to hear it speak, but in the universal animal language she heard, "Mrs. Deer, please hear what I am about to say."

Hollyhock stood and stared at the fairy. Her long eyelashes blinked slowly, and her body relaxed.

"My name is LindaMay, and I am your butterfly fairy. My colony of fairies has been sent to this forest by Mother Nature. We are here to help the weary, wounded, and distressed plants and animals."

Hollyhock stood as the fairy hovered and examined the condition of her body. The fairy seemed to know that winter had taken a toll on the deer and felt her pain.

"Let me soothe your pain," said the fairy. Throwing her hands up, she twirled three times in the air and smiled. When she did that, a mist surrounded the deer. "I have showered you with healing mists. In a few moments, your body will heal, and your pain will disappear."

As the mist landed on Hollyhock's body, it permeated her hide and had an immediate effect. She felt better; her gashes and the blood from the thorns disappeared, and her body felt pain-free.

"Is that better?" asked the fairy in a sweet voice.

"Yes, it is, thank you," replied Hollyhock, speaking for the first time. She raised her head as high as she could and stretched her body, loving the feeling of being pain-free.

"Wonderful! Consider yourself butterfly fairy kissed." The fairy laughed and twirled upward again, pleased with herself and the deer's response.

Hollyhock watched as the fairy made another lifting motion with her arms and seeds fell to the ground around them. She watched them land, and in an instant, sprout.

Hollyhock was amazed and looked from the new shoots to the fairy.

The fairy flew over to a nearby stem, neatly folded back her wings, and said, "Now, please tell me your story."

Hollyhock told her about her ordeal with the beast. She explained how cold it had been, how she and the other deer huddled together to stay warm, and how during snowstorms they lay with their heads buried down against their chests. At night, they felt safer and ventured out for food together, but food was hard to find buried under the snow.

After spending time with her, the fairy giggled and twirled again. LindaMay explained it was time to be on her way and waved. She wished her good luck and flew off. As she did, the scent of wildflowers lingered in the air, and Hollyhock noticed more new growth beginning to appear on the ground. She stood and sniffed, enjoying the scent, and hoped it would linger all day. It reminded her that better days were ahead.

The Fairy Heroes

By mid-afternoon of the second day, each fairy in the colony had visited at least five of the inhabitants above or below ground. Plants, however, were a different story. Plants outnumbered the animals, but most still slept dormant underground. The fairies threw healing mists on the above-ground plants' dried stems with the hope they would penetrate their roots and revive them. They visited all the trees, shrubs, climbers, and creepers. From towering to squatty, they visited them all. Each got their fairy kiss, a kind listening ear, and a handful of new seeds.

There was a soft breeze that day, and the fragrance of fairies filled the air. The scent was intoxicating, and the forest was relishing and reliving their visits.

Light was fading, and the fairies were tired. They started to gather in the appointed rest area, laughing and telling each other about their experiences there. This forest would soon be producing new growth, and the animals would find more food. The fairies wished they could stay to witness the new growth, but could not, as the next morning they were expected to depart for Flitterdom.

Three fairies named Edna, Ivy, and Rosalyn were best friends and were resting in a different part of the forest. A short sprinkle came through, and they took cover under leaves until it passed. They looked at each other and laughed because each of them was dirty from head to foot. Soon their laughter became contagious and they couldn't stop.

The rain stopped, and they held down the tips of the leaves to pour water from their cradles. They were splashing it on their faces and wings and taking long drinks of the fresh water. Edna started singing, and the other two joined in:

> *"We three butterfly fairies,*
> *Lifelong friends are we,*
> *We'll always be together,*
> *Throughout eternity."*

They sang the verse repeatedly until they settled back on their leaves, each reflecting on their time there. They loved being there and helping, but they also looked forward to returning home with all the other fairies and, of course, Mother.

While they sang and enjoyed the fresh scent after the rain, they didn't realize it was late and past the appointed meeting time. As the air chilled, the light began to fade. The three shivered as the cool air crept over their bodies. The fairies, now concerned, decided there was no harm in spending the night huddled together. At sunup, they would fly and meet up with the others in the morning before the roll call.

As the sun went down, the three fairies put their arms around each other and gathered on a leaf. Their body warmth was distributed between the three. The air was cooler than they liked it to be, but they had the others to keep them warm.

> *"We three butterfly fairies,*
> *Lifelong friends are we,*
> *We'll always be together,*
> *Throughout eternity."*

Tears of the Fairies

Back at the flutter, Zelina watched the multitude of fairies gathering on the ground, talking among themselves. As the body heat circulated throughout the group, she sensed a wave of drowsiness sweep over them. They positioned themselves in rows, and the flutter fell asleep. Zelina closed her eyes as well, but her thoughts lingered on their plans for leaving the next morning.

Zelina was again the first to stir in the morning. She stretched and did a quiet count of the sleeping bodies. Her count showed three fairies were missing. She felt a knot form in her stomach and wondered if she had miscounted the day before. Thoughts went through her mind: *What if*

I'm right? What if something happened overnight? She resolved to take a precise count when the fairies were all awake.

In a firm voice, she called out, "Wake up fairies! Prepare for roll call." Wings rustled, and a minute later the fairies were lined up. Zelina counted the fairies twice, and, yes, three fairies were missing. Her chest tightened. *Please let them just be late.*

Knowing which three were missing, search parties flew out to look for them. Zelina stayed behind to wait, every part of her body tense. When the searchers returned, their solemn expressions told her the truth.

The missing fairies had been found on a leaf with their arms encircling each other, their bodies still and cold. She had feared this, but hearing it confirmed made her wings feel heavy. The fairies were gently swaddled in leaves and carried to the ground. Prayers were whispered, and Mother Nature was notified. Zelina knew their fairy souls were already in Mother's care. That brought some comfort.

Zelina knew the ritual well: Back home, the fallen fairies' names were already recorded in the great journal. There was a place for fairies to write sentiments and adieus. If they wanted, tears could be dropped; butterfly fairies left quite a few.

Before they left for home, Zelina felt a responsibility to have an impromptu meeting. She felt she couldn't leave for home without saying a few words. Chatter faded as faces turned toward her.

"Before we leave," she said, her voice steadier than she felt, "there is something I want to say. If you haven't heard, three of our sister fairies did not survive the cold." She watched as more sorrow showed on their faces. "This is why none of us should sleep alone on missions. Our bodies are not made for cold nights. That is why we live in warm Flitterdom. Please, don't take chances. We want every fairy here to live long enough to become an old fairy."

As she spoke, she felt better giving them the reminder they needed to hear. Vigilance could save their lives, and she silently vowed to never let this happen unnoticed again.

Late Spring,
A Day in the Life of Fairies

The fairies led active lives in Flitterdom. Their days were highly regimented with class assignments each day. All the colonies lived by a simple rule: Classwork had to be done before they could play.

Every morning, the fairies washed and dried their wings with dew from leaves and groomed themselves. Then, they waited for their leader to call for attendance; each hoped they would be a leader someday. They stood in line with wings neatly folded back, as the leader counted every head. Each day, she recorded their daily number, but this ritual was always dreaded.

If there was a change in number from the previous day, it was a reason for sadness. If a fairy was missing, a search commenced immediately. If the fairy was found alive, there was happiness; if not, the name was recorded, and the soul went home to Mother Nature. All fallen fairies were considered heroes because each was courageous in their own special way.

Three weeks had passed since the flutter returned from their northern mission. The roll count had been taken, the fairy count was the same, and they were eager to start their lessons.

Seated in rows in small groups, they recited their names. In one small group there were DebAnna, Zelina, and Beulah. Seated across from them were LindaMay, JudyMar, and Joy. Just like when they were younger, they still made faces at each other and loved to annoy the other fairies.

For millions of years, exercise and education were their top priorities. Fairies needed to be smart to preserve their kingdom and be strong to be able to fly on missions. Each fairy had three books placed before them. They were required to read all three books within one hour. When they were done, they would sit with their hands clasped in their laps. Reading was their favorite subject as they knew they would be smarter by doing so.

What happened next was amazing. The fairies chose one of the books and placed it in front of them. They folded their hands in their lap, looked down, and read the book from start to finish without opening the book. When they had grasped all the words and envisioned all the pictures, they selected their next book. By the end of the hour, all the fairies had read three books.

With reading over, the fairies unfolded their wings and all the fairies from all the flutters flew to meet in the great meadow. This was an amazing sight as young and old converged from every direction. Sunshine made their wings sparkle and the influx of bodies, bumping and swiping when they came together, always caused laughter. They quickly found a comfortable spot on the ground and waited. Excitement increased as it was time to hear the morning message from their great maker, Mother Nature.

They never knew what she was going to talk about. She liked to keep them abreast of important news from the outside. It saddened them to hear of droughts and floods, areas having had excessive heat, and others with excessive cold. Mother reassured them that she was monitoring the situations but only interfered in extreme cases. She liked to tell stories about the different forests they visited on their missions.

That day, her voice sounded serious and urgent. She took a few minutes to tell the backstory that involved a special request for volunteers.

"The forest that Flutter Five just visited has undergone a traumatic event. I'm not talking about their hard winter. Last fall, as they were getting ready for winter, they experienced weeks of loud noise and earth trembling. It caused a lot of damage and hardship in their forest. They wanted to know the reason but decided to wait until spring to try and reach me."

The fairies listened but whispered among themselves, asking if anyone knew about this.

"I could have gone to them, but I don't normally interfere with these matters. Besides, I do not show myself to anyone except to you, my butterfly fairies."

The fairies all smiled at her, all feeling special.

"The forest doesn't know this yet, but I am going there very soon to select a group of animals who will act as ambassadors from the forest to meet with me. This will involve a long journey on their part over several days to reach me. Once they reach me, I will give them answers to their questions."

The fairies hoped to get more information about the source of the noise and trembling, but Mother didn't offer it. They didn't know she had held back that information for a good reason. She wanted to know which fairies would volunteer for another mission having just returned from their spring mission. She also wanted to know who would put the needs of others over her own without knowing what it entailed. This would show their commitment to their duties, who was flexible, and who were truly committed to helping others.

"I am asking for four volunteers to go on a special mission. This will involve flying two days there, doing the mission, and flying two days back." She provided little information, which puzzled the fairies. Having just returned from their spring assignments, many were reluctant to volunteer again so soon.

There was a moment of silence as fairies contemplated her request. Then, many hands rose. Mother was pleased with the response, looked over the hands raised, and made her selections. She thanked everyone for listening and especially those who volunteered. She would speak privately to the volunteers to give more details.

The fairies flew back to their village as more activities were planned for their day. As they flew back, many wildflowers called out, "Please, stop and smell my bouquet," as each flower thought their scent was the loveliest. The bees looked up as the fairies passed by and then continued flying from flower to flower. Each flutter reunited to resume their day's activities.

When they returned, it was time for exercise. They spaced themselves apart to practice their acrobatics. With great speed, they flew up high as if thrust up by an air current, twisted and turned in the air, and practiced falling as if dropped. Every day they flew laps around the compound to increase stamina. After two hours of exercise, they were exhausted and sat and rested on the ground. It took only a few seconds before they were back gathering petals and seeds for their magic. So many supplies were needed, and there were never enough to spare.

After lunch, with work and exercise behind them, it was time for cleanliness and mending. The girls took this time to bathe and fashion their hair. They wore flowery head wreaths while they went about their work. If buttons were missing, they found seeds, fashioned two holes, and attached with spider's silk and a makeshift needle. This was the time for repairing clothing or to stitch together new dresses.

There was time before supper for fun and games. The young fairies loved to play hide-and-seek in the flowers. They took turns covering their eyes and counting to ten. The fairies flew off and hid. Whoever found the most fairies in the flowers in twenty seconds was the winner. The winner would get to pick a fairy to ride piggyback to the dining hall for supper. There was cheering by the fairies when they were not picked to give the ride.

As soon as the sun began to set, the fairies gathered in the great dining hall. Places were set and a bountiful display of food awaited them. Before eating, they bowed their heads and gave thanks to Mother Nature and the Almighty Creator for life and everything good they had been given.

With the moonlight casting its gentle light and the fairies settled into their sleeping positions, they thought about the natural world they had seen and their efforts to keep it pristine. They loved their home and their purpose as Mother Nature's helpers. Life here was so good; they wouldn't have traded it for anywhere else.

Looking up at the stars, they noticed brighter lights coming from Jupiter and Mars. Their minds swirled with all the knowledge they possessed of the world, plants and animals, and of all humanity. Goodnights were whispered, and soon the fairies were fast asleep.

CHAPTER NINE
Spring's Changes

Year Three, Spring,
Max's Awakening

THE CROWS WERE YELLING again, causing a disturbance outside. Something was happening, and it woke Max from his hibernation. He made out the words *lost* and *missing* but couldn't make out who or what they referred to. He hadn't planned to come out of his den so early, but the crows made the decision for him. *Why are they always so noisy when I'm trying to sleep?*

He then heard another irritating voice. Through half-opened eyes, he pushed forward on his belly and looked through the brush covering his den opening. It was Tate, Frederica's mate, sitting in a nearby tree making all the racket. *Oh, what now?*

Max thought he might as well get up since this racket wasn't going to let up. He pushed forward, stopped, pushed again. *What in the world?* Max was stuck in his den. Last fall, he remembered having trouble backing into it and now regretted not making it wider. He clawed forward on his belly and shoved aside the stems and brush he had packed in to close the opening. Finally, he was out. He stood and stretched his body.

The bright light made him squint until his eyes adjusted. The noise he made pushing out the brush, and his sudden appearance, startled the birds. They were silent until they realized it was just the bear coming out of his den. He shook his head, and drool flew in all directions. He was thirsty, and his stomach was telling his brain it needed food.

Tate was upset about something and was flying excitedly around the area. That meant Frederica wasn't too far away. For some strange reason, Max looked forward to seeing the bird again. Tate flew down to a closer branch but didn't say a word. His eyes darted back and forth, and he looked worried and concerned.

Max wanted to ask Tate what was going on, but his mouth was parched from thirst, and he was weak from not eating; his tongue felt like it was glued to the roof of his mouth. First things first, he needed water and food, and fast. The snow was dirty from animals traipsing through it, but he didn't care. He put his head down and ate it. Each mouthful was held until it partially melted and then he moved it around his mouth and tongue before swallowing. It was lumpy and hard to swallow, but he ate snow until his thirst was satisfied.

The bear walked away from his den to look for something to appease his hunger. He dug through the snow looking for leftover anything but found nothing. He nibbled on dead stems because he found nothing better. He longed for anything green—flowers, dandelions, new buds, leaves. The beast's wrath had taken that all away. He told himself he had to be patient, go without plants for now, and give them time to grow. He knew there were no walking ants yet, but he thought he'd tip over some nearby rocks to luck into sleeping ants or dead beetles.

The woods looked bare and unfamiliar. Every spring this happened; the beast walked around and rearranged everything as it saw fit. He found the birches but couldn't find his bed. Then he stumbled upon it. His stick bedding was strewn about, and what remained was covered with dirty snow. He didn't care. He lowered his big frame onto the snow, looked around, and waited for Frederica to show up.

Frederica is Missing

Tate sat on a branch, constantly scanning the area as he waited for Frederica to fly in. This tree beside the bear was the cardinals' usual meetup place in the spring if they became separated during the winter. Three days had passed since Tate had seen or heard her calls, and he was concerned. Usually, if they were apart, he could hear her distinctive call from a long distance away, but he hadn't heard it in days. He was worried about his Frederica; it wasn't like her to make him wait this long. After all, they had bonded for life.

Tate had been calling out to other birds, asking if anyone had seen her. So far, nobody had. He knew he had woken Max, but he didn't care because it was time for him to come out anyway.

Last year had been their happiest year together. They had successfully hatched two batches of eggs after two seasons of failure. He'd never seen Frederica so happy, and he wanted to see her joy again after having endured this terrible winter.

He called out again, then waited, but no return call came. He continued calling until his voice was hoarse, but still nothing. The trees knew he was on edge and watched for her. His bird friends flew the area and looked for her, and the animals were venturing out further than they usually did in the hope of finding her.

Everyone had given up looking for her and told Tate they were sure she would show up soon with a plausible excuse. But it was now the middle of the afternoon, and Tate was beginning to wonder if she ever would. He waited at the branch to be there if she returned. Then he saw those three crows flying overhead. Two stayed in the air, but Stu, the obnoxious one, flew in and perched next to him.

Tate was shocked at the nerve of the crow coming to sit beside him. He was about to fly off when Stu said, "Don't go. Stay."

Angrily, Tate replied, "Just leave me alone. There is nothing you can say I will believe. Nobody here likes you, just go away!"

"Yeah, yeah, I know you hate us. I just came to tell you that your missus is lying on the ground close to that old apple tree. I saw her a minute ago. Might want to check on her." Saying that, Stu immediately flew off.

Max was sitting below the tree and heard the conversation. He stood up and looked at Tate. "I'll go with you, meet you there."

The bear started walking in the direction of the old tree while Tate flew ahead. Tate got there first and was walking in circles around Frederica. Max arrived and sniffed her.

She was cold, certainly deceased.

Max spoke first. "I'm sorry, Tate. I wonder what happened. Last fall she looked fine."

Tate just stood there, in shock. Finally, he asked, "What am I going to do, Max? I don't want to go on without her."

"It was just her time. None of us know when our time will be up. She was a good bird."

"That she was. I'll miss her. Max, would you do me a favor and dig a hole for her? I don't want those nasty crows picking at her."

"Of course." With that, Max scratched the ground and got a hole started. The ground was hard, but he continued pawing until it was six inches deep. Then, with one movement of his paw, Max rolled her body into the hole. Tate walked over and looked at her. "Goodbye, my dear." With a sad expression, he flew off.

Max looked at Frederica and thought of everything she'd gone through with her eggs because of those crows. Her concern about his eye problem that day showed him she was a caring bird. Because of her helping him, he had changed his perspective about being part of this forest community. He was glad he had been able to help her by protecting her two batches of eggs. He took one final look at his friend and pawed dirt over her body. Tapping it down, he was sure nothing would get at her. He walked back across the field to the birches.

Tate Reflects

Back on his branch, Tate was upset about Frederica's unexpected passing. He was confused about how and why it had happened. He missed his talkative mate and felt lost and alone.

Over the cold months, she had never complained of any ailments and seemed as spry as a bird half her age. Maybe she had eaten too fast and choked on seeds, or in her haste eaten something poisonous, or maybe her heart had given out due to old age. He would never know the true reason, but he did know now he had a hard decision to make.

He was now in a predicament. Frederica had been his first love, and they had vowed to be lifelong mates. He had worked hard to claim this part of the forest for their nesting site. Driving off other cardinals who wanted to claim the woods had been time-consuming, but he had done it all for her. Now she was gone.

Tate calculated he was four springs old. He wondered if he was too old to take another mate or should he live out his life and be content alone. His body was telling him otherwise. The urge to mate had pestered him even before Frederica disappeared. The urge was still strong, and it told him he was not too old.

When he thought he had made up his mind, he changed it again. He still imagined her flying back at any moment and greeting him as if nothing had happened. The cardinal had never been in a situation like this before. The decision felt monumental, and it frustrated him. One moment he was confident; the next he hung his head, unwilling to let her memory go. Not knowing the right thing to do, he sat and did nothing.

But then he considered the big picture: he had the area, a good tree, and Max for protection; he just needed a mate. *What to do, what to do?*

Deciding what to do was hard, or was it? He didn't want to tarnish Frederica's memory by moving on too soon, but his mind kept urging him to go for it. He'd be forced to look out of the area, and he might get driven out by another cardinal, but it was an unpleasant chore that had to be risked. His nesting urge was too strong to ignore. His decision was made.

That evening, he roosted again with cardinals from other forests. He decided he would begin looking for a new mate in the morning. Most females were likely already taken, but he would try. Maybe he would get lucky.

The next morning, after eating seeds and several bugs, he started his quest. He flew through the trees until he judged he was a couple of forests away. His energy level was falling, and he knew he needed to rest and find food again. Their tallest tree stood out, and he landed on the ground under it. If this forest was anything like his own, he knew the trees were watching him. If news of his arrival had spread underground, and if the trees whispered his presence, he didn't care. He spied a few missed seeds, snatched a bug from a spider web, and ate a cricket and a beetle. That was enough food; now he just needed to rest.

He flew up to a low branch on the tall tree and perched to look over the area. It was very quiet here. It appeared there were no birds at all, or the birds were quiet and hiding because of him. Silence could be good for the soul, but not all the time. *No animals, no birds. What a strange place.*

A large shadow appeared on the ground under him. It took him by surprise. He froze—it hadn't been there a minute ago. It looked menacing and beastly, and then he looked up. Dark clouds had been moving quietly and stealthily toward the forest, hoping to catch the inhabitants unaware. Well, they certainly caught him unaware. Now he knew why everything had been quiet—everyone else had sensed the threat and had already taken shelter.

His bird instincts should have kicked in, but they hadn't because he'd been preoccupied with finding food. By then he and Frederica would have been huddled together in the thicket by Pippen.

Drops began to fall, and Tate noticed the wind picking up. He had to move from this branch or risk being blown away or seriously killed. Just then he heard another bird's voice.

"Hey, you, get over here!"

He looked around to find where the voice came from.

"Over here!"

He followed the voice to another tree with a split branch hanging down. In the crook of the branch sat a female cardinal, protected by a leaning trunk. It didn't look like a very safe place to take cover and could come down with the slightest wind shift. But it was raining harder and the sky rumbled, and it was probably the nearest shelter he could reach.

He dared not go over because her mate would beat him up. But a loud clap of thunder changed his mind. About this time, Frederica would be frightened, and he'd be by her side. Since this bird's mate was nowhere to be seen, he flew over and joined her. She moved aside to make room and made eye contact.

"Hello," she said as she dug her feet back into the torn branch.

She was shaking and jumped every time she heard thunder. He couldn't help himself and opened his wing to let her in beside him. It was a bold move on his part, but he felt the need to protect her. She didn't object, and the two birds huddled together through the storm.

The dark clouds moved on, and the sky finally cleared. They relaxed in awkward silence.

After a few moments, the other bird asked, "Where'd you come from anyway? I noticed you sitting there. You looked lost."

"I came from another forest. I had to get away after I lost my mate."

"Oh, I'm sorry."

"What about you?" asked Tate.

She looked away and was silent. Then she answered, "He wasn't a good mate. I finally kicked him out. I couldn't trust him. He wanted a different life. I'm by myself now."

"Wow, what a jerk. I'd never be like that."

"No?"

"No."

"Come here, sit by me," she said, "Then, we'll go look for something to eat."

He liked this bird. She was more reserved than Frederica, maybe a little younger, but just as pretty. *She might be the one.*

Tate learned her name was Kitty, and she was two years old. He figured she had at least three good mating years in her. She told him about her past: last year she'd bonded with a male named John, and they'd hatched a nest of eggs together. He was never happy and always wanted to go on long flights, but she preferred staying close to home. Sometimes he would take off by himself, and she wouldn't see him for days. But he always came back, sometimes a little battered. Other birds said he had gone into other forests pestering females until their mates chased him off. She didn't trust him and never felt loved or wanted. A few weeks ago, she asked him to leave, and he did, and never came back. She had been waiting for another male cardinal to come around.

He told Kitty about his seasons with Frederica and how she had died unexpectedly a few days ago. He told her about their problems with hatching eggs and how their bear, Max, had guarded their eggs from the crows. Last year they had successfully hatched two nests. He told her about his forest and how many years he had lived there.

She was excited to hear all this and wanted to visit his forest and that bear. Tate sensed she wanted to mate with him as much as he wanted to mate with her. They planned to leave in the morning to go back to his forest and find out if she wanted to make it her home as well.

Dance of the Buttercups

The yellow buttercups were among the first flowers to appear every spring. Just like the butterfly fairies, these little gems were cherished because they were a sign of spring's awakening.

The plants thought if those little girls could survive the winter and bloom, they deserved to be cheered on. Just seeing their five little petals, mimicking the color of the sun, put a smile on weary plants and animals.

This spring, the buttercups were out in abundance. If there were any sunny areas on the forest floor, they were peeking out. Mothers had been busy over the winter making clothes while their daughters slept. Making all those yellow dresses was quite a task to have ready by spring, but the mothers didn't mind. And when their daughter's dresses were damaged, new outfits were always waiting to be worn.

What a beautiful sight it was to see the buttercups dance. They stood on their tiptoes, pointed their faces to the sun, and twirled their skirts in the spring breeze. The girls were not the least bit shy. They laughed and giggled, and their silliness was contagious to everything around them.

When their mothers said it was time for bed, they carefully folded away their skirts and offered prayers of thanks. They thanked Mother Nature for the rain, the sun, and for life itself. They were eager to unfold their skirts in the morning for their next recital.

The buttercup families had good manners and didn't seek more than their share of attention. They were the first to display and dance in the spring, but daffodils also waited for their turns to dance under the sun. After the daffodils' performances were over, it was time for the daisies, violets, and lilies to dance. The flowers all took a bow and retreated to their bedrooms until it was their turn to dance again next spring.

The Voice

Since coming out of hibernation, Max's surroundings had been unusually quiet. For the past two years, his days had been filled with Frederica's constant talking. He knew Tate had gone out in search of a new mate. Max thought it was funny that it hadn't taken Tate long to move on after losing Frederica. *Birds were strange.*

Max waited for Tate to return because he had no one else to talk to. Being a solitary bear, he had never spoken to anyone before the cardinals came around. Tate had only been gone a few days, but Max was already curious as to how his mate quest had turned out. He just sat and waited to see who Tate brought back.

Before Tate left to look for a mate, he had brought Max up to date on how angry the beast had become and how relieved everyone was when he moved on. He also said the butterfly fairies had been there for two days during their spring visit and were widely welcomed. Max always received fairy visits each year, even though he'd be sleeping in his den. It was the same every year: a fairy slipped in, whispered a few words, and thrust healing mists on his body. Frankly, he wished they'd also bring snacks.

But this year had been different.

Only half-awake, he vividly remembered hearing a voice in his den. It hadn't been the sweet, timid voice of a tiny fairy, but a mature, motherly voice coming from something with a much larger presence. How the source of that voice had gotten in through the piled brush and snow, he'd never know.

The voice had said something that day he'd never forget:

"You are destined to lead, oh sleeping bear, to help get a mission off the ground. When you're awake, gain your strength. You will hear my voice again, which will summon you and a group of animals to gather about a mission. Just sleep. I'm sprinkling healing mist on you and leaving behind a scent to remind you of spring."

He hadn't felt the mist, but the fragrance of fresh green leaves combined with the earthy smell of soil after rain had lingered in his den.

He remembered the voice and had been thinking about it every day. *Destined to lead? That's silly. Me lead? Ridiculous. Meet about a mission? Absolutely not.* He remembered the terrible noises last fall and ground shaking and all the death and destruction it caused for many weeks. He remembered the community meeting and everyone deciding they needed answers—from Mother Nature herself, no less. He assumed with spring here, there would be another meeting to discuss how to do that. *Could that have been Mother Nature speaking?*

Nothing the voice said made any sense. He thought about it, decided to put it out of his mind, and went for a stroll around the area. He was hungry, maybe something new had grown overnight that he could eat.

He met Mr. Mole on his walk. The mole was picking up sticks and miscellaneous junk around his home's entrance. Mole was a nice guy but a little strange. He was always preoccupied with doing fix-up projects around his place. Mole waved. Max grunted and kept going. Max didn't have time for niceties. He was hungry but had no appetite for the animals he knew personally. Instead, he wished tasty plants would just jump out and ask to be eaten. *Humph, only in my dreams.*

He walked back to his bed and settled in, ready for a full night of doing nothing. Suddenly, he thought about the lovely female bear he had met and mated with last spring. He wondered how many cubs she might have now. He toyed with the idea of trying to find her again, keeping a distance, of course, just to watch her and the cubs. If she had cubs, she wouldn't let him get close to her anyway. Going on those long walks took so much of his energy, but he threw the idea around anyway.

Brothers Disbanding

This was the crows' third year together, and their partnership had begun to fray. Stu was still giving orders like nothing had changed, but Jack and Bobber were tired of Stu ordering them around. And Stu, well, he just didn't want his brothers around anymore, period.

Jack and Bobber were surprised when Stu said, "Brothers, we are all equals and not one crow should be the boss of all crows. It is time for we three crows to part ways. Let's go out on our own, live our own lives, and find some female crows."

Jack and Bobber exchanged a look—half shock, half relief. Stu had never spoken rationally to them before, and for once, all three agreed wholeheartedly. The crows were pleased to hear Stu wanted to mate and settle down as much as they did.

"We agree," Jack said. "But how shall we divide the contents at Wazoo? We each own a share of it, and it should be split evenly."

"Yes," Bobber added. "Very complicated… not going to be easy."

"Come on, crows, let's fly to the tree and decide." Stu took off first, as he always had, and the others followed. They flew straight to the tree and stepped into the hole. There sat their enormous pile of accumulated junk, but to the crows it was a pile of priceless treasures.

The food stash was piled off to the side. That pile was an easy division. Two lines were drawn in the pile, and it was easily divided.

The real issue lay with the treasures. Bobber had an idea. "Let's take turns and pick one thing at a time to put in our pile until the pile is gone." All three nodded.

"Who wants the first pick?" asked Bobber.

There was feigned hesitation. All wanted to go first but none of them wanted to say it. Stu looked up at the ceiling, pretending sudden interest in imaginary bugs. While he did that, the other two just shrugged, knowing what Stu wanted.

"You go first, Stu," Jack said. "You're the oldest."

That made Stu happy, but he tried to hide his satisfaction.

After an hour of choosing, the pile was divided. Stu would keep Wazoo, along with his share of food and treasures. Jack and Bobber would have their belongings out as soon as they relocated.

The three had once claimed this forest together, chasing off male intruders and acting united. Now, being independent crows, they divided up the woods and agreed not to intrude on the others' territory. They also agreed their brothers' females, eggs, and nests were off limits. Each would be responsible for chasing away crow intruders in their own areas.

Stu said, "All right, brothers, it's been fun, we'll see each other at the roost."

They raised their front claws, tapped each other to seal their pact, and flew off.

The next morning, Stu stood and stuck back in untamed feathers and deliberately fluffed his body feathers to show he was an available beau. "I'm here, girls, I'm ready for you." He puffed out his chest and spread his wings to show his great reach, all to impress any female onlookers. Then he waited and waited.

Word soon got around that Stu was out making a fool of himself by flaunting his body and showing off. Several girls sat together on a branch and watched him.

"What a loudmouth," one muttered.

"He's part of the gang that yaps every day," said another. "I heard they went their own ways."

"He steals bird eggs," a third chimed in.

"He lies and begs," added the fourth. "From what I can tell, he's got bowed legs."

With nothing nice to say, they flew off.

Stu continued flaunting his feathers every day, but word traveled fast. No female wanted anything to do with him. In fact, they seemed to despise him.

One girl, as she was flying away, yelled, "Hey, move out of these woods!" That stung. His search for a mate looked grim.

Meanwhile, his brothers had success and found mates. In their own sections of the forest, they were given the green light. They weren't treated like pests at all. They found their females and passed the female's strict mating tests with flying colors. The couples were building nests with their partners.

Weeks passed, there was Stu, still alone in the forest. The girls weren't even in earshot anymore. He wondered if he would be alone for the rest of his life. Now he had no mate and no brothers and regretted his decision to break up.

Then one afternoon, a voice from the next tree got his attention. He looked, and it was a female crow he hadn't seen before. She was studying him with amused eyes.

"Hey, I've been watching you for a while. I like your style. You're funny and sort of cute. You make me smile."

Stu didn't dare push his luck. He just smiled and nodded his head to invite her to join him. She glided to his branch, and they talked without any pretentious behavior on his part.

Over the next few days, they foraged together, chatted endlessly, and found they genuinely liked each other. Stu passed her mating test, and soon they spent all their time together.

He was happy and realized he and his brothers had wasted a lot of time being musketeers instead of settling down and having families. He had found something real at last.

PART
THREE

Under the Shadows:
The Age of Change

CHAPTER TEN
The Great Animal Expedition

Winds of Change

FORESTS WERE ALWAYS CHANGING and adapting. Plants and animals expected changes with the seasons along with the consequences of change.

When the blackberries ripened on the vine, the bears, birds, and deer all took turns eating them. They gorged on berries one day, but when they returned a week later, those same berries had dried up. When their time in the sun was finished, they withered and died. This was expected to happen, and animals went without blackberries for another year.

If storms and strong winds came through, they forced change. The winds bent over the young trees and, if the trees survived, they would be forever misshapen. Weak and sickly plants perished in storms. Branches broke off, and whole trees were uprooted and died. Storms with strong winds always left changes. This was expected to happen and plants adapted.

In shadier parts of the forest, moss thrived as it spread along the cool ground, up rocks, and over fallen trees. It disliked bright sun and craved low light instead. If a tree bent or went down in a storm, it opened the area and more sunlight streamed in. With all that sunlight, shade-loving moss neighborhoods eventually withered and died. If the moss was able, it relocated to another shady area. An overabundance of light for shade-loving plants changed the forest floor. Plants knew this happened, and they either adapted or died.

Rain, of course, was the forest's friend. Plants and animals required regular doses of rain to soak their roots to survive. However, an overabundance of rain was their enemy. Rain day after day in large amounts was not good. If roots became too soaked, their plants could drown. Worms were forced up because their tunnels flooded. Aboveground, they were often washed away, and drowned or hungry birds picked them up. Water changed the appearance of the forest above and below ground. The forest had been through this before and had adapted.

A forest always changed and adapted from natural demons. These demons came and changed the landscape, but the forest understood the reasons. Change had happened before, and it would come again.

But it was the sudden, never seen, unnatural sights and sounds that perplexed this forest. If there was no history of it, there were no answers.

They didn't know how, or if, they should adapt to what they'd been through last fall. Would a disruption like that happen again? If so, should they prepare for it? Did they need to move to a new home? Distressed and full of anxiety, the entire forest lived on pins and needles.

Summer,
The Secret Trip Began

The trees knew that Tate and Max were having a conversation, but they couldn't make out what they were saying. The cardinal was perched directly above the bear as they talked in near whispers. Max looked around constantly, to avoid anyone hearing them. The trees didn't *need* to know what was being said, but they *wanted* to know because they were nosy and felt entitled to know everything. They watched as the pair raised their heads and sniffed the air. The animals then lowered their heads and looked worried. The trees were confused by their actions and didn't like not knowing.

What in the world are they discussing? Why are they being so secretive? This was unlike the two of them. They rarely spoke, and when they did, it was always loud enough for the trees to hear.

The trees continued to watch Max and Tate, both with their heads down. They appeared to be listening to someone, but there was nobody else around. Their heads drifted upward and back as if searching for the source of sound, puzzled looks on both their faces. The trees saw Max whisper something to the bird, then got up, and shook himself off. The bear walked forward, following the bird as it flew ahead.

When the trees lost sight of the pair, they alerted their neighboring trees to continue eavesdropping. The trees monitored them as they walked to Mr. Mole's hole. These three animals barely spoke to each other, yet here they were, besties meeting for tea. It even appeared that Mr. Mole had been expecting them, because as soon as the bear and bird arrived, he came out and walked away with them.

Bear, bird, and mole walked over to Benji's house. Benji had obviously been sleeping because he came out rubbing his eyes. The four sat close to each other and spoke in muffled tones. The group talked for half an hour and then stopped. The trees heard cordial "goodnights," after which Benji went back inside his hole, and the others went their separate ways.

As soon as the sun came up, Tate, Max, and Mr. Mole met at Benji's hole. Max crouched flat on the ground as Benji and Mr. Mole climbed onto his back. They clumsily dug their claws into his fur, as Max stood. Because Benji was blind, he sat closest to Max's neck and held on to his fur. The mole kept eyes on Benji in case he fell off. Tate took to the air and slowly flew west, stopping occasionally on a branch to let Max catch up.

Now the trees were thoroughly confused. These animals were going on a trip, and the cardinal was leading the way. If this trip had anything to do with the forest, the trees felt they should be in the know. They were not happy, not knowing where these animals were going.

Day One, the Animal Trip

Max had been on his feet for five hours, walking and following Tate. The bird said he had the route engrained in his head. Max hoped he did. He had a good sense of direction and thought he could find his way back home if he had to, but he'd rather rely on Tate and not make the effort to pay attention.

He was already getting tired. If the mole and rabbit weren't riding on his back, and if he didn't know they had a destination to reach that day, he would have stopped to rest.

Max heard the mole and rabbit constantly talking. The mole had taken it upon himself to describe everything interesting he saw to the rabbit. He had found a way to describe colors and shapes to the rabbit, which Max thought was clever. Mole told Benji to let familiar scents guide him. Grass became green because it meant something good. When he smelled an apple or strawberry, they were red and tasted sweet. When he sniffed the earthy scent of the ground, he was to associate it as dark brown, like dried leaves. Benji quickly caught on, associating colors with scents he already knew.

By listening to their conversations, Max was kept alert. He occasionally warned the two to hang on when going under a branch or going up an incline. Max thought about how terrified Benji must have been to go on this mission. Without sight, birds and animals of prey could pounce on him. The same with the mole, especially because he was leaving his family without any explanation.

This whole trip had come up so suddenly, and Max still couldn't believe he was part of it. He had never been one for impetuous behavior, yet there he was. He also didn't really have a choice.

It had started yesterday when Max was taking his afternoon nap and was awakened by a voice.

"Wake up, Max," the voice said.

At first, he thought it was a fairy because this spring, he'd heard a voice while he was sleeping in his den. He recalled that first voice had said something about leading a mission and being summoned for some nonsense. He hadn't given much thought to those words since then.

But this was a different voice—a mature, female voice like none he had heard before. She sounded mystical, other-worldly, and authoritative. He recalled waking, looking into the low light, but seeing no source for the voice.

"Wake up, Max," he'd heard again.

He opened his eyes again but once again saw nothing. Confused, he finally sat up to find the source of the voice. He heard it again and this time it was right next to him.

"I know the terror your forest experienced last fall from that disturbance, and I'm very sorry for all the hardship and destruction it caused. When your meeting was held, I watched, and I knew you had questions for me. I understood the decision the forest made to find me because your forest wanted answers."

Max had been stunned, suddenly wide awake and alert. Knowing the source of the voice, he'd been shocked and petrified, knowing Mother Nature herself was speaking to him. At first, he thought it was a dream, but after closing and reopening his eyes, he knew it was real.

"Big changes are coming to this forest. There are things I must show you that will seem unimaginable and very confusing but seeing them will explain who will be making these changes. You must see these things to understand what I will be telling you. It must be done in person, and you must come to me. When I show you, I will tell you why these changes are being made. I have selected you, Mr. Mole, Benji, and Tate, to meet me at a specific location to receive an explanation. Don't be afraid; you will all be protected."

After last fall's meeting, the forest hadn't known how to initiate contact with Mother Nature. They postponed everything, intending to rethink it in the spring.

He remembered she'd said, "Today I am informing all the parties involved of a mission. I would like you four to leave as a group tomorrow morning at sunup. You will meet with the others tonight and discuss the mission but keep it to yourselves. I have placed in each of your heads a map that will guide you to me. You will hear me speak, and I will lead you to points of contact along the way that will assist you. The trip will be long and grueling, but fuel will be provided. I will talk to you next when you arrive. Max, I have confidence in you and each of the animals' abilities."

That was all Max knew. That was all any of them knew.

Their First Help

Around mid-afternoon, the animals heard Mother Nature's voice while enroute to meet her. They were told where to find a stream and a certain fish to get their first piece of help.

They heard, "You will come upon a winding stream. Walk upstream along the bank until you see two turtles sunning themselves on a branch in the water. Next to this branch is a deep pool where a trout named Brookie lives. Ripple the water to wake the fish, he will swim up to the surface to meet you. Don't move too quickly or act agitated, or you may scare him away. He will provide you with further instructions."

After hearing her words, Tate flew ahead to find the stream. Five minutes later, he flew back to the others to let them know.

"I found the creek up ahead where the turtles are sunning themselves. It's about a hundred yards upstream. Keep walking straight until you see the patch of grass next to the water. You will see me in the tree above the grass."

Max acknowledged Tate's directions and watched him fly ahead. "Hang on, guys, I'm walking to find that stream and Tate."

He walked for ten minutes, following the stream. Finally, he saw the grassy area up ahead with Tate sitting in a tree waiting for them. Max had to rest for just a minute. When he plopped down, Mr. Mole and Benji jumped down to stretch their legs.

A few minutes later, Tate flew down to get them moving. He said, "Let's go rouse that fish. Remember no quick moves."

The mole and rabbit climbed back onto Max's back. Once they were ready, the bird flew and waited for them by the stream.

When Max arrived at the stream, he swirled his paw in the water to let the fish know they were there. They waited with no reaction. He swirled again and waited. He wondered if the fish even knew they were there. It occurred to him that the fish might be ignoring the rippling because, like himself, he didn't like company.

Max didn't know that the fish struggled with tasks like this. The fish was insecure and was unsure whether he could come to the surface to fulfill his task. He was near the bottom trying to build up his nerve to swim up.

Facing Insecurities

Brookie liked the deep pool for the peace it provided. Nothing visited him down there except for an occasional snapping turtle or slow-moving sucker fish. They were the only deep-water dwellers who passed through on their way to new feeding grounds, and they never paid any attention to him. When he was done feeding, he spent his time alone in the dark.

Earlier, he'd been thinking about the voice he'd heard yesterday and how that was even possible. Fish were supposed to pick up vibrations, not conversations. He couldn't speak or send thoughts the way land animals did. Hearing words come out of nowhere made him freeze midwater. With a flick of his tail, he vanished into the shadows below. His fins had trembled as if the current had turned against him. He didn't know who or what the voice belonged to or how he was able to hear it, but the request had sounded urgent.

Brookie felt the water quiver strangely. He hesitated. He wondered what going to the surface would accomplish. He wouldn't be able understand them, nor they him, and it all seemed like an enormous waste of good hiding time. His common sense told him to stay where he was, yet he impulsively started ascending. Remembering the urgency of yesterday's voice, he didn't dare ignore it.

As Brookie neared the surface, he saw faces looking down at him. Then something unexpected happened. He hadn't even opened his mouth, but he heard his thoughts being passed to the waiting animals.

"You must walk two miles north, as the crow flies. Look for the largest oak tree in the area. Stop when you see it and eat the food waiting for you. Rest and sleep. At dawn, continue your journey."

The animals seemed to hear and understand. Brookie wondered how this was even possible. Then the big animal raised a paw in what seemed like agreement and turned around.

What an experience! Brookie had stressed about this moment all day. Just thinking about it had made his fins tighten. *Why had that voice chosen him of all the fish in the stream? Why hadn't it spoken directly to the animals?*

But it was over, and he was proud of himself for doing it. He had accomplished something outside of his comfort zone, and it hadn't been hard at all. It occurred to him that maybe this was why the voice had chosen him to relay the message. Maybe it wanted him to do something he normally would have been afraid to attempt. The voice wanted him to face his fears, and he had.

He swam back down to his deep hole—down to his lonely pit of a home.

With that experience behind him, he felt more confident and surer of himself, and decided to swim higher to where the other fish swam together. The other fish glanced at him but paid him no mind. For the rest of the afternoon, he swam among the other fish and looked for food. It appeared he was accepted as one of them. When he finished feeding, he rested in the warmer water where he could see through the surface. He found all the new shimmering colors quite intriguing.

During the day, fish were in their own little world, exploring, and feeding. Brookie noticed their camaraderie and sense of family. He wished then to be a part of that and decided he would conquer his fears, come out of his self-imposed exile, and try to be a more social fish.

That night, Brookie joined the other fish under the sheltering branches in the water which served as their hideout. They floated together and rested. In the morning, they went about their normal routines of exploring, nibbling, and socializing. This time, Brookie swam right along with them.

A Week Earlier,
The Four Fairy Volunteers

The fairies woke up early, excited to be heading out on their mission that day. None of the them had ever been chosen for a special mission before. Mother Nature had already met with the four fairies and had told them what the future held for this forest. They were surprised to hear it was the same forest they had visited earlier that spring. When they heard that death and destruction would come to the forest, the three younger fairies were shocked and saddened. They couldn't imagine why Mother would do such a thing.

JudyMar, the youngest fairy, had begged, "Mother, please don't do this. Isn't there some other way?"

"Why must it be this forest?" DebAnna had asked. "This forest is still so beautiful."

LindaMay remembered visiting the two apple trees and knew they were related. The old apple tree, Great Apple, was the father of Pippen. "Please, Mother, don't hurt the apple trees, especially that young one named Pippen. He just started making good progress with his growth."

The oldest fairy on the mission was Beulah. Mother Nature had chosen her because of her wisdom and mother-like demeanor. She was thoughtful and calm, and Mother knew the younger fairies could learn from her.

Beulah interrupted the younger fairies' pleas. "Girls, remember, Mother would never do anything that wasn't in the best interest of the forest. We must have faith in her decisions and do our best to fulfil her wishes."

Mother Nature explained that four animal ambassadors from that forest would soon be on their way to meet with her. She had a dismal scene to show them, one that couldn't be described and had to be seen to be believed. The trip would be dangerous for the animals, and she wanted her fairies to use their magic to prevent any accidents or injuries. The animals couldn't know they were being watched and shouldn't be any worse for wear by the time they returned home.

Mother Nature read their name and their assignments. "DebAnna, you are assigned to watch over the bear." She had been the fairy who visited him in the spring while he slept. "Make sure he stays sure-footed and doesn't get confused."

"JudyMar, I'm assigning you to the blind rabbit. Please watch that he doesn't tumble off the bear and get hurt." JudyMar was delighted because she had always thought that bunny was so cute.

Next, she spoke to the older fairy. "Beulah, I'd like you to watch over the cardinal. He becomes excited easily, often acting before he thinks. Do your best to keep pace with the bird and ensure he stays on track."

LindaMay received her appointment last. "I'm entrusting you to keep an eye on the mole. He's the smallest of the group and could be easily misplaced or stepped on. Don't let that happen."

The day of departure was here, and the fairies were fully briefed and prepared. Beulah woke them early, and soon they were in the air, heading north. They estimated they would be away from Flitterdom for eight days, longer because of the time it would take the animals to reach Mother Nature. They were all in good spirits, laughing and singing their favorite songs, while keeping their eyes on their leader for any change in flight direction. That night, Beulah would scout the woods for a safe place for them to rest. They would eat, comb their hair, and repair any damaged wings. After a night's rest, they would resume another full day of flying.

On the third morning, the towering tree once again guided them safely into the forest. They flew through and were pleased to see how well the plants and animals had bounced back. Normally, they never saw forests during the year after their spring visit; they remembered only how downtrodden everything looked at winter's end. What they saw that day was quite an improvement. The fairies were all smiles, knowing they had helped bring about that change. They bedded down again, aware the next morning they would fly beside the animals unnoticed.

Day Two, the Animal Trip

After thanking Brookie, the animals followed Tate to the large tree and saw the large pile of food. They were all hungry and thankful to see food put there to eat.

After having eaten better than they had in weeks, the bear, mole, and rabbit sat stuffed and exhausted and huddled together for the night. The cardinal sat alone on a nearby branch and watched them nervously. Normally, about this time, Tate would be perched with the forest's other cardinals high in a tree for their nighttime safety. But this night he was alone and he felt uncomfortable. He thought that as soon as he fell asleep, a snake, an owl, or even a raccoon would grab him off his branch. Now he couldn't fall asleep.

Tate saw the two small animals resting comfortably by Max and he wanted to have that same safety net. He flew down and stood between the mole and the rabbit. They felt him fly in, separated, and made room for him between Max's legs. He was used to perching on one leg, his foot tucked around a branch. Tate dug one foot into the soil to firmly grip twigs and tucked his head and other leg into his feathers for warmth. He could also feel the warmth of the small animals and the bear and thought this was much better than perching alone. It wasn't long before the four friends were all fast asleep.

The next morning, the animals opened their eyes when they heard the irritating voices of crows overhead.

"Caw! Caw! Wake up! Caw! Caw! Wake up!"

Tate, still standing, spotted them first. "It's those crow brothers! I wonder why they're back together and out here?"

Max and Mr. Mole looked up and saw them while Benji sat in fear, afraid to move.

They heard, "She's waiting for you guys, get up, get moving!"

Mother Nature had instructed the crows to shout down a wake-up call, which was what they were doing now. Stu, Jack, and Bobber had been interrupted in their roost the other night by a mysterious voice. They were told to wake and relay directions to the four animals on the second morning of the trip. If there was anything the crows feared, it was a spooky voice without a body. That morning, they knew they had no choice but to take leave from their mates to find the animals.

"Why can't they ever leave us alone?" asked Tate, exasperated at the sight of them. "C'mon, guys, I guess we have to get moving."

Benji was a year old now and a fully grown rabbit, but he still depended on his neighborhood friends to give him danger warnings. Mr. Mole had drilled into him how dangerous birds were, especially since a hawk had killed his mother. He knew he couldn't depend on the warnings of others to protect him all his life.

There were times when he'd been outside and heard that "Caw! Caw!" sound without any warning. It scared him to death, but he always made it back to his hole in time. So far, he had never strayed far from home. This sound of crows frightened him, but he knew both he and Mr. Mole were safe if they stayed near Max.

Benji wondered again what help he could possibly be on this trip. Being sightless, he felt like he was in the way. He couldn't give any warnings, and, if there *was* danger, he couldn't run to hide not knowing where he was going. *What was Mother Nature thinking choosing him?*

Benji didn't realize it, but because he had been blind since birth, his other senses had been heightened. He was able to hear, smell, and feel danger before the others were even aware. She also knew that his whiskers were sensitive and could help navigate them if they got off track. On top of that, he had an excellent memory and could store what he learned in his little file cabinet in his head. He would be a big asset and Mother Nature knew this—that's why she chose him.

Mr. Mole had always hated crows. Moles lived in constant danger of being snatched and eaten. Crows flew in unannounced, scoped out the forest, and did their dirty work. They sat in trees, waited for small animals to show themselves, and then pounced. Moles had to be constantly aware of their surroundings, have sharp ears and eyes, or risk living short lives.

Like Benji, Mr. Mole wondered how he could contribute to this outing. He was the tiniest of the animals and not able to hold his ground against anything. He felt useless.

Mr. Mole didn't know it, but Mother Nature knew his eyesight wasn't the best. She also knew he had a great sense of touch and was good at detecting sounds through ground vibrations. If there were danger at night, Mr. Mole would be the first of the group to detect it. He was also a quick thinker, seeing how he thought through problems and came up with solutions. Yes, he was a necessity to have on the mission.

Today the crows were cordial, having been ordered by the voice to not attack the small animals and to look elsewhere for food. They were to relay the instructions and leave the area.

Another crow shouted down to the animals, "Walk in a straight line, don't veer. Keep walking until you hear the voice again." Saying that, the three crows flew off.

The animals quickly ate the leftover food from the previous night. Benji, in one quick leap, was up on Max's back and in position by his neck. Mr. Mole struggled to get up. His front feet couldn't grasp Max's fur, and he kept sliding to the ground. On his third attempt, he was sliding back down again when he unexpectedly found himself sitting on the bear's back behind Benji. *Humph, how'd that happen?* They didn't know how it had happened but were relieved it did. With his passengers situated, Max opened his mouth, yawned, and began walking.

To walk in a straight line, they needed to walk up a steep incline. Tate flew ahead, leading the way. Max was making his way up when he forgot he was carrying two passengers. He put weight on his back legs and pushed through brush in his way. If he walked around it, he wouldn't be going in a straight line.

The bumpy ride unexpectedly caused the mole and rabbit to fall off, and they went tumbling down the hill. The bear came to his senses, turned his head, and saw them lying on the ground. They were covered in debris and looking confused. Before Max could even turn back to get them, the mole and rabbit were back up on his back, free of debris, and hanging on. All were surprised at what had just happened, but the bear continued walking.

Max walked in a straight line for what seemed forever and began to wonder what he had gotten himself into. The animals were tired, hungry, and wanted to rest. Just then, Tate flew down and pointed to a large field ahead. They walked closer, stopped at the edge, and looked out in amazement.

The field was filled with beautiful spring flowers, dancing and swaying in the wind. It was a glorious sight after seeing only trees, brush, and darkness this whole trip. Max stood and stared. Mr. Mole described to Benji all the colors they were witnessing and asked him to envision the scene. After today's walk, it was a wonderful thing to see.

Off in the distance they saw what looked like butterflies flying. Thousands of butterflies of all colors flitted gracefully from bloom to bloom. They danced and mingled without a care in the world. The animals all wondered at the same time if these were butterfly fairies and if they had happened upon their homeland.

The aroma of the field was intoxicating, and the flowers and butterflies were so beautiful that the animals stood awestruck. Mr. Mole hurriedly described the scene before them to Benji as the rabbit's nose wiggled to sniff the scents in the air.

But something was developing to disrupt this beautiful scene. Quite unexpectedly, their awe turned to uneasiness as the animals felt a change in the air movement. Just moments earlier, the air held a gentle breeze, and the flowers were swaying with it. The breeze had stopped, and the flowers and butterflies were completely still and statue-like. There was no movement whatsoever over the field. The lighthearted feeling was replaced with a sense of anticipation. Their uneasiness now turned to fear.

Then the grass flattened and the plants kneeled to provide an entryway. The flowers bent and curtsied, seemingly in respect to an approaching entity. The butterflies alighted onto the flowers and sat still. The animals were afraid and instinctively tucked their tails and flattened their ears. They trembled when they saw a sphere with glowing light in the distance. As it approached, they felt a pulsing sensation, which added to their uneasiness.

Benji could feel the pulsing but didn't know what was approaching or what his friends were seeing. The mole pressed his whole body hard against Benji's, shaking in fear and not describing anything.

The Entity Approached

Mole's trembling told Benji he should be afraid, but he wasn't. He heard the pulsing, and because he had become accustomed to the similar pulsing of trees near his home, he didn't fear it. He liked to think of pulsing as the tree's heartbeat, a calming and tranquil sound.

He considered this pulsing now and compared it to a tree's heartbeat. The sound was similar but not the same, but neither frightened him.

Benji knew the others were seeing something more, but since he couldn't see it and nobody was telling him anything, he decided to stay calm. He felt he needed to be the voice of reason and reassurance and calm these guys down.

Tate flew down and was standing on the ground beside the bear. He stood with his wings tucked back and head down, his way of showing fear. Tate slowly raised his head and looked up. He saw Benji standing up on the bear sniffing the air, looking relaxed and unafraid.

Then Benji said, "Guys, whatever is happening, I don't think we have anything to fear. It's nothing bad. We shouldn't be afraid. It feels like the moment before a surprise... the nice kind." Saying that, Benji sat back down and waited.

Max was about to walk under the trees and hide, as was Tate, but when Benji spoke so calmly, they stayed where they were. He was right; this approaching sphere gave no sign of being a threat, and besides, the colors emanating from it were beautiful.

Mr. Mole told Benji a deer was walking up to them from the left and that it was Hollyhock from their forest. She wasn't afraid, in fact, quite the opposite. She walked up and stood confidently a short distance from them and watched the sphere as if waiting for a cue.

The sphere hovered fifteen feet away, shutting down the lights and pulsing. Then they heard the same voice they had heard on their walk earlier. The voice didn't come from the sphere but came directly from Hollyhock's body.

The group of animals heard the deer say, "Thank you for making the long trip to see me today. I am Mother Nature, and I speak to you today from our friend, Hollyhock. Please don't be afraid and don't run away. You cannot see me, but you will hear me through the deer."

The animals looked from Hollyhock to the sphere, puzzled at what was happening.

The voice continued, "I brought you four here to explain what happened last fall when the loud sounds and earth-jarring took place. I know everyone was afraid, and it disrupted the lives of the plants and animals in your forest. You wanted answers; I'm here to give them."

The animals' eyes were on Hollyhock, in shock to hear the familiar voice of Mother Nature coming from the deer.

"I must tell you about the changes that will be happening in your forest. You may feel you are being picked on, but don't be, because you are not alone. Sooner or later, these changes will happen in all forests. You must accept the changes and not reject them. Believe me when I say it is for the continued health of your forest."

What she said sounded ominous, but all wondered if the changes could be worse than putting up with the beast for months on end. Max wondered if the changes would be worse than the pain he endured when his stomach was hungry in the spring. Tate, Mr. Mole, and Benji had all endured the pain of losing loved ones and wondered what could possibly be worse than that. With Benji having to navigate the forest blind, he wondered what could be worse than trying to stay alive without sight and depending on others just to find food and stay out of sight of predators. None of them could think of anything worse than what each had already endured.

Her voice continued, "Walk with me for a short way. There is something I must show you. You will be shocked when you see this, but I will explain. Hear me out and keep an open mind."

Hollyhock pointed her head to indicate direction and started walking. Tate flew overhead, and Max, carrying the little guys, followed the deer through the forest. The sphere rose again and hovered invisibly over the trees. Max followed the deer up another hilly incline, and again the little animals lost their grip on his fur and fell off. Within seconds, they resumed their positions on his back unhurt, with Max unaware he had lost them. At the top of the hill, Hollyhock stopped and pointed for them to look down through the trees.

They stood and looked at the weirdest animal they had ever seen in their lives. It was puzzling how it walked on two legs, not four.

Unraveling the Mystery

Mr. Mole immediately described to Benji what they saw on the bottom of the hill. Benji's eyes widened with surprise as he visualized the scene. The bird, the bear, the mole, and the rabbit were confounded, not knowing what species of animal they were seeing. They knew every animal in the forest, and this wasn't one of them. It didn't have fur like a fox or a bear; it walked on two legs like a big bird, yet they didn't see wings. It was tall, much taller than any animal they knew existed.

More of the same animal came into view. On two legs, they took long strides and covered the distance quickly. They walked up to the first animal and stood with it. Small, skinny, leg-like protrusions came out near the tops of their bodies, with even smaller protrusions wiggling on the ends, which pointed at things. The animals in the group made strange sounds and appeared to be talking to each other through their mouths. The forest animals watched and strained to hear but could not understand any of the words.

The group, including Hollyhock, watched for several more minutes. The newcomers had unnatural coverings over their bodies and heads. The sight of them all covered up was so strange.

Finally, Mother Nature started speaking again through Hollyhock.

"A new creature is visiting this forest. This creature walks on two legs, and the species is called human. Humans have lived on this Earth for a very long time; you just haven't seen them before. They come here now as part of my plan."

The animals watched the creatures with looks of shock and continued listening to her voice.

"Humans don't normally live in forests. They live with their families in homes outside the forests, where they are happier and more content. The ways of humans are very different from what you know. You won't be able to understand what they are saying, and they won't understand you. Like you, they can only speak to and understand their own kind."

A few minutes later, all the humans walked out of view and disappeared into the forest. The animals were nervous, looking around and wondering if other new species would appear. They noticed the humans had left behind a distinct scent, and it now filled their senses and memory. The strong scent indicated to the animals that humans would not walk through their woods undetected.

Mother Nature continued speaking through Hollyhock: "When you heard the rumbling and shaking in your forest, humans had arrived in *this* forest, and I watched them walk about. They measured the trees, and on the larger, older ones they placed X-marks. The trees here were confused as to why marks were being put on them."

Tate, uncomfortable alone, flew down and joined the others on Max's back.

"I explained to this forest what would happen, the same way I am explaining to you today what will happen in yours. Humans returned to this forest and cut down the trees with the X-marks. Tree trunks were cut down and placed on big hauling machines and taken out before dark. It was the sound from their cutting machines that was heard in your forest. The sound was carried by the winds and heard for miles around. The crashing of trees was the great disturbance you felt on the ground for days on end. You were not alone; other forests felt it too. I am sorry for what the forest went through, and Mr. Mole, I'm very sorry your children died."

Mr. Mole sighed. He still felt the loss, but it was softened with the birth of new children this spring.

"As you can imagine, this forest was completely devastated. When the trees perished, the animals hid from humans and machines. When the humans left, my fairies arrived and offered words of comfort and hope. The forest knew this was coming, but they still did not understand why I was so cruel to let humans do what they did."

The group looked at the roads made for the machines to go through the forest. They saw the stumps of trees and many brush piles, but no animals.

Mother Nature explained, "This is what is due to happen to your forest. I don't know exactly when it will happen—only approximately—but it *will*. The humans will make that decision."

She paused, giving the animals time to think and look around.

After a moment, she continued. "Let me tell you a story that you may pass on to your forest: I was with your Oakren when he died. He spoke to me and asked why he had lived that long. He said he was ready to die years ago, not wanting to live without Victoria. Like Oakren, many of the old trees here had spoken to me. They had wanted to go; they were old, broken, and ready to return to the earth. I listened to their final words and heard their goodbyes. When they were felled, I saw their stumps kiss the falling rain."

But Mother Nature wasn't finished talking yet. The animals were surprised that she was taking as much time as she did to explain this to them.

"In all forests, death brings renewal. This was an old forest, too thick with big, old trees, and their canopies were shutting out all the sunlight. The smaller trees were starved for light and were unhealthy. Plants were drying up and dying because they needed the energy from sunlight to survive.

"With the plants dying, animals had less to eat. I explained to this forest why this cutting was necessary. With fewer big trees, sunlight will stream like never before, giving all the trees the light they need to grow taller and wider. Plants here now have the light to grow and provide food for the animals. There is more room for the seeds my fairies threw out. All types of berries will begin growing again, making all the animals happy. Everything has a better chance of survival in the years to come.

"Humans were back here today to check on the forest's progress. What you see are the remnants of last fall's cutting. My fairies have already been here, and seeds have already sprouted. It will take a few seasons, but forest life here will be healthier and happier."

Everything Mother Nature said made sense. It explained their lack of food, but they were still tentative about her plan.

"As you can see, many tall trees remain standing. Of them, one is the tallest tree, and one of the others will take its place years from now when that tree passes. The tall tree is needed to oversee the forest and to guide the fairies every spring. It's part of my plan for every forest. The other tall trees remaining were selected because they are healthy and strong and were needed to support the ground.

"Return to your forest with my words. Tell everyone they have nothing to fear for a few years. Get on with your lives and be happy. If you don't, I won't be happy. For now, your forest will be untouched but know that it *will* be changed. You now know the reason why.

"When humans appear, be wary. It's all right to be afraid when they're around. Coexisting with humans will be scary, but you must. It cannot be avoided, and it is my wish."

The group watched as the sphere lowered to the ground again. Mother Nature said goodbye to the animals and explained she was on her way to visit her next forest that day. Tate and the animals bowed and watched the sphere rise and move away. When it disappeared, the animals looked at each other, humbled by this experience.

Exhausted, they ate the food that had been provided and hunkered down before beginning their journey home in the morning. Before sleeping, they made a pact that when they returned, nothing would interfere with the friendships they had made on this trip. When Benji hiccupped, they all laughed and fell asleep.

From the Forest

Up and down,
Back and forth,
Movements every day.
Daily matinées,
Of graceful ballets,
Forest gifts are displayed.

Close your eyes,

And listen closely,
To the voices and the sounds.
The forest speaking,
Squeaks to creaking,
Communication abounds.

Old trees eagerly,
Tell their tales,
To the horseflies and the bees.
Wildflowers look up,
Ants line up,
Stories told by elder trees.

Told are stories,
Of flowers and trees,
And loved ones now departed.
Things they saw,
Birds that caw,
And how some were outsmarted.

Nighttime falls,
No time for sleep,
Nocturnal creatures rising.
Owls on high,
Flickering fireflies,
Food search preoccupying.

From the forest,
A final hush,
Animals bedding until dawn.
Birds are nesting,
Trees are resting,
Except for a few hangers on.

CHAPTER ELEVEN

Lost and Found in the Woods

Three Years Later,
The Puddle

THE STORM STARTED IN THE MIDDLE of the night, and it woke Finn's roots. He could tell the storm moved closer because the thunder was becoming increasingly louder. A loud warning crack of thunder reverberated underground. It shook him to the core, and he braced himself for another long night, wondering if he'd still be standing in the morning.

The storm rolled in, and with it came high winds and pelting rain. He didn't know what was going on aboveground, but down here the ground was getting very soaked, and the noise was deafening. Every time thunder shook the ground, it rattled him, and he prayed that each shaking would be the last. He'd been through storms many times alone, but this one seemed unending. He felt his trunk pulling on his main root and knew it was having a hard time fighting the wind. His roots veered off in every direction, trying to keep his trunk stable.

Finn was a three-year-old apple tree, growing just a short distance from Pippen, his father. He tried to act brave during storms because he knew that was expected of trees. This storm was just too loud, and his young roots were succumbing to fear. He wanted to go by his father's long roots to seek safety. He slowly inched his way over to Pippen. *Please, please, please, be awake.*

As Finn got closer, his dad saw him and reached out and gathered him in. Only one of Finn's smaller roots could come; the larger ones had to stay back to support his trunk during the storm. The embrace was enough to give all his roots the confidence they needed to hold tight for the rest of the night. Every root heard Pippen's voice, "Don't be afraid, little roots, I'm right here."

Finn trembled as his father held him. He heard the constant *boom, boom, boom* of thunder and couldn't stop shivering. With every boom, he hoped the thunder beast was finished, but it never was.

"When will the storm tire out?"

"Don't worry, it'll be over soon."

While they lay there, water was everywhere, but it was slowly seeping deeper.

"Dad, why do storms have to be so loud? I just wish it would rain without all that noise. A law should be passed, and done very fast, that thunder isn't allowed to scare little trees."

Pippen and Finn finally drifted off, their roots finally managing to fall asleep.

In the morning, Finn woke first and tapped his father to wake him. "Dad, wake up! The storm is over. Let's spread out and hear the talk about it."

They did just that. Pippen found out that there were no tree casualties, but one tree had been struck by lightning, lost two big branches, but survived. Many other trees had dropped debris, which trashed the forest floor. Many plant stems broke and perished, and worms were clinging to life above ground after being forced up by the water. As the water seeped deeper, the worms tunneled back down before hungry birds could snatch them. The forest would be in chaos for a few hours this morning until all the injuries and deaths were tallied.

By mid-morning, a large puddle of water remained in the middle of the commons area; the storm had left something good in its aftermath.

The trees watched birds come in pairs to the water. First came the cardinals, then the blue jays, then the chickadees and canaries. Each took a turn swishing water over their wings. They jumped and flapped, making a spectacle of themselves; you'd never think they had just survived a vicious storm. The trees enjoyed watching the birds splashing in the water.

When the birds cleared, a mole ran to the puddle. He walked in slowly, turning his head, checking for animals who might be waiting to pounce. It looked safe, and he took a quick drink. He turned and saw his family waiting by their door. He signaled for them to join him, and they ran over. Mother mole ran over last and took a long drink, then tiptoed in and did a splashy happy dance. The mole just shook his head and sniveled at her behavior. He motioned for the whole family to get back to their hole before somebody saw them.

One by one, more animals came over. The raccoons, who usually slept during the day, walked over. The fox and squirrel families came in, drank apprehensively, and ran off to look for food.

A doe and fawn timidly walked forward, their ears twitching at unusual sounds. They heard there was a puddle, and they wanted a drink too. Mother deer signaled her fawn to drink first while she stayed back to stand guard. Since it was clear, she advanced and drank beside the fawn. A minute later, they heard crashing in the brush ahead of them. It was probably just a quail, but, out of caution, both deer bolted into the woods. Another forest dweller was making his presence known.

It was the resident bear on his daily walk. The trees fixed their gaze on him as he approached. The bear took a long drink and rambled out again.

Around midday, the temperature got warmer, and the water diminished. The puddle was nice while it lasted. Tomorrow, the animals would return to their normal search for water, and it would be harder. The animals and trees would all remember last night's storm, the terror they experienced, and the nice puddle it left behind.

Max Reflects

Max lay half-awake under the birches. He opened his eyes and saw Pippen standing there. He thought back to five years earlier, when the same tree asked for help to stop the deer from eating his branches. He was glad he had played a role in outsmarting those deer. He looked at Pippen's height now and saw a strong, straight apple tree. But beside him stood a little apple tree, a scrawny lad, just a sliver of a tree. Max was glad Pippen had become a dad.

Max closed his eyes again to reflect on how much his life had changed since he returned from that trip four years ago. The animals didn't fear him anymore; in fact, they treated him like their grandpa. He had become thick pals with Benji, Mr. Mole, and Tate. They had spent many good times reminiscing about their experiences on that journey. It had been the trip of a lifetime for all of them. Benji had even grown into a wise old rabbit.

Sadly, those friends had all passed; Benji had been the last to go. Max had outlived them all. With each loss, a void had grown in Max's life. He had made friends with the new animals, but he missed his old friends. Life held less meaning now, and he saw little point in going on. He spent most of his days alone and reclusive, much like his early years in the forest. This last winter had been another rough one, and he didn't know how many more springs he would live to see.

He had lost count of the number of times he had hibernated in this forest. So many memories, both good and bad. This was where he was born, and this was where he wanted to die. Until then, he would live out his days under these same skies.

"Look here, everybody! There's that bear sitting in his nest!"

The crows spotted him, poked fun, and flew away. The crow brothers from years ago were long gone; these were their noisy offspring.

Hearing these crows brought back memories of the old days. Those old crows were the reason he had made friends with the cardinals. If he hadn't helped Frederica and Tate that year with their beloved eggs, he wouldn't have been a good bear. That year had been the best of his life. Drifting in and out of sleep, he felt tapping on his paws.

What was going on? He opened his right eye to see what was waking him. *For heaven's sake, I'm trying to sleep.* He turned around and was gobsmacked to see a baby raccoon dangling from a tree and tapping his foot.

"Hello, Mr. Thing. I'm a little lost. May I sit by you?"

Max rose to his feet. He lifted his head and sniffed the raccoon, who didn't seem to fear him.

A Day Earlier,
It Was the Toad's Fault

In that short moment... A mother raccoon was clawing at the ground trying to dig up a meal of worms for her children. It just wasn't her day. The worms she managed to dig up squirmed out of her claws and wiggled back into the ground. They went just out of her reach, and she didn't see them again.

In the blink of an eye... The raccoon kits were waiting, watching their mother struggle with the worms. They patiently sat where they were told to sit. Then out hopped a toad.

It happened so fast... The toad wiggled his rear and teased, "Come and catch me!" That did it. They couldn't stay put any longer and chased after him. The toad hopped behind a rock and hid.

They couldn't help it... The kits scratched at the rock, trying to find the toad. Finally, the rock moved, and the three kits expected to see the toad. There was nothing there but a pile of dirt.

Since she was still busy... Then they saw the toad crouching under a sheltering mushroom. They ran up, but before they reached the mushroom, he disappeared into the dark. They almost had him.

They decided they should go back... The three baby raccoons took off in the direction of their mother. Sissy, the smallest raccoon, was left behind in the rush. She tried to follow but could not keep up with her brothers. They just ran too fast.

It happened every time... She stopped and waited in the dark, hoping her mother would find her. She already knew she was in trouble. This would be another raccoon family reminder to stay put when they were told.

Alone in the Woods

The night was dark, so dark. And cool, so cool. And quiet, oh, so quiet. With her ears cocked, she didn't hear anything. She looked around for something familiar but saw nothing. Sissy was lost.

Normally, darkness wasn't a problem for Sissy. She liked roaming the woods at night with her mother and brothers. They looked for food together every night. It was fun. But that night being alone in the dark was not fun.

Suddenly, she heard the high-pitched sound of a coyote. This haunting sound frightened her, and her body shivered. Her mother had repeatedly told her, "Coyotes are not our friends. They love baby raccoons for a snack."

She wished her mother was there right now. She wished she had paid attention to her mother's rules. Sleeping trees tried to cover her view, but she could still see the moon. The moon cast its light down on her and for that she whispered, "thank you." Sissy looked up and saw the light from the stars as well. The light cast from these familiar sources helped her navigate the woods alone tonight. Tonight, light was her friend, and she did not feel quite so alone.

There was no sense standing here by herself. She needed to find her mother or her dumb brothers, who had left her stranded. *One step at a time. I'll be fine.* She convinced herself that her mother was waiting right around the corner. *One step, two, three. Keep going.*

She stopped walking when she saw an odd-shaped object on the ground ahead. Her eyes were good at identifying familiar daytime shapes at night, but she hadn't seen this object during the day. It wasn't the usual rock or log; it was rounded and black and stood out in the murky darkness. It occurred to her that it might just be her mother and brothers all sleeping in a pile.

Tiptoeing closer, she heard snoring and knew it was an animal. Going even closer, she stopped just feet away. No, it wasn't her family. Without moving closer, she strained her head forward, trying to make out the animal.

What was this big black thing, anyway?

The Disappearance

Sally struggled to keep the worms together. As soon as the mother raccoon dug a few out and added them to her pile, others were already pushing their snouts back into the earth to get away. It was frustrating, and she wanted to give up, but her children were hungry. They were behind her, waiting for their supper. The pile was finally big enough, but the worms were all squirming to escape. She needed to act fast and get the children over here.

"Come here you three and eat before they get away!" None of them came forward to eat. When she turned around, they weren't there.

Where did they go?

She was irritated that her children weren't sitting where they had been told to sit. Exasperated, she forfeited the pile of worms to look for them.

Why did they always disobey her? Why didn't they listen? They knew the rules! Her heightened anger mellowed and turned to worry. She knew they were just children; she had been the same curious raccoon at their age.

"Sissy, where are you?"

"Jon, come out of hiding."

"James, come here—you know better!" she shouted.

There was no answer. She wasn't going to panic yet, because she had taught them what to do if they became lost. She walked around, calling their names, but there was no sign of her children. *They couldn't just up and vanish!*

A moment later, the light given off from two sets of eyes darted erratically and looked at her in the darkness. She'd seen these eyes in the dark before and knew she had nothing to fear as they were her children's. The eyes that ran up belonged to her boys, but little Sissy wasn't with them.

Before she could ask about their sister's whereabouts, she heard, "Mother, Sissy's coming, she's following us." They acted like nothing was wrong and she shouldn't worry.

Sally held onto the boys as she scanned the woods for Sissy to appear. She prayed her littlest would walk in at any second, but she didn't. She wanted her daughter home, safe and unhurt with the rest of the family. The boys were now whining because they were hungry. Their whining might call in danger, which meant she had better feed them now and look for Sissy afterward.

After the boys were fed, they searched for Sissy together, roaming the whole area and calling out her name. They climbed a tree; and as three sets of eyes looked out for a better view, they hollered her name. When they didn't hear or see Sissy, they climbed back down and walked the area again, all the while calling her name.

Where was that girl?

Then, quite by accident, they came upon the bear sleeping under a tree. It looked like Sissy was in his grasp.

Sissy and the Bear

Her mother always told her, "Listen to your mother and don't talk to strangers. These woods are filled with danger." *But she liked to take chances.*

Sissy climbed out onto the limb of the tree directly over the thing. She turned upside down and dangled from her tail to get a closer look. Whatever this thing was, it looked old, and had dirty, matted fur. She had never seen this sort of animal here. Its head was down, covering its feet as it lay there. *Was this thing even alive?*

Still dangling and with her front legs hanging down, she got up the nerve and poked it with one front paw. Something her mother once said popped into her head: "Never, *ever*, poke a sleeping bear." *But was this a bear?*

It didn't move, so she poked it again, and again. The thing slowly opened its heavy-lidded eyes and stared back with small, round, beady eyes. If the animal was smaller, she would have thought these were friendly eyes, but she knew better. *Holy smokes, this thing was big!*

The thing lifted its head and looked up at her. Then it spoke in a low snarly voice, "Do you want me to eat you now or shall I eat you later?" As it spoke, drool dripped from its large crater of a mouth. *Oh, how gross!*

Being in danger hadn't occurred to her before this. This thing was big and smelled horrible, and there was icky gunk dripping from its mouth. These were all signs of danger, but she hadn't felt it until now. *Did it really mean it would eat her and find her a tasty morsel? She hoped it didn't mean that.* It hadn't pounced yet and lay looking at her.

Sissy took a deep breath and said, "Hello, Mr. Thing, my name is Sissy, and I'm a baby raccoon. I am lost and afraid. May I sit with you for a while? Please, sir, don't be mad."

The thing's face seemed to mellow, and it sat up and leaned against a tree. She thought that if she asked nicely enough, maybe it would let her sit there beside it. Then she heard, "I'll think about it." *It sounded like he might let her.*

"Let me introduce myself," it said, "My name is Max, and I am a black bear. I don't like being disturbed in the middle of the night, but you may stay."

So far, she liked this black bear thing.

The Rescue

Sally stood balancing on her back feet, trying to get a better view of Sissy sitting between the bear's legs. Of all the animals to meet, a bear! She had told her children many times not to talk to strangers. Yet here was her little Sissy talking to a bear who, if so inclined, could make her his next meal.

Sitting beside her, Jon pointed and said excitedly, "Momma, I see her!"

"I know, I see her too," replied Sally.

Sally and her boys sat looking at Sissy and the bear. Her heart was racing with fear for her child.

Jon, not giving up, whispered, "Will he hurt her with those big claws of his?"

"Shush, be quiet now. Go sit by your brother."

Sally had taught her children to give a particular bird sound if they were ever in trouble. She had been listening for the sound from her daughter but hadn't called it. *Didn't she know she was in trouble?* Since her daughter hadn't called it out, Sally made the sound herself, hoping the girl would recognize it.

She saw the Sissy raise her head above the bear's paw and look straight at her. Jumping up, Sissy immediately ran to her mother, who was happy to see her.

The baby raccoon rubbed against Sally, glad to be found. Her brothers were there with worried looks on their faces. She made a face at them, even though she was also happy to see them.

"Momma, I'm so hungry," said Sissy.

"Let's go home, we saved food for you," replied her mother.

Sissy waved to the bear and yelled, "Goodbye, Max. Thank you for letting me stay by you tonight."

The little raccoon watched Max's ears bend back in acknowledgment, but he didn't say anything. Then she ran off with her mother and brothers, leaving Max alone again as he lay back down.

Back at their home, Sissy began telling her story. "When I got lost, I sat all alone waiting to be found. I was very afraid when I heard strange night sounds." She told her mother and brothers how she accidentally ran into Max.

"He pulled me in close to protect me. We just talked and laughed. He was funny. We heard an owl, and he told me not to be scared. He said if I ever needed help again, I should yell for him, and he would hear me."

Sally listened to her kit as she ate. She had never met this bear named Max, but she'd heard about him through the grapevine. He was the bear that came back from that trip to meet Mother Nature a few years ago, before her kits were born. She thought she should thank him for what he did.

CHAPTER TWELVE
Farewell and Return

Things We Take for Granted

MAX LEANED AGAINST THE TREE and studied the moon in the sky. He had seen the moon every day of his life, and its presence was taken for granted by everything in the forest. On nights like this, the moon was big and brightly colored. Something caused its change of color. He liked to think it changed color when it was happy. On other nights, it looked sad because it appeared to have lost its size and color. On those nights, it was dull colored and looked as if a chunk had been bitten out of it. It was a strange and curious thing because the moon always seemed to grow back to its normal size. He took the moon and its size changes for granted.

Besides the moon, Max realized there were many other things in the forest he took for granted. After coming home from that trip, he knew that when the time came, life here would change fast. He wondered if he would still be around to witness it. Four years out now, nothing had happened yet. He knew that just waking up every morning was something he took for granted.

Little things in the forest were taken for granted. The trees, for instance, did not magically grow tall overnight. An acorn had to fall from a tree and take root in the ground. It took many years for them to grow to the stature they reached. Tree growth was taken for granted.

He paid no attention to the yips of a coyote or the lonesome hooting of an owl. The sound of animals prowling at night was commonplace. They did their own thing, and the nightly noises of their foraging escapades was paid little attention and taken for granted.

He took for granted the air he breathed every day. He had breathed in air from the day he was born. He couldn't help it and felt good when he did. When the same air made movement, it was either happy or trying to warn of something. He was grateful for air and took it for granted.

Rain came down or it didn't, but it usually rained at the right time when the forest was thirsty. Sometimes, for whatever reason, Mother Nature deprived them of water for long stretches of time. When that happened, they didn't complain; she was the boss. They looked forward to the rain when it finally came and took for granted it would fall sooner or later.

And the sun was constantly there. Unlike the smaller moon, he knew why the sun was there. The sun appeared on one side of the forest and woke the forest in the morning. As it appeared, it slowly brought light and heat. When it was bedtime, it slipped through the trees on the other side of the forest and turned off the light and heat. Everything liked to watch the sun's light show as the forest and the sun readied for bed. The different colors in the sky made by the sun's light were the forest's entertainment before it got drowsy.

The actions of the sun all made sense, except for one thing: Why did the sun keep the light on but turn off the heat for three months every year when the beast was here? That made life miserable for the plants and animals in the forest. But it happened every year and he and the others all took the lack of heat for granted.

In his many years of living here, he had figured out that the big sun has a hand in making his shadow as he walked. He knew the flowers loved light and it helped them to grow bigger. He knew the light and heat from the sun helped his beloved berries to grow. He pushed himself to get to them on time. He also knew the sun reduced its light and heat which made his berries fall to the ground and the stems die. But it was all expected and taken for granted.

So many things in this forest had been taken for granted. When their time for the change arrived, he wondered what things would be affected by it, and whether they would ever take them for granted again? He was afraid to think about that and lay back down to sleep.

The Inquisitive Apple Tree

Four springs ago was the first time Pippen saw the little rabbit sniffing around under his tree. At the time, he had no idea the animals were watching the rabbit to ensure his safety. He didn't know then that the rabbit couldn't see and that this was the reason that the little guy never noticed or talked to him.

Thinking back to that year, Pippen recalled that his last apple from the previous fall had finally detached from its high branch. It had stayed because the deer couldn't reach it, the wind couldn't budge it, and it hung on precariously. It seemed defiant, unwilling to meet the same fate as the other apples. One by one, other apples let go, or were forced to let go, and sacrificed themselves to the forest's common good.

After lying on the ground for a week with only a few ants investigating the dried-up apple, the rabbit came by and started enjoying its sweet taste. After many nibbling sessions, the rabbit eventually consumed what remained, leaving only two seeds to find their own way in the world.

Pippen remembered the bear coming over and pawing the ground in the vicinity of the seeds. It was then that he knew the seeds would have a chance at life. Weeks later, one seed sprouted and looked up at the light. He waited for the other to sprout, but it never did.

The single seed had rooted close to him, and as the little tree grew, they became best friends. Pippen named him Finn because his father had explained that Finn, according to some traditions, meant being interconnected with living things in the forest and having respect for nature. He wanted his son to grow up with that respect.

Pippen told Finn the story of the year he had been Finn's age—when the deer had eaten his branch tips and the animals banded together to feed the deer instead. He knew Finn hadn't had that problem because the story had passed down to all the deer offspring. The deer all had compassion for Finn due to guilt, knowing they were partly responsible for his father's lack of growth.

Finn was Pippen's only offspring, a wisp of the apple tree he would someday be. At a young age, he was already an inquisitive tree. He liked to unravel how and why things happened in the forest. The most insignificant things he pondered for days. Most of the time, though not always, he could figure out the answers if he thought about them long enough. This watching and pondering filled his days. When he felt he had things figured out, he went to Pippen to discuss his ideas. Pippen was amazed at Finn's thoughtful explanations about life in the forest.

When Finn wondered why the ants were always moving dirt, he thought the only probable answer was to avert death. Their tiny bodies couldn't take the heat, so they had to dig deeper to cool off. He had reasoned they took turns going in and out of the hole to cool off. Finn said they seemed to be such insignificant little creatures, but Pippen suspected their mothers would disagree.

Finn also wondered why the trees always moved. He concluded that they communicated through their roots. He claimed to know this because his own tiny roots had felt tapping and whispers to tell him something. The winds, he reasoned, made tree branches thrash about, but he knew the trees enjoyed the exercise because movement helped them to see more of the world.

When Finn watched the leaves fall, he figured out that after they landed, the ground collected them and let them dry and crumble. The decaying process provided food for the soil and the wiggly worms who lived below. Pippen was pleased that his son grasped the cycle of decay and renewal.

Some days the forest seemed sad. Finn noticed that the forest was darker now under the canopy than when he had first sprouted. He remembered the loving feeling of light and warmth when he first sprouted. That was four springs ago; now he saw that sunlight was scarce, sometimes with no sun for days on end. On those days, plants felt sad and drooped with little energy. But when the sun came through the crowns, they received a burst of energy. Finn watched plants eagerly stretch into the light and revive.

At first, it saddened Finn to see fallen branches, and he knew the same could someday happen to him or his father's branches. But he also understood that when a branch lay dead on the ground, mice or other small animals chewed through the wood and made holes for homes. Pippen had already taught him about the circle of life, and Finn seemed to accept that death in turn brought new life for the forest.

There were days the animals wandered aimlessly because food was scarce. Some days they walked in circles and passed by Pippen's tree several times. They hunkered down hungry, knowing they needed to conserve energy for the next day's search.

When Finn saw the animals sniffing around, he guessed they were investigating their surroundings just as he liked to do. He listened to their questions and the answers their parents gave. Like Finn, they were eager to learn.

While Pippen watched Finn's curiosity, he found he was also watching and learning from different things. Both trees spent their days always looking for something new. Neither wanted to miss a thing in their little part of the forest.

Pippen and His Dream

How time had gone by so fast was a mystery to Pippen. It seemed just yesterday he had complained to his forest friends about those deer eating his branch tips. They had come up with that ingenious plan that helped spur his growth. That had been fifteen years ago, when he was a young tree. He was an older tree now and had a son to help through life.

He didn't have anything to complain about in his life. His body felt strong, and his tree produced many apples that the animals loved. His own father, Great Apple, was well over one hundred years old. He creaked a lot and stood crooked, at least that was what Pippen had heard. Pippen and his father hadn't spoken to each other much since his seed blew there and sprouted. They communicated with each other through the root system, which passed messages between roots. The system had worked well for millions of years and would for millions more.

Many times, his bird friends brought and sent news to him. News sent by bird express was faster than root mail. If his own roots had had the ability to stretch the distance to his father, that would have been perfect, but they could not go that far. The worms and other small animals had also volunteered their services, but he hadn't taken them up on that yet.

He felt fortunate to have Finn growing up next to him. With this closeness came the satisfaction of watching him grow and witnessing his life's milestones. He saw Finn's first flowers, his first apples, and the first time his leaves turned colors and fell. He also shared in Finn's excitement when Finn passed on his first root message to him.

Each year, Finn's friends threw a birthday party for him, just as Pippen had enjoyed at his age. Now he was an older tree, and didn't get that attention anymore, but deep down he still liked to be remembered.

Pippen rarely dreamed, but on those nights he did, the dream usually vanished from his thoughts as soon as he woke. A few mornings ago, however, he had woken from a dream that had stayed with him for days. It had been a beautiful dream, but disturbing for a tree. He wondered if either a butterfly fairy or Mother Nature herself had planted it in his dreams as an omen of something to take place in the future.

In the dream, he had stood near a large field. The weird thing was that his lower trunk had split, and he was standing on two legs. He'd been shocked, but once he realized he could move on those legs, he'd felt exhilarated. He remembered walking and feeling the different textures on the ground—soft grass, bumpy stones, and the cushioning moss. It was surreal; these were all things he could never have imagined. He had raised his legs to touch other plants, twisted his torso to see around him, and drank in the sunlight that spilled over the field.

The field had been huge and stretched as far as he could see. Wildflowers were everywhere, swaying and dancing in the warm breezes. Their heads were tilted to the sun, grasping the light they adored.

And bees! Up ahead, the field was covered with them. They hovered everywhere; the pulsating wings created the sound of *"hmm,"* like a sigh of contentment. Flying from flower to flower, the bees flew carefree in their beautiful flower playground.

And the smell! As he walked into the field, he remembered the wonderful fragrance. It reminded him of the spring fairies, freshly opened flowers, and the sweet fruity scent of ripe berries. The aroma was dizzying and intoxicating as he walked.

The flowers and the bees noticed him there and were extremely polite. Rather than let him bump into them, they opened a path for him to walk, which made him feel special. The bees were fearless and rested on his branches. They enjoyed the new vantage point as they looked out over the field.

In the dream, there hadn't been a cloud in the sky, and the light and warmth had felt wonderful on his bark. The field seemed a perfect place for flowers and bees to live. The bees flew, gathering nectar from the plants, happy and content in their work. With their heads high, the plants were happily drinking up the sun without a care.

But then he woke up. *If only this were real.* A sudden realization hit him: Those weren't bees at all; those were thousands of butterfly fairies!

Of course! He had dreamed of butterfly fairies! Those sweet little girls who visited the forest each spring had found their way into his dreams. It had all been very pleasant.

A week after that dream, he had been roused early from his sleep, when he had felt a tapping on a branch. "Pippen! Pippen! Please wake up!" A real butterfly fairy had been trying to get his attention.

Late Summer,
The Berry Thief

The air had been damp and stagnant, much like it felt after a rain, except it hadn't rained. For the last week, the temperatures during the day had fluctuated between hot and very hot. If there had been a way to take off his fur for a day or two, Max would have done it to get relief from the heat. It was hard to get a full breath, and he felt tightness in his chest as he lay there.

With these miserable conditions, Max was lazy. His mind gave him excuse after excuse to stay down: His body would be stiff from not moving, and if he got up, it would be difficult to walk. His fur would be matted and sticky from bugs under him, plus he stank. He didn't want to smell his own stench, let alone his neighbors smelling him.

But he had to get up, sitting here was suffocating him and his common sense. On days like this he didn't want to walk around, but he couldn't ignore his hunger any longer.

Max moved his front shoulders up and down to loosen his joints. As he leaned his head back, he waited for the crack—the sound that indicated his neck would feel better after hearing it. He sighed, a*h, that was better.* He slowly rose to his feet and turned his head from side to side.

The forest didn't move and trees were still, and, obviously, all the animals were doing what he'd been doing—hunkering down, waiting for the insufferable air to dissipate.

All right, I gotta do this. Max knew what time of year it was. His good bear sense told him that the blackberries should be ripe. The breeze always brought their scent through the forest, catching the animals off guard. Each one followed their nose until they tracked down the berries to satisfy their craving.

But that day was different. There wasn't any breeze, the forest felt dead, and the sweet berry scent wasn't there. But he *knew* it was time. His mind imagined berries calling, *come here, bear, pick me, eat me.* He envisioned them on the vine just waiting for him to show up. He could be first if he got there today. He had to get there before any intruder bear had the same idea.

If he remembered correctly, a long walk was ahead for him. With this thick air, it would take him longer to get there, but he must; he wanted to be first. As he trudged through the brush, his anticipation grew for the taste of blackberries. He didn't need anyone to show him where they were because he took pride in his sense of direction and smell.

Shuffling through debris on the forest floor, Max walked over dead logs, ducked under low-hanging branches, and pushed ahead through brush that tried to hinder his advance. *I'm hungry; get out of my way!*

He stopped to rest. By his recollection, he should be seeing the bushes. *Yes!* He saw the patch through the trees. He recognized the leaves and the height of the plants.

Max continued his trudge through the trees and stood in front of the patch. Turning his head from side to side, something was off; this was not what he expected to find. The plants were trampled down, with wide paths going up to the bushes that once held berries. Those stems were on the ground with the ripe berries eaten and the rest smashed. Some other animal had been there and carelessly trampled the bushes. Where feet had gone through, the vines were dead and already brown. He was disappointed and angry at the unexpected sight. *Dang it! Another bear ate here before me!*

The lower stems within his reach were stripped of ripe berries; only the tart red and green berries remained. The lower stems were always the easiest to reach, leaving him to work to find the juicier black ones. He raised his head and looked around; but as expected, no ripe berries were within reach. The higher stems, with their wickedly long thorns, were filled with blackberries. They were calling him, but he had no way to get to them.

He stood on his back legs to try to reach the berries. A thick stem with long thorns brushed against his nose. Jerking his head back to try from another angle, he tried again, but this time the stem's buddies ganged up on him, stabbing their thorns into his hide. His head and side were cut, and he backed up when he felt the pain.

Max gave up and sat down, out of breath. He thought that somewhere out there, another bear from another forest had walked here and was licking his chops.

Upset and tired, he knew he should calm down and not overdo it. At his age, too much activity would be bad for a bear. He decided to rest and try again when he woke up. His legs buckled, and he dropped to the ground in exhaustion.

Tired from the morning walk and the fight to find berries, he slept. Max finally roused, opened his eyes, and realized where he was. He forced himself to his feet again to search for any accessible berries he had missed. As hungry as he was, even half-ripe berries were now acceptable to eat.

His ears went back when he heard crows squawking up ahead. They were not playing around; they were warning of an incoming threat.

Two-Legged Creatures

The forest floor woke from its lazy slumber at the sound of crows flying overhead. The screeches were usually annoying, taken-for-granted sounds, but that day their voices carried a tone of urgency. Crows detected trouble before other birds or animals, and on this day their warnings sent shivers through the forest.

"Watch out! Strange creatures in the forest!" the crows cried. They followed with, "Danger, danger!"

The plants and animals stared up at the crows, not knowing if they needed to take shelter. They waited in fear until they knew more from Little Tree.

Little Tree looked off into the distance, past the meadow to where the daisies grew. It was his job to warn the forest of danger, and sometimes he relied on birds to see things before he could. He strained to see what the crows had spotted and finally made out the shapes of the creatures the crows were seeing. Two tall beings moved slowly and silently approached the woods. Creatures he had never known existed.

The crows flew another pass over Little Tree and cried, "Something approaching, our woods encroaching!" The crows looked alarmed by the unusual sight, yet excited that something exciting was happening.

The creatures entered the woods from the field. Little Tree sent warnings down through the roots to spread the news. Those messages spread to the animals, who told other animals and were warned to hide.

As the creatures walked into the trees, their footsteps made crunching sounds that alerted the forest. Animals took one look at them, ran for cover, and disappeared. Baby animals huddled close to their mothers and stayed very quiet.

With strange creatures in their midst, there was complete silence. The beings pointed at trees with their odd appendages and walked up and inspected them. Their movements were unnatural, and they spoke to each other in an unknown language. They left peculiar footprints— one long indention with no sign of claws. A brave bee flew up to inspect one of the strangers and was swatted away.

Little Tree watched curiously as the creatures stood at the base of his trunk and looked up. One of them held an object that was wrapped around his trunk. To measure it, perhaps? He could not be sure. After a few minutes of walking through the area, it looked like the creatures were preparing to leave. But then they approached the blackberry bushes, walked around, and quickly left the area.

Creatures in the Woods

The sound of crunching leaves alerted Max that something approached. The thick blackberry bushes obscured his vision, but he suspected it was the intruder bear returning for round two of eating. He stood there and waited, ready to reveal himself to his nemesis. He walked forward and looked through a small opening in the bushes. He wanted to see the intruder before it saw him.

It had been years earlier when he first stood in shock seeing these same creatures. That day when Mother Nature explained what would happen to their forest, had become the most significant, life-changing day of his life. When he returned to his corner of the forest, he held all that knowledge and shared it with everyone. Almost overnight, his status in the forest changed and he'd become someone the animals trusted more.

The prophesied appearance of the creatures was here, and he stood in shock to see two, two-legged beings approaching the berry patch. *What was it Mother Nature had called them? Oh, yes, they were called humans.* That first encounter on the hill, looking down, seemed a lifetime ago, something he'd remember for the rest of his life. Mother Nature's words that day about humans and their impending arrival in the forest, also stuck with him. She said to be wary and learn to coexist. To be wary would be easy; to coexist would be impossible.

He didn't know the reason for their being there that day or whether they meant harm if they saw him. In his younger years, he had never been afraid to stand up to anything to defend himself, but with advanced age and dwindling strength, he couldn't anymore.

Unsure of what to do, he decided that the sensible and safest action was to slowly turn and walk away. He turned around and walked through thorny bushes, exiting to the trees, out of view of the humans. Not sure if he had been seen, he turned to see if the humans were still there. They were and were bent over studying his tracks on the ground at the entrance of the patch.

He wondered if they were afraid of running into a bear, or if only he feared them. Max felt no animosity toward humans or other bears, at least not yet, and he started walking home. There appeared to be no blackberries on the menu for him today.

Before he arrived back at his home in the birches, he walked into animals standing together and whispering in the commons area. The deer were irritated and fussed over the strange two-legged creatures they saw. Sally, the mother raccoon, was tearful, overwhelmed by the whole experience. As soon as Max walked in, they asked him to tell everything he had seen and what he knew about the creatures.

Max sat on the ground and faced the other animals. Birds were lined up perched in trees. Moles came out and sat in rows on their knees. The sudden hush silenced the bees. For this meeting with Max, they let go of their petty differences.

The trees had paid close attention to the day's happenings. The animals' perceived threat had brought this impromptu assembly. Only the oldest animals still living there knew of the other meeting after the terrible forest disruption and the decision to contact Mother

Nature. The older trees saw the same fear on the animals' faces that day that they remembered from years earlier. The trees also knew that Max was the only animal from that original mission still living, and only he could answer their questions.

Max tentatively sat and looked at the animals. All these years he had avoided public speaking, but there he was, expected to speak to this frightened group of animals. It finally hit him that perhaps that was what Mother Nature had intended for him to do all along. He had gone on the mission as a leader and would attend this meeting not as a listener but again as a leader. She had foreseen him as the explainer, the voice of reason, and the one to calm their fears. He thought he had better take the time to do just that.

He sat and rested and was almost ready to speak. The group waited patiently to hear words of reassurance that there was nothing to fear. He took his time as they watched him brush flies away from his head.

He knew that what he would tell them would break their hearts. He'd never had to deal with this sort of thing before, but here they were, waiting. They had to know what he knew, because the future events Mother Nature warned about were going to happen.

Max began, "Several years ago, Mother Nature spoke to a group of animals here about the day creatures called humans would appear in our woods. She said they would come in and walk on two legs and speak their own language. We were told they meant no harm, but it was all right to fear them. They had an unusual scent that would warn us when they are here. We were also to heed the warnings of the crows and hawks."

Max told the animals that they would be seeing many more humans in the days and weeks to come. He explained to this new generation of animals what would happen to the large trees in the forest. He said Mother Nature was allowing this to happen so the forest could become strong and healthy again, which would make all their lives better.

The animals waited for Max to continue. The bear was tired from his day of walking and his encounter, but he had to finish and tell them the rest.

"When humans come again, life here will be tense. The ways of these strangers won't make sense. If you are afraid, your legs and speed will be your best defense. Keep alert, help each other, and think clearly."

Max stopped talking and looked at the sky. He could see the sun getting low in the trees. "Go home now, go home to your beds. In the morning, tell others what I've said. I want everyone prepared for the next arrival of humans."

He was tired and done talking for the night. He walked to the birches and settled down to sleep.

What was all the whispering?

He looked around to see all the animal families tiptoeing in and settling around his bed. Parents and their children were coming in to hunker down with him.

The trees watched and were in awe of what they were witnessing. Sally, the raccoon, and her family crept very close to the bear. Sally's children were whispering and asking her questions.

"Momma, what if those humans eat all our food? Do we have to watch for them all the time?"

"Shush, go to sleep now, I don't know all the answers." She was also afraid but didn't speak of her fears in front of the children.

Sally looked up at the moon overhead. The light it sent down touched the ground and was comforting. With that light and with Max here, she and her family were safe. All this talk of intruders and the need to run worried her. She knew she wasn't alone; it was the same for all the animals. At least with the old and wise Max here, they had less to fear.

The trees watched as the raccoons slept comfortably against the snoring bear. They saw a family of foxes huddled on his left side. Three deer stood for the longest time but eventually dropped to the ground behind the bear. Owls and owlets were cuddled together, sleeping on a branch overhead. The plants and animals all had humans on their minds and had trouble falling asleep, but they finally did.

The next morning, the animals sniffed the air before leaving. There was no unusual scent to indicate human presence. One by one, they disappeared into the forest. Once again, the foxes and moles sneered at each other but went their own way. The crows flew over and yelled, "All clear!" So far, it looked like another normal day.

All thoughts of humans vanished from their heads. Their immediate concern was searching for food, after which chores had to be completed. The same old arguments resumed, and some got heated. Confused bugs got caught in spider webs, and the spiders busily packed them away to eat later.

The Last Apple

Pippen and Finn had listened intently to Max speaking that night. His son already knew most of this because he had told him the tale of Max's encounter with Mother Nature. Max had only reinforced to Finn that the stories were true. But hearing it again made Pippen apprehensive and concerned about the forest. Pippen knew that their peaceful forest was on the verge of being upturned and destroyed. He wished there was something he could do to help calm fears, but what? He was only an apple tree.

Weeks had passed since humans walked into their forest. There had been no return visit, and life returned to normal. The signs of fall approaching were everywhere. The days were getting cooler, berry bushes were dry and withered, and leaves were changing to their fall hues. These changes were a reminder that the animals needed to plan again for the beast's return. Amid their preparations, Max's words of warning were always on their minds. Animal senses were on alert for another human appearance.

That dream Pippen had a few weeks earlier never left his thoughts. The beauty of the field, the aroma, the carefree atmosphere and, of course, his ability to walk made it unforgettable.

He knew in real life this stuff could never happen. How thoughts like this even entered his dreams was beyond him. Walking the valley on a moving torso? *Pfft, that would never happen to a tree.*

But yesterday he'd been awakened by a distinctive floral scent. He looked around and saw a bee hovering beside his trunk. The morning sun pierced its wings, giving the illusion of near invisibility. The tiny body had been close enough that he saw two tiny arms and legs folded back, clothing glued against its body as it hovered. He looked closer and could see very fine, brownish-red hair dancing in the air. As the small creature sparkled and hovered, it emanated happiness. Pippen knew this was not a bee but rather one of their beloved butterfly fairies.

Fully awake, he'd been surprised to hear a voice. Plants talked through their roots but also spoke through their trunks to other plants. He heard the fairy speak to him as if he were hearing another plant speak. He listened as she spoke her mind. None of the other trees, including Finn, were aware of her presence or their private conversation. Her voice came to him squeaky and high-pitched, like that of a bee. While friendly, it also sounded authoritative.

The voice said, "Good morning, Pippen, my name is Miss Laurel, and I am a butterfly fairy. I have flown a great distance just to see you. I am here at the request of Mother Nature to tell you more about her plan and how these woods will be affected by coexisting with humans. I have been asked to help you understand what and why it will happen. We have a great many things to go through."

Pippen listened carefully as Miss Laurel spoke. After a minute, he noticed her voice quaver and her wings no longer moved in unison. She said, "I'm sorry, but I must rest. My energy reserves are low from the trip here. My body tells me I need a five-second recharge."

She flew over and sat on a leaf, neatly tucking back her wings and straightening her clothing. Miss Laurel closed her eyes while Pippen waited. Suddenly, her eyes opened again, and her energy was renewed.

Pippen asked, "Are you okay?"

She smiled at him, indicating she was fine, and resumed her business at hand. "I am aware that a few weeks ago humans visited your forest, and I know that many of your trees will be cleared in the spring. The clearing is being done to help your forest. You will see. After clearing the trees, humans may eventually build homes. Right now, they live elsewhere in their own habitat, but they have taken a liking to your forest. The forest is geared to have a long existence with humans, but don't be afraid, because they will become your neighbors. They will come this spring with machines which will produce ground disturbances and loud sounds. The animals should temporarily move deeper into the woods and get out of their way, as their activities and noise will make their lives miserable."

So far, Pippen already knew much of what she said. Max had already told them that humans were coming; he just didn't say when.

"Pippen, this is where we need your help. We need someone who is brave, strong, and likable to contact all the plants and animals here to let them know what will happen this spring. Many already know, but the vast majority do not. When it starts, we don't want anyone saying they didn't know. They also need to know that these humans come as friends, and that what they do to the forest is for the forest's overall good. If animals want to have contact with humans, that is their prerogative, but we advise hiding and blending out of sight until humans leave the forest."

Pippen had been silent, confused by her last words. He'd known he couldn't question Mother Nature's plans. His purpose was to carry out her wishes—but he wondered why she'd chosen him, a tree, to do this.

It's not as easy as she thinks. I'm a tree, I can't move. Can I refuse? Why doesn't she ask someone who can walk? It is just impossible for me to do this! As he thought this, he forgot she could hear his words.

Miss Laurel heard his thoughts and continued, "Pippen, we know that over the years you have developed a kinship and trust with your forest. We've seen how you are with Finn. You are a thoughtful and attentive listener. That's what we need; someone to explain the change but also someone with the patience to listen to concerns and calm their fears. It won't be fun, and it won't be easy, but she has faith in your ability to walk and navigate through these woods spreading the message."

Huh? What did she just say?

"This fall, when your last apple falls from your branches, you will be free of extra weight. You will wake up from sleep, and you will have two legs upon which to walk. Don't be afraid. You will be able to walk through the forest to speak directly to groups of inhabitants. Say goodbye to Finn and be on your way. This must be completed before the beast arrives."

Pippen had been shocked. He knew then that his dream had been a premonition. That was why he couldn't get it out of his head. His walking on two legs was really going to happen.

"Walk the entire woods. Speak quietly in groups. Don't worry, plants and animals will all understand your voice. Come in, set up meetings, and tell them the facts. Don't be a gloomy Gus but explain the upside of life after tree removal. Don't disappoint Mother Nature. You were her first choice."

Miss Laurel had completed her meeting with Pippen. She wished him good luck and said farewell. Within just a few minutes of her arrival, she was ready to return home, and she took to the air.

He was honored to be chosen by their beloved Mother Nature, and he understood his task. The woods needed to know that Mother Nature had their backs and that they shouldn't be worried when humans became a distraction.

He hoped Miss Laurel would be his visiting fairy again in the spring before all the commotion started. All he could do now was wait for that last apple to fall.

Dang! I'm going to be a walking tree! He was not looking forward to telling Finn.

Loving the Land

In her invisible sphere, Mother Nature's job was to nurture life in the natural world. A higher creator had given her the power and resources to perform her work. Her job included being a provider, nurturer, teacher, and healer. She was the force behind and the interconnector of nature.

Although never seen, Mother Nature might have been happy and content or might have been worried and sad. One day she might have been righteous and powerful and the next meek and timid. Though she seemed to hide when disasters struck, she was everywhere. Every action had a plan, and every plan was carried out with purpose.

She had been pushed forward and then pulled back, swept along by ocean currents. Whale pods were heard calling out to each other. When mothers breached the surface, she enjoyed seeing the calves breach alongside, learning as they grew. The whales lined up, fed, and swam together. She followed for hours; watching the oceans was a test of her endurance.

From high in the sky, she looked down on the land. With outstretched arms, the winds guided her over treetops. She and her millions of fairy helpers visited the forests every spring. They sat and listened, and took note of growth, deaths, and progress. They healed the weary, thrust seeds for new growth, and marveled at the strength the forests possessed. Tears sometimes fell as raindrops.

> *Feeling joy in her heart, she shouted out loud,*
> *"I love this land! Yes, I admit it!"*
> *For millions of years,*
> *And for millions more,*
> *To the natural world she was committed.*

From a high vantage, she saw the land in its full glory. As she looked down on the Earth, she was a proud mother. Carefully choosing which cloud to embark, Mother Nature often got tossed about when the sky turned dark. Her best decisions and ideas were formed while she sat on the clouds.

Mother Nature watched as rivers meandered and flowed, viewing the routes from up high or from the ground. Sometimes, while marveling at a scene, she got lured in by the water. She stood on riverbeds and talked to the fish. Her feet were enchanted by the delightful squish of the bottom. The fish all swam to her like bees to their queen. Her wish was for all fish to be healthy and strong so they could populate the waters.

> *Feeling joy in her heart, she shouted out loud,*
> *"I love this land! Yes, I admit it!"*
> *For millions of years,*
> *And for millions more,*
> *To the natural world she was committed.*

She watched the geese migrate to their wintering ranges. They flew with strong wings, with self-preservation in mind. Flights were long and hard as they concentrated on their destinations. She loved seeing each flock's different but well-aligned V-formation. When new leaders were assigned, there was only a minor change of pace. They were unsure, but they sensed Mother Nature flying along.

When darkness settled and the world slept, she took a break from her busy merry-go-round of life. Her days were filled as a busy globetrotter, taking notes on mountaintops and calming the storms. She gave water to the thirsty and rest to the weary. Her flowers bloomed year-round, giving joy to the world and nectar to the bees.

Her life was a constant teeter-totter, seeing the good one day and the bad the next. But there was no need to prod her to do her job, because her life's work had her completely spellbound.

> *Feeling joy in her heart, she shouted out loud,*
> *"I love this land! Yes, I admit it!"*
> *For millions of years,*
> *And for millions more,*
> *To the natural world she was committed.*

Finn's Questions

Finn thought it was awesome that his father had another encounter with a butterfly fairy. Finn was excited when he heard what Mother Nature had asked of his father. If a tree could jump up and down, Finn would be doing it. He was proud that his father had been picked for such an important job.

He repeatedly asked his father to tell the story of meeting the fairy to him. Finn had noticed that with every retelling, his father remembered new details he'd left out. He was an observant apple tree and noticed the slight variations in stories but kept asking because he wanted to know everything.

Finn couldn't help feeling sad that his father would be away from home for a few weeks. The thought of something happening and his father not coming home, made him uneasy. Finn didn't want to imagine growing up alone.

Pippen told him everything he knew about what would happen when the humans came, but Finn still asked questions nonstop. The fairy had said patience was one reason his father had been chosen. Finn could tell his father was trying hard to show it. He answered Finn's questions with *great* patience as if Mother Nature might be watching him.

"Father, when humans come, will *we* be okay? Do you think our trunks will be left in shambles? What about Great Apple? Will they cut him down? Will they frighten the birds, the bear, and the deer? Will humans trample the berry vines and brambles?"

Pippen answered as best he could. Finn wished his father knew more. It seemed Miss Laurel either didn't know the exact details or had purposely left them out. All Finn knew was that they had a month before fall arrived, and after fall, the beast would be back. The humans were due to return once the beast moved on.

For Finn and Pippen, it was a waiting game for his last apple to fall. When that happened, Finn knew his father would be on his way. That is, if he got his legs.

Saying Goodbye

A month had passed and summer had ended. The wind had dropped Pippen's apples onto the ground, where they were eaten or stolen by the animals and birds. He didn't mind because he knew they were beginning to stock up for the beast's arrival. Every day, Pippen looked around and counted the number of apples that still hung on his branches. As the apples decreased, his apprehension increased; he was good at keeping his fears to himself.

A final apple was teetering high on a branch. Finn watched it constantly, waiting, and ready to report its drop. The squirrels seemed to know the last apple was there, and the surrounding trees predicted the race to grab it first. Pippen and Finn both knew the apple would disappear by morning.

That night, Pippen and Finn were saying their goodbyes.

"Dad, do you promise to come back?"

"Yes, Finn, I do promise."

"Do you really, *really* promise?"

"I do, I really, *really* promise. All I can say is that I'll be back when the job is done. It shouldn't take very long."

"Okay."

"If I can, I'll get messages to you that I'm all right and when I'm coming home."

That pacified the young tree, and he relaxed. They talked long into the night, and Finn's roots slept beside his father's. Finally, Finn drifted off to sleep. Still awake, Pippen thought being the chosen one was highly overrated.

Pippen Departs

That morning, Pippen looked at his son's root as it slept near the base of his main root. He looked so peaceful, and he hated to wake him to say goodbye. His son was young, but smart and levelheaded. Pippen hated leaving him but trusted the promises of nearby trees to watch over him, and Finn had his friends to keep him company for a few weeks.

At that moment, Pippen could feel his body changing. He wondered if the nearby trees or any animals were noticing. His weeks of apprehension, fear, and dread were ending today. The last apple had fallen during the night, and a passing raccoon had hastily run off with it.

The day to start on his appointed task was here. The promises he'd made to the fairy, Mother Nature, and to his son, came to mind. He prayed he would be able to keep them. In addition to having a son, this would be his greatest life achievement; that is, if he lived through it. He knew he needed to think positively or he might fail.

I will not fail, and I will not let Mother Nature or the forest down.

He was confident and ready. The tree knew what he was supposed to do but had no idea of the hardships he would meet. He was about to find out.

He felt more movement; someone or *something* was messing with his life support. A moment ago, he'd been watching Finn and feeling normal. Suddenly, all feeling had gone away. When he tried to communicate through his roots, he couldn't. He had lost contact with the entire underground root system.

He knew his incapacity was Mother Nature's doing. Looking down at his trunk, he realized his change was complete. His torso and roots were disconnected, resulting in his loss of feeling and nourishment. Not being connected to his roots, he should have been dead, but he wasn't. He was alive and stood on two wooden legs. He wondered if he was *truly* alive or if this whole thing had been one long, crazy dream.

What had formerly been his sturdy, straight trunk was split from the ground up, forming two strange wooden legs. He thought his legs were ugly, and his appearance repulsed him; he tried not to look down. He thought, *how am I ever going to walk on these hideous legs*? He knew he had no choice.

His fruit-bearing branches had all disappeared, presumably to make it easier to walk through the woods. Last-minute questions raced through his head: *How will I drink without my roots? Should I practice walking a little or just head out? How will I speak to animals? Will my roots still be alive when I get back?*

There was no more time for questions; he felt the urgency to start walking.

He and Finn had already decided the best route to take. Since their immediate community already knew of the humans' return and had the explanation from Max, he was going to start talking in groups assembled by Little Tree.

Pippen took his first step, then two, then three. It was surprisingly easy. With the weight of his apples and top branches gone, walking felt effortless. So far, he loved this feeling of movement with nothing holding him down. His trunk felt awkward as he made his way out of their little community and over to Little Tree. The tall tree was shocked as Pippen walked over on two legs. Little Tree just stared at him, curious about what had caused this change.

When Pippen walked in, all the birds and animals gave a collective look of shock and bolted.

All the trees were just as shocked when they saw him, not believing the forest's apple tree had just casually walked in. He heard a tree whisper, "He should be ashamed of himself. He's not doing his job of keeping his birthplace sturdy." He heard the admonishing, "tsst, tsst, tsst," sounds and looks of horror.

He stood alone, not knowing what to do. The community was hiding and all he could do was wait. After a few minutes, he saw small animal eyes peeking out from behind bushes and heads sneaking looks at him from behind trees. Sensing no harm from this strange tree with legs, the curious crept over to inspect him. As they circled him, they sniffed, poked, and kicked at his bark. More animals came in as curiosity got the better of them.

When they heard the tree speak, plants and animals were shocked, as was he, because they magically heard his thoughts. They understood him; he only had to be careful what he thought. On that first stop of the first day, he stayed all day. The forest stopped its daily routine and listened to his warning. He slept well and at first light walked to the next part of the forest.

Day after day, he walked into a different part of the woods, and each day brought the same scenario: at first, they were afraid of him and disappeared. When he showed no harm, they curiously came forward, and he introduced himself. After telling them of the advent of humans and their plan for the forest in the spring, the expected resentment, loathing, and anger erupted.

"How dare humans invade our home!"

"They'll be stinking up our forest with their poking around!"

"And cutting down our beloved trees—we won't tolerate that!"

"I don't believe it; it can't be true!"

Convincing the plants and animals that the arrival of humans would be a blessing, took a great deal of talking. He explained that large old trees would be sacrificed, but it was for the good of the entire forest to enable light to stream in. The new sunlight would produce energy for plants to grow healthier and happier, which in turn would provide more food for the animals. He said that culling the unhealthy, sun-hogging trees would be difficult, but it would minimize overall suffering. The old trees were alarmed but understood the reasoning. It meant their selflessness today was what they would be remembered for tomorrow.

Wherever he went, Pippen arrived as the bearer of bad news. He never knew what to expect and sometimes felt he risked his life to be there. Some animals were hostile and hurled obscenities, while others went further and threw rocks or tried to claw off his protective bark. The bark on his trunk became sparse, giving woodpeckers the access they needed to peck his insides for insects. When he walked, some animals snarled angrily to scare him away, but he stood patiently through all the harassment.

"Hey, I'm as surprised as you that I can get around. Mother Nature changed me. I've been instructed to visit you. Every living thing here must know and understand why this will happen."

After they calmed down, they listened to his message and reluctantly accepted his words as truth. Because of his calm demeanor, they trusted Pippen and often begged him to stay. But he couldn't; he explained he had more communities to visit with the news.

Pippen was exhausted from walking, and the job seemed never-ending. The more he walked, the more frustrated he became, losing enthusiasm and energy. At night, he would stand and tell himself he should forget about the rest of this work and let the pieces fall where they may. The forest would either survive, or it wouldn't. It wasn't his problem. And with the beast approaching, he was worried about getting back to his son before it appeared.

By the end of his second week, Pippen's spirits were at an all-time low. His trunk was in extreme pain and stripped of bark, and putting one leg in front of the other was becoming very difficult. As he stood there, he didn't want to do this anymore. His pain was almost unbearable. He didn't want to take one more step and just wanted to quit, shut down, and die right there.

But then he thought of Finn and remembered he had him to live for. He didn't want his son to hear that he had perished. He thought of the promises he had made and did not want to let down the fairy, Mother Nature, or his son. He did not want to die a failure.

Looking ahead, he saw a large open area. Every step took effort, but he managed to walk out of the woods into it. He stood on the edge of the field and stared out. The field was familiar; it was the same one from his dream weeks earlier. In his dream, it had been summer, and filled with beautiful, dancing wildflowers. What he saw that day was a different scene. The stems lay flat on the ground, having succumbed to the colder temperatures and the dread of the coming beast. In his dream, butterfly fairies danced in the air, laughing and playing in the warm sunlight. But now the sky was dark and overcast and there were no fairies. It was just a bleak and chilly late-fall scene without activity.

He turned to walk back into the forest when a slight movement on the ground caught his attention. Looking down, he thought it was a small animal wanting to say hello. But it wasn't. Instead, he saw a lifeless stem slowly pushing and moving, trying to come back to life. The clouds cleared, the chilly air warmed, and sunlight broke through. In seconds, the entire field exploded with color as flowers came back to life and swayed in the breeze. Butterfly fairies appeared everywhere, dancing from flower to flower; their scent and the sun's warmth filled the air.

Pippen watched the scene in awe. As he stood looking out, he could feel his trunk repairing itself. His bark reappeared, hardening, and a renewed flow of energy surged through him. He stretched and felt like kicking his legs up in the air, but he resisted, not wanting to make a fool of himself in case anyone was watching. He looked up and thanked Mother Nature. He knew she had heard him and was behind this dream experience coming to life. It was exactly what he'd needed to lift his spirits; his body felt renewed, and his sense of purpose was restored.

After leaving the field, he continued walking. He surprised a mother bear and her cubs as they were bulking up for hibernation. The family was shocked, as usual, to see a walking tree approach them. After convincing them he was no threat, they trusted him. He took the time to explain what would happen in the spring. The mother bear was initially upset, not wanting her cubs to face it. Pippen reminded her of all the positive things to come for her and her cubs and that the disruption would only last one spring. Her cubs watched her anger rise and then dissolve. After an hour, he took his leave and continued his walk, letting the mother bear soothe her cubs' fears.

Moving on from the bears, Pippen noticed three crows watching his every move. When he walked, they flew overhead and tried to follow inconspicuously. When he stopped, they perched in trees and whispered. They hadn't ventured over to him yet, but Pippen knew they were curious and wanted to check him out.

"Hey, you crows, come here, I need your help." The crows heard him shout and were dumbfounded. They flew closer and perched in a tree but hesitated to approach.

"Get over here, now!"

Surprised at his tone, they flew in.

"I know you already know that humans are coming in the spring with their machines. I need your help to be the warning system for the forest. If you see or hear humans coming, shout, shriek, and be shrill. Call down and tell the animals to take cover and the birds to take wing. Be loud, but not too loud. We don't want to break the ants' eardrums."

The crows understood and flew off.

After walking the land for over a month, he learned how vast their forest truly was. Standing in his little corner, he had never realized its full size. The fact that Mother Nature managed all these forests, fields, wetlands, and marshlands, astounded him. Pippen hadn't known that this forest was just one of millions of forests around the world that she tended.

The Homecoming

Finn missed having his father around that month. He tried to be brave and handle things on his own, but he still wanted his father there. There was nobody to talk to or snuggle with when he was afraid.

Several storms came through, bringing thunder and lightning that shook the underground. The nights had become very cold, and he missed the warmth of his father's roots. And he missed the tickles. He loved being tickled awake in the morning. He knew that going through this stuff alone was helping him learn and grow, but he didn't care about that, he still wanted his dad there.

He wondered why it was taking him so long when he had said he'd only be gone a few weeks. Over a month had passed, and he still hadn't received any messages from him. Finn started to worry that something had happened.

The neighborhood bear walked by his tree several times a week. Finn knew the bear would soon go down into his den. He'd been out walking more than usual, looking for last-minute food to fatten himself up. Some days, he just sat and stared out, taking in the whole area. The beast would be arriving soon, and Finn thought perhaps that was what the bear was thinking about. He knew the bear was old but didn't know how old. Finn wondered if the bear was thinking about his younger years and all the fun he had once had. Finn thought he'd never know because the bear never talked to him.

Finn hoped that someday the bear would warm to him and come over to talk. These days, the bear seemed to want seclusion and wasn't interested in talking to anyone. With his father away, Finn was lonely by himself.

Just as he thought that the bear stood up. He walked over to Finn's trunk and started sniffing it. Finn wondered why he was doing that. Had he heard what Finn had been thinking about him? The bear circled the tree, still looking at him. Then he stopped pacing and looked up.

The bear let out a loud growl to get Finn's attention. It worked because it almost scared him to death. The trees were also surprised at the bear's outburst.

Finn said, "Hey, do you think that making loud noises will make you friends? Believe me, bear, it won't! Just keep it down."

For the first time in his life, the bear spoke to him. "Pay attention, squirt. It's about your father. I have some news. I ran into him yesterday at the stream. He was wading in the water talking to the fish, turtles, and dragonflies. He asked me to tell you he'd be home soon. He's got a few more places to stop at, but he should be home in a couple of days. Don't be surprised when you see him; he's going to look very different."

Finn was happy hearing what the bear said, and almost at once his sour disposition cleared. He thanked him for the news, and as soon as he did, the bear lowered his head, walked back to his bed, and plopped down.

Then Finn wondered, *how different could he look? He had to have exaggerated his appearance.* He was sure he would recognize him immediately. He couldn't wait.

Finn waited for his dad to walk in and surprise him. Every time a bush rustled, or an animal walked by, he hoped it would be his father. But it was never him, and Finn was always disappointed.

On the third morning, Finn woke up and saw what he thought was a tree standing in his father's place, though he wasn't sure it was a tree. This intruder stood naked and looked dead, completely devoid of bark. It resembled a tree, but it couldn't possibly be one. It didn't move and holes were bored into its trunk. All the branches were broken off, leaving ragged stubs. He wondered why this hideous fraud of a tree was standing there.

He was distracted when he felt a tapping on his main root and then a tickling sensation.

The tickling continued, and Finn tried to ignore it, thinking it was those wiggly worms playing tricks on him again.

He looked over at the intruder tree and suddenly recognized that two of its lower stub protrusions were in the same place as his father's branches had been. *What? No, it couldn't be.* But it was.

He felt the tickling again. *That's him! He's back!* His father's unexpected arrival surprised him, and he intertwined his roots around his father's and squeezed tightly. One of his father's big roots had come over to say hello. Finn was so happy he was back.

It *had* been his father standing there after all. Finn was shocked, it looked as if something had ripped him to pieces and left him to die. Finn felt sad for his father's condition, and his own roots started shaking.

He heard deep, pitiful-sounding vibrations traveling through his father's roots to his own. Then a raspy, gravelly whisper was heard, "Finn... stop... shaking."

Finn stopped shaking as his father's root rested on him. Just feeling the weight of his root, eased his sadness. They lay together and rested.

Hours later, Finn heard him speak again, his voice sounding somewhat stronger. "I will heal from this. I am happy to see you standing and looking good. Don't worry about me. I know I look bad now. It might take me a few seasons, but I'll get back to where I was. You'll see."

Over the next few hours, his father told him that when he arrived back, Mother Nature had reconnected his trunk to his dormant roots. Several hours later, he had felt his root-to-tree life returning. During the time he'd been away, Pippen said he'd gone without water, but Mother Nature had magically provided sustenance to keep him alive. His body ached, and he had been cold, but he was alive. And that was all that mattered, that and being back with Finn. Finn and Pippen clung to each other.

Pippen is Home

Pippen stood there, a shell of his old self. Word spread rapidly through the community that he was back. The animals rushed over, stood around him, and gawked.

"Are we sure this is him?" asked a mole.

"It looks like he's been in a fight, and lost," said a squirrel.

"Oh my, he must be in pain," moaned Mrs. Blue Jay, "I hope he makes it."

To know that one of their own had completed a task for Mother Nature filled them with pride. The fact that he came back at all left many teary-eyed. To them, he looked as if he had aged a hundred years.

The miles of walking had taken a toll on his trunk. Walking through the thick brush and thorny bristles had left him bruised, bent, and broken. His bark was stripped nearly bare from the abuse. Pippen looked blank and confused, nothing like the vibrant apple tree they once knew and loved. The animals returned home with broken hearts.

For days, Pippen simply stood, rested, and healed. He thought about everything he had gone through and the amount of woods he'd explored. *So many trees, so much land! Oh, to be a bird, and be able to see all this from the air!* That experience taught him that his little patch of forest he called home was only a tiny speck in the grand expanse Mother Nature oversaw. He had gained a new respect for her work.

After several more days of rest, his strength returned. He felt almost fully hydrated, and the pain had finally subsided. He was ready to tell his story to the curious plants and animals. He suspected they would be bored long before he was done.

Pippen began his story as interested animals gathered around and nearby trees eavesdropped.

"One day I was out walking, and I tripped on this log. I didn't see it; it just snuck up on me. I went down hard, headfirst. I couldn't move my legs, and that was when I bent my trunk. I was badly hurt and just lay there moaning. I stayed on the ground for days, thinking this was it for me. I was ready to give up and die."

The mice and moles leaned closer and listened intently. Such suspense!

"But then I heard crow voices laughing at me, coming out of nowhere. I thought: *How dare they!* I went through all of this for their good, and they laughed. But their laughter gave me strength. I pushed myself up to stand—oh, it hurt so badly. They didn't know I had it in me, but I cussed out those crows with swear words I didn't even know I knew. When they heard my voice, they were rattled and flew off. There was no way my life was going to end after being heckled by crows!"

A young raccoon timidly walked up to Pippen and gently patted his trunk with her front paw. He felt the warmth of her touch, and it soothed him. She shyly asked, "Mr. Pippen, where are your legs now?"

Pippen looked down at her. "When I came home, Mother Nature took them away. Now I'm back holding up the land again."

"Oh." She ran back to her mother.

He continued, "Everywhere I went I was met with resistance and fear—even hatred. I just stood and waited while the animals gathered to check out the strange tree. They sniffed me out and did things they didn't think I could see. Finally, when a group assembled, I'd shout, 'Hello, I'm Pippen!' Every time I did, they jumped and ran away. But they always came back, curious about the tree with legs. Then I'd say, 'Hello, Mrs. Deer,' in a friendly tone, or 'How are you, Mouse?' They realized I wasn't a threat. That was when I began explaining why I had come."

Pippen was surprised to see that Max had wandered over and was sitting under Finn's branches and listening. He hadn't known yet that Max and Finn were now friends.

"I walked in streams and made new friends there, too. Frogs and turtles swam over, and fish rose from the depths to hear me talk. I was amazed they could understand me underwater. I got to feel the mud squishing on the bottom of my legs. That was *so* soothing. I even talked to a fish who said he was the offspring of that fish named Brookie, the one who helped Max years ago." Pippen saw Max's ears perk up at that. "All the water creatures took turns swimming between my legs."

He went on. "I got spit on by foxes, and bears rubbed against my trunk. My bark got chewed on by raccoons and mice. One time, a blue jay tried to make a home in my trunk but flew off after seeing a better tree. An owl perched on me during one of my talks and asked what diseases I was carrying. I thought that was rude. If I were ever asked to do this again, I'd say *I-don't-think-so.*"

Pippen described finding the field that burst alive with summer wildflowers and butterfly fairies. He told how the sight had cheered him and how Mother Nature had healed his aches just enough for him to continue his work.

He spoke of meeting bears, foxes, and coyotes, and animals he had never known existed. He talked to them all. He even mentioned he ran into Max. Max raised his head and one paw in acknowledgment.

The animals listened intently. Now they finally knew where he'd been and what he'd endured for five long weeks. They said goodbyes to Pippen and Finn and returned to their homes.

CHAPTER THIRTEEN
From Farewell to Renewal

Another Fairy Departure

THE BEAST'S INCESSANT DESIRE for annihilation made it even crueler than in previous years. It had an unyielding urge to knock down and devour whatever was unprepared for its arrival. When it finally moved on, it was a time of sadness and despair as families picked up the pieces of their shattered lives.

After the beast disappeared, plants and animals awaited the arrival of the butterfly fairies and forest rejuvenation.

A few days later, the air was filled with fairies. Those little stewards of goodwill listened and comforted, grieved for the lives lost, and gave hope for better days ahead. Upon receiving their healing mists, pain dissipated. When the seeds were strewn, new life would soon burst from the ground. With their aches and pains alleviated and the welcome forest growth, there were always improved dispositions that lifted the weight of hopelessness.

The day of the fairies' departure arrived, and the great multitude of wings were flying to their assigned rows and positions in the sky. The great assembly took place in the air over the daisy field, and the plants and animals watched in wide-eyed amazement. They saw the leader fly through each row, looking for unoccupied spots, which meant a missing fairy would cause a delay.

The leader shouted, "Everyone is here!" and cheers of relief were heard from the rows of fairies. It was time to leave the forest for another year. The fairies looked down and, turning their heads to the side, blew kisses to the forest. Then, poof, they flew off leaving their sweet aroma wafting down.

Now on their own, it had been a waiting game for humans to arrive. The animals had been concerned, as they had a lot of work to do in rebuilding homes and finding food. The wrens and chickadees were already having a war of words; each claimed the other had stolen their winter rations. Life had already returned to normal.

There was, however, a general feeling of uneasiness as they knew the future would bring humans and destruction. In addition, the animals had been expected to relocate at a moment's notice.

Spring,
The New Road

Just as the temperatures were getting warmer, the animals were busy finding mates and getting ready to raise their young. The forest was alive with activity, with no time to think about the prophecy of cohabitation with humans coming true.

One day there was an unusual knocking, clunking sound and nobody knew where it originated. Mother raccoon thought, *those woodpeckers were making their racket again.* The trees thought, *oh no, the older trees are cracking and falling.* The deer were apprehensive, thinking another walking tree would come strolling through at any moment.

The noise was intermittent and unusual at first. It started to frighten the animals when it changed to a constant grinding that grew louder. They still didn't see anything that could be making the sounds.

Then they heard the crows flying over, squawking something about, "Machines... humans... take cover." Some animals remembered Pippen's advice and immediately ran deeper into the woods. Those who had never seen a human didn't run, waiting instead to see them appear first.

Curious and straining to see the clearing, the animals watched machinery being unloaded and human creatures climbing up and sitting inside the big machines. The machines appeared to be hungry because they now made loud, grinding noises. The animals thought that as fierce as the machines' hunger was, it would be wise to stay unseen because they could get eaten in one mouthful. They ran deeper into the woods to join the others and avoid being eaten.

The trees watched the goings-on with interest. The machines appeared to be making a road across the field. They went back and forth pushing dirt, resting, then back and forth again. By sunset, a rough road had been cleared across the field, and the machines sat unoccupied and sleeping.

The next morning, the humans returned, and their machines were hungry again. Soon after they arrived, two big machines came carrying their back ends full of small rocks. The contents were dumped, and the other machines moved back-and-forth, pushing the rocks over the road until it was blanketed with rocks. With the rocks down, the machines seemed to have an easier time traversing the field. The trees found this all very interesting, and it caused only a few gasps.

The machines entered their forest and continued going back and forth, making roads, and pushing down brush that got in the way. The trees were aghast when that happened but calmed when they saw the trees themselves were unharmed. The animals became accustomed to the sound but remained deeper in the forest.

Several humans entered from the field into the forest and walked into their midst. They advanced and looked at the trees, appearing to study their size. They held an object that, when pressed near the top, released a red spray. Red X-marks were sprayed on many of their larger and older trees. But the trees were still not alarmed because many thought the splashes of red beautified the forest.

Each night, when humans left and machines slept, the trees conversed through their root systems. The young trees brought up the X-marks and their possible meanings. Pippen had been silent, thinking surely someone remembered the prophecy he spoke of last fall.

Little Tree's roots listened to the other roots' questions and speculation about the reason for the X-marks. He found it hard to comprehend that, after all the meetings, announcements, and other efforts to notify the forest of what would happen, some in the forest were still clueless.

He thought again about why he was given the honor of being the tallest tree. He'd heard it was because of his good qualities of being likable and patient but also friendly to everyone. He knew that now was the time to show patience and speak to the roots once again.

"Ahem. I'd like your attention please." The roots and their trees aboveground quieted when they heard the tallest tree speak.

"I know many of you weren't around four years ago when our animal delegation came back from a firsthand meeting with Mother Nature. That was when this forest learned of humans coming here and the reason.

"I'm sure you remember Pippen going all around the forest last fall, telling us the humans were coming when it warmed. He came home all busted and bruised from that excursion for all our sakes. With all those meetings he held, weren't any of you paying attention to him? *Please,* listen to me now."

The roots had his complete attention and waited respectfully for Little Tree to continue.

"The red marks show which trees they are going to cut down. The trunks will be harvested, removed, and put to good use." There was silence. If you could hear snow falling, that would be the sound.

Little Tree explained once again the purpose of the cutting and how it was for the long-term health of the forest. This time, they seemed to grasp his words.

"Each tree with an X-mark is owed our gratitude for its sacrifice. In the coming days, let's express our thanks to each tree with the marks. The remaining trees will forever be in our debt, and they will never be forgotten."

For the next week, there were no sightings of humans or loud noises. This gave the roots and their trunks time to thank the marked trees for their upcoming sacrifice. These trees were grateful to be recognized for their service to the forest.

Everyone wondered if human plans had changed. The animal families took advantage of the break in activity and returned to their homes. The children played, but the adults were still on edge.

Then one day their feeling of apprehension came back. From his tall vantage point, Little Tree saw that a single smaller machine was approaching the woods on the new road. Two humans got out of the machine and walked into the woods.

One human was taller and stockier; the other was shorter with hair blowing to the back. As they walked, he saw the two humans hold each other's higher appendages, much like roots liked to touch each other's ends. One of the humans walked with the aid of a tall stick, perhaps to swat at bees, he didn't know. This time, he didn't see their eyes as they were covered.

For those that didn't already know, he sent a message down to the roots announcing the humans' arrival. Little Tree waited for their presence under his tree.

A Walk in the Woods

Todd and Grace drove out to the land because they knew an access road had been completed from the county road to their property. The new road had been built to give trucks and heavy machinery access across the field and into the woods. The couple wanted to drive on the finished road and take another walk through this part of their land.

They knew the forester had recently come out and walked the property to assess its health. Besides wanting to see it again herself, Grace also wanted to show something to Todd. She wouldn't tell him what it was; she only said she wanted to surprise him.

There were several trails leading from the field into the woods. Deer and other animals made these trails to make it easier to move through the dense woods more quickly. Some led to food and water sources, others to bedding areas, and some were used as an easy route from danger.

The couple found an opening in the wood line with a trail leading from the field into the trees. In the evening, when deer fed in the field, this was one of the trails they used to go deeper into the forest to bed down.

"Here we go—just follow me," said Grace.

They walked in, ducking under low-hanging branches and pushing past plants that didn't seem to want their intrusion. They walked single file into the woods, with Grace leading the way.

Todd watched as she pushed forward, her ponytail swinging through the hole in her hat. He stayed close in case either of them tripped on exposed roots or dead wood along the path.

After a short time, he tugged on her jacket to slow her down. "Come on, how much farther is it?"

"Not far now. Don't be a baby. It's right up here," she replied.

They arrived in an area with unusually tall trees. The ground was cleaner, allowing them to see soil instead of the usual covering of fallen limbs and branches. Even though it was midday, the area was darker with the tall trees casting long shadows. The air was stagnant and damp. It carried the scent of last year's decomposing leaves and plant matter, awakened by the warm spring.

Grace stopped and held her hand out to stop Todd. Ahead of them stood the tallest tree they'd ever seen. They stopped and stared upward.

"Man, just think of all the lumber we could get from that tree." Todd was thinking about money, but Grace was thinking about how majestic the tree was and how it overlooked the whole forest.

Unknown to them, Little Tree looked down and saw the humans at his base looking up. He thought that because of their differences, there were many secrets humans would never know about this forest. They'd never know that he had a name and that Mother Nature had grown him tall for a reason. They would never know about the fairies who came every spring and the magic they left behind. They would never know that their presence was always detected, or that plants and animals lived in communities and knew each other.

"We'd better go before it gets too late," said Grace, "I want to show you the perfect building spot I found for our cabin."

"When did you come out here without me?"

"Oh, about a week ago. You were working and Kevin had the day off. He brought me out, and we walked some of the trails. With the new road, he wanted to get in and look around." Kevin was their oldest son and liked to come to the land whenever he had free time.

Just ahead, Grace pointed to two lone apple trees growing about twenty feet apart, their branches not yet touching. They grew in a sunnier spot where a little light managed to break through.

She threw up her arms and said, "Here it is. I love this spot! I love these apple trees. I hope they can be saved. Look at this little guy trying to grow. I think with the trimming or removing of a couple of the close-by trees, we could get more sun in here for these two."

Todd walked over and looked at the older tree. "My goodness, it looks like this tree has been through a war. There must have been a bad storm or something else traumatic. We can probably get him pruned and fixed up though. Yeah, I like this place. Good choice."

Grace continued, "I thought maybe a half-acre plot for our building project—our own little cabin in the woods where we could sit and stargaze. Nobody will be able to see us. We can watch the animals walk through, feed the birds, and watch their drama. Kevin said the trout stream isn't far. You can make a path there with the four-wheeler. We have all the firewood we'll ever need. I'll even help cut and chop it."

This time, Todd led the way back to the truck. "Hold up, I have something to show you too. I know a shortcut." He pointed to a new path and started walking it.

"Surprise, surprise, surprise," Todd said in his best Gomer Pyle imitation. He spread his arm out and pointed to a patch of thorny bushes. Grace laughed at his imitation, then recognized the blackberry bushes.

"The forester found these when he walked through the area and told me about them. He remembered you mentioned you loved blackberries, cats, flowers, books, chocolates, and yellow canaries. He says they'll stay away from all the berry patches they find."

The Plan

Todd and Grace had owned their eighty acres of wooded land for fifteen years. After his father died, Todd's mother had turned the land over to him. Without her husband, the enjoyment was gone and visiting the land wasn't the same.

His mother had known how much he loved the land and wanted him to take over managing it as his father had.

Forty years earlier, Todd's father had bought the property as a hunting investment. Over the years, the men in the family had hunted only ten acres, leaving the rest untouched. Now, again, Todd and their two sons also loved the land, hoping it would remain in the family for generations.

One small area of the land had a short driveway and a clearing. This was where Todd's family of four camped and spent time together. They grilled food, found star constellations, and when the boys were young, they helped them collect lightning bugs in jars. They liked being out in nature, sitting by the campfire talking, and listening to the night sounds.

Every fall they walked into the thickest woods when the raspberries and blackberries got ripe. Grace never went in alone; she knew that bears passed through for the berries. Last fall, they entered to pick blackberries twice. The first time, they filled a gallon bucket. The second time, they left empty-handed after spotting fresh bear tracks outside the patch and walked away immediately.

They were back to the land now, waiting for the state forester to arrive. Todd drove his truck to the end of the newly constructed road and parked just outside the tree line. Todd and Grace were going to walk with Phil Stevens, the State Forester, one more time. The big trees in all their majesty were on the line.

They watched the 4Runner cross the field and pull up beside the truck. Phil Stevens got out and shook both their hands.

"Hello, folks, it's good to see you again," Phil said warmly.

"Hey, Phil," Todd replied. "Thanks for coming up again. We're looking forward to hearing what you've come up with."

Grace smiled politely, though inside she was bracing herself. She had been fearing this meeting ever since their first walk-through with the forester.

Stevens opened his back door. He removed and set up three collapsible stools. He offered the couple a seat, as he sat and faced them.

"As you know," he began, "a colleague and I walked your land a couple of weeks ago. I'm aware that you and your father select-cut the land twenty years ago and took out many mature trees. It looks like it has rebounded nicely and is full again with mature growth."

Todd knew where this was going. He remembered his father making the same decision twenty years ago; it had been devastating to see the forest's appearance afterward.

"Your woods are thick, and we saw many trees sick or dying. The old-timers' canopies are taking the sunlight for themselves. They flourish while the smaller trees struggle under the shade. There are many crooked, stunted youngsters, classic signs of insufficient sunlight. Growth is being held back. Let's walk in, and I'll show you."

They followed him into the woods. Stevens pointed at various trees. "You've got a nice assortment of trees." They walked in further until they reached a towering oak.

"Look how tall this one is—straight and confident."

"I love this tree," Grace declared. "Don't you dare cut this one down." She shot Todd a look that needed no translation. Todd nodded in agreement; he loved it too. Stevens smiled, he wasn't going to get into the middle of that.

"We found apple trees, sugar maples, several oak species, aspen, birch, poplar, and pine, and others," Phil said. "I suggest keeping the apple trees because the animals feed on them. We want happy animals, right? As you can see, we've marked the trees we recommend removing."

Grace was relieved to see there was no mark on the tall oak she wanted saved. She and Todd had already talked about saving the apple trees.

The forester continued, "We have put together a fifteen-year reclamation plan. Select-cut forty acres this year, the remaining forty, five years out. Then, every five years, we go in again and remove a few of the larger, poorer quality trees, leaving the little ones to have a good go at life. Clearing excess brush will help too, making way for new growth. This will keep the trees and wildlife happy and healthy for many generations."

Todd and Grace looked at each other and nodded. Everything Phil said had made sense.

"I know your family is a family of sportsmen. If we wait until next spring, the deer will have time to adapt before fall. Improving habitat will help the deer and bear populations, and you'll also see some income from the cut. If you agree, I can coordinate everything and ensure the work matches your goals."

After walking for a half hour, they returned to their vehicles. They agreed that the plan should move forward. Papers were signed agreeing to Phil Stevens' plan. He was going to contact a logging company and get their land on their calendar.

As Todd watched Stevens' truck disappear, he thought of the weight of stewardship placed on their shoulders. He knew they had made the right decision and was sure his father would also agree.

The World According to Finn

He heard Finn's voice, which sounded frustrated. "Dad, this is *our* land, they're trying to claim it. Why don't they move to a place they already own? We were here first. How would they like it if we claimed *their* land?"

Pippen listened, as Finn's concerns and distress rippled through their roots. Poor Finn. He remembered the same feeling when he was younger. He had been just as fiery before he learned what things could and couldn't be changed.

Pippen knew that what the humans had in mind was inevitable; there was no changing anyone's minds. Mother Nature had given her blessing for this, everyone knew of it, and they had to accept the outcome. He had to try and explain this to his son.

"Finn," he began softly, "just remember we are here for a reason. We are the foundation of this ground—the bricks and stones that keep it steady. Trees have done this since the start of time. But while we stand and do our work, we must share this place with many kinds of visitors. Humans are our new visitors here.

He felt Finn's leaves shiver, uneasy.

"Mother Nature has approved of their being here, and we must trust her judgment, even if we don't yet understand it."

Finn hesitated, then asked, "Dad... we can talk to everyone here. But humans can't speak to us. They don't understand us at all. How can we live with them if they can't understand us?"

He felt a familiar ache tug his trunk. If only he could give Finn all the answers that would quiet his fears, but he couldn't.

"I don't know all the answers, son. Some things just depend on trust."

Finn wasn't finished. "I just hope they don't stay long. Maybe they'll get tired of all us trees and go back to wherever they came from. Then we can go back to doing whatever we want."

Young trees just think the world revolves around them.

"Come over here. Just sit by me and relax." Pippen's roots reached out, coaxing his son in closer. "You're getting way too worked up about all of this."

Finn moved in closer, already feeling better with his father's words.

"Remember, this is not our land. We don't own it. Mother Nature decides who and what may live here. Humans have just as much right to this ground as plants and animals do. Finn, the forest is always going to change. It always has. Our job is to accept those changes and find a way to live alongside them."

He could feel Finn's tension ease, if only a little. Pippen hoped the rest would come with time.

The Five Senses

Max lay on his bed resting on his paws after his early morning foraging. He knew, without even seeing them, that two humans had walked through the forest that afternoon. He didn't get excited; there was no reason to leave. With the noise of the machines and the humans marking trees, their presence every few days became commonplace. From where he lay, he could almost feel their presence settling into the forest floor.

If he could speak to them, this was what he would say:

"You don't know it, but we hear you. You make unexpected, unfamiliar sounds in our woods. With every twig you break, plant you shake, or words spoken, our quietude is broken. The forest listens to every sound you make.

"You don't know it, but we feel you. We feel every step when your feet touch the ground. When you leave your footprints, ants die and grieve. Every plant you crush, there is a silent hush. We have no defense against the harm we receive.

"You don't know it, but we see you. There are many eyes watching your every move. From the berries you waste, to the apples you taste, showing disdain would be in vain. Each time you walk in our presence, our trust in you is placed.

"You don't know it, but we smell you. You are detected every time you walk in our midst. The scent you emit when you walk or sit, animals surmise without opening their eyes. When we detect a new smell, we don't easily forget it.

"Finally, you don't know it, but we taste you. Your presence drifts in, brought by the wind. Our tongues taste your tears and fears. When humans are present, this sense is intense. We stand and wait until the taste of man clears."

The words settled inside him as the evening air shifted. Tonight, Max felt a strange mix of uneasiness and contentment. Times had changed in his twenty years of being the dominant bear here. He'd been content living in this forest and had made a few good friends over the years.

But something in him stirred; his body was telling him something.

He wasn't sure what it was. When that happened, there was only one thing to do. He needed to take a walk.

The Transformation

For several weeks, humans and machines brought a flurry of activity to the woods. The trees adapted to the constant noise until it became a part of their daily life.

The animals, however, found the noise unbearable and were driven back into unfamiliar parts of the forest. They brought what food they could carry but left behind their homes and worldly goods. Many families and entire neighborhoods were uprooted. With their homes being torn apart, leaving was all they could do. Even the animals who intended to stay were eventually forced out. The mood of the forest was somber and humbling.

Humans cleared the already-fallen trees from the ground to make way for their machines. Clearing the debris made it easier to walk without tripping or falling. Trees marked with the red crosses were cut down, leaving behind only their stumps. Limbs were removed, and the trunks were sawed into smaller lengths.

As their beloved older trees crashed to the ground, the standing trees took note of each fallen companion. With every crash, news was relayed underground to the remaining tree roots who were ready to record the deaths. They documented each tree's attributes, years of service to the Earth, and the families left behind.

As the cutting continued, the forest stood speechless and numb. Each night, the decimated forest lay shattered when the machines finally drove away. Every morning, they hoped the destruction was over, but humans and machines always returned.

As the culling advanced, the machines drew closer to Great Apple, who wore an X-mark. Young trees were prepared for the worst. Humans walked back and forth under his branches. One human was looking at a sheet of paper, shouting orders. The forest held its breath. Then, unexpectedly, the group climbed into their machines and drove away, leaving Great Apple untouched. The trees were relieved but baffled.

Great Apple had been spared for reasons unknown. The root system immediately conveyed the news to Pippen and Finn. The two were overjoyed, and sent word back that they, too, had been spared. It confused them that many trees around them went down, while the apple trees remained standing. They had no idea who was behind it, but somebody cared. After everything that Pippen had gone through last fall, he suspected Mother Nature had spared him, his father, and his son.

Little Tree had also been spared. He watched in horror as trees were felled and their trunks loaded onto machines. Large trees around him were felled, but the younger ones were left standing. His mother and father's trunks had been cut, but the two had expected this fate and accepted it. His roots reached out to theirs to say goodbye. Everything that happened was exactly how Pippen described it would happen during his walking visits the previous fall.

Within a matter of weeks, the forest had been transformed. The trucks and machines, loaded with wood, finally left. The forest floor was littered with branches and chunks of cut wood.

Several humans the forest recognized came back in the evenings and began stockpiling wood on the ground. One moment, plants and animals grumbled about the harsh, open look of the forest; the next, they commented how pleasant the new sunlight felt on their backs.

There was no time to waste on tears. Life had to go on. The animals came back to find their old homes smashed, and almost immediately, they began rebuilding near their former sites. Food had to be found, and families needed to be fed. Most chose to get on with life without harboring bitterness. Some words were simply better left unsaid. The forest had changed, but it was not their ruination. They and their families were still alive.

Many trees saw beams of sunlight for the first time in their lives. Lifting their heads, young trees were utterly beguiled. Never in their short lives had they ever felt such warmth and affection. Sunlight felt like their mother's roots as she stroked them with love. As their treetops took turns basking in the rays, they felt the surge of energy flowing from their leaves to their roots. The older trees watched proudly as the young ones stood awestruck.

Hollyhock, followed by her two fawns, tentatively stepped from the shadows into the light. They returned from the deep woods to see the destruction but also to see the light everyone was talking about. Her two fawns were afraid and clung to her. Hollyhock felt exposed and uncomfortable, preferring the safety of cover. With a swift forward motion, she ushered her family back into the thicker woods. They would return later to the field to feed.

During the weeks of human occupation, many noticed Max's absence. He had never been away for more than two weeks at a time. Max was a fixture of their community, known by all. Not being seen throughout the whole ordeal left many worried that something terrible had happened to him.

Max's Disappearance

When Max came out of hibernation, he didn't feel like himself and was disoriented. That happened every year when he sensed milder temperatures and knew it was time to stop sleeping and start feeding again. He'd been confused this time because the warmer air had coaxed him awake, but when he opened his eyes, there was still snow covering the ground. Shuffling through cold, wet snow was unpleasant and it made finding food nearly impossible. Sitting outside his den, he contemplated his options and briefly closed his eyes.

Suddenly, he opened them and stared out. He remembered dreaming about Belle. It wasn't the temperature that woke him but that he'd been dreaming about her. He thought again about the last time he saw her with the cubs. That had been three years ago. *Surely, they were on their own now, and she was free of motherly duties. Hmm, I wonder...* As he daydreamed about Belle, he imagined how nice it would have been to wake up beside her after hibernation. Finding food together wouldn't have been so frustrating.

Feeding was always such a chore when there was nothing to eat, but he had to start because he needed energy. *How old am I? What year is this? I don't know anymore.* He remembered some of the forest talk about humans coming this spring, but somewhere along the line, he had lost all track of time.

The snow was dirty and full of animal footprints. He was obviously the last one up again and was weak, ornery, and hungry. There was never enough food in the spring, and this one had been no different. Day after day he walked and foraged but there was next to nothing to eat. He couldn't remember a spring so empty of food for a bear. He wondered if he was facing his last days.

One day he was particularly bummed out and decided to try and find Belle. If he was going to die, he wanted to lay eyes on her again first. In the back of his mind was that lush green grass that she had that they didn't. That would have been so good right then.

He started walking aimlessly with Belle on his mind. He wasn't yearning for a tryst but simply for bear companionship. At his age, that was all he wanted. This time, if he found her, he was going to stay with her; that is, if she wanted him around. He considered the possibility of never coming back.

After making his way through forest after forest for many months without a sighting, Max lost hope. He was in a state of mental exhaustion and, without hardly any appetite, physically unwell. Belle had either moved on or something had happened to her. Wherever she was, he had made the effort to find her and had failed. His body felt drained, the trip had consumed him, and he wanted to go home to his forest to see what remained of it.

Max walked into his home forest late one night after walking and resting most of the day. The walk back had become a great ordeal and he was very weak.

There were many familiar trees and landmarks as he came into the forest. He looked up as he passed that hill that he climbed to look for ants under the rocks. He couldn't imagine ever climbing that hill again. The commons area, where the animals held their forest festivals and meetings, was still recognizable. But many trees had been cut and stumps stood in their place. It was eerily quiet. No animals revealed themselves and the usual sound of night birds was absent.

He turned in a circle to get his bearings because everything felt unfamiliar and rearranged. He wasn't sure where he was or which direction to walk. He began following an unfamiliar road that did not look animal made.

He thought it was probably made by one of those machines he had heard about. Then he recognized the silhouettes of Pippen and Finn's trees in the darkness and knew he was in the right area. His cluster of birches, if they were still standing, shouldn't be far away.

When he'd left to find Belle, he had never said goodbye to the apple trees. He should have, but he hadn't, and now he felt guilty about it. Those trees had been his friends, and just then he didn't know how to approach them, or whether he even should.

Max saw a strange structure in the dark that hadn't been there before, and it looked completely out of place. No animal he knew would live in such a thing. It sat a short distance from the apple trees. When he was younger, he would have investigated it, if something smelled good inside. He might even have found a way inside to settle his curiosity. But that day, he didn't care what it was or who was inside. He would leave it alone.

Taking a few steps forward, he stopped, exhausted. Each step left him short of breath and his legs didn't want to take him further. His body told him that his end of life was near. He'd known it for some time but, strangely, he wasn't afraid of death. He knew that tonight the stars weren't aligned in his favor.

He saw that Pippen was still awake and had heard his rustling and struggle to walk in. Pippen whispered, "My friend, we were hoping you'd be back."

Max lowered his head to acknowledge his greeting. Finn was also awake and staring at him. Max saw their surprise as they took in his thin appearance. He lay on the ground between them.

Max felt his heart rate slowing as he drifted in and out of sleep. He knew his body was failing. For now, he only wanted to be close to the apple trees—two of the only friends he still had. He was tired and wanted to sleep; in the morning, he would talk to them.

But Max was gone the next morning. He had vanished once again without a word. Pippen and Finn suspected he hadn't gone far after seeing how gaunt he had looked the night before. There were sounds of movement coming from inside the building, and Pippen suspected Max had heard them, forcing him to go to another part of the woods.

Just before sunup, Max had gathered his remaining strength and ventured to his old home under the birch trees. He lay his body down for a final time. He was tired of living, closed his eyes, and let nature take its course. He relinquished all pain and memories.

Later in the morning, there was a tapping on Pippen's roots. The maple tree next door told him Max's body had been found in his old bed under the birches. Several small animals had noticed his lifeless body and spread the news. The roots heard and had already recorded his death in their records.

By then, every living thing in the forest knew Max's history there. He had been the only animal still living who had ever met Mother Nature. He was the brave bear who, years ago, made the journey with three other animals to learn the truth about the terrible noise and their impending danger. Because of his great size, the animals had felt safe around him when they were frightened, and he had never turned them away. Max had his peculiar ways that sometimes didn't seem normal, but the forest accepted them as Max being Max. He was a bear they would never forget. He would go down in history as the legendary bear who displayed courage, wisdom, and friendship in their times of need.

Plants and animals understood the circle of life, and Max's death was part of it. His passing wouldn't be for naught. To survive, animals consumed any food found; to this law of nature, all were bound. The animals took turns visiting his body, and within a matter of days, no trace of it remained. The bear named Max would live forever in their hearts.

Three Years Later,
Cleanup and Renewal

Three years had passed since the land was select-cut. Initially, the results were devastating for both the forest and the landowners. Todd and Grace knew what to expect, but they were still aghast at the terrible mess the loggers had left behind. An unimaginable amount of brush, branches, and debris lay strewn everywhere. Their beautiful woods looked destroyed, and they wondered if they had made a terrible mistake. They were discouraged and worried about all the animals that had lost their homes.

It was disheartening at first, but Todd remembered the same scene twenty years earlier when his father had the land first logged. His family's reaction back then had been almost identical.

Years ago, Todd, his father, and other family members spent two entire summers trimming, piling, hauling, and raking, just to be able to navigate the woods. It had been hard, backbreaking cleanup work, but they knew it had to be done if their efforts were to be rewarded. By fall of the second summer, plants had rebounded, and bear and deer sign had returned. Little by little the animals came back.

This time, with the cutting completed, the forest resembled nothing of their once-beloved woods. When Todd and Grace came in, they sensed tension. Many young, straight trees were now exposed after being hidden for years due to overcrowding. The large trees were gone, replaced by the newly revealed ones.

They imagined that if trees had feelings, they would be angry at having no say in this matter. If trees could speak, they imagined words of contempt being directed at them. The young trees had lost their protective cover of elders and seemed not to like being exposed. As they maneuvered carefully over the brush-covered ground, the remaining trees seemed to watch them with scorn.

So many big trees had been removed that only stumps remained as clues that a tree had ever stood there. The forest was so silent you could hear a pin drop. The birdsong was gone, and no trace of animal life remained.

The deer, with their habitats destroyed, had moved deeper into other woods. To avoid being seen, curious deer walked through when humans were not around. The once-dense forest, formerly their safety net, was gone. Many trees, including Little Tree and the apple trees, still stood, but nearly everything else familiar had disappeared. It had been replaced with mess and mayhem that animals wanted no part of.

The fairies arrived during those first two springs and found no animals in the forest. They spent their time with the existing trees and emerging plants and spread handfuls of seeds everywhere. They missed not meeting with animals, but experience in other forests told them they would return soon.

Todd, Grace, and their two sons began cleanup almost immediately. The discarded tree limbs were trimmed, cut, and piled. The sound of chainsaws filled the air every weekend for two summers. Ground branches were cut to manageable lengths and stacked. Everywhere they looked, there were piles of wood. All of it was cut, chopped, and used as firewood. Todd built a woodshed next to the new cabin, and it was filled with wood left behind from the select-cut. Many weekends were spent at the cabin to give them easier access to their work.

Grace helped by walking the woods and picking up smaller branches and debris. They were put into large containers and dumped in a designated area of the forest.

The second summer, a woodchipper was rented, and the men had the laborious task of feeding piles of branches into the machine. The weeks and weeks of chipping left everyone dreaming of chainsaws, tractors, and woodchippers.

Phil Stevens returned that second summer to inspect the woods. The forester was pleased and surprised that the family had accomplished all this work. He suggested spreading the wood chips across the forest floor to nourish the soil and feed the roots and worms. As the wood was chipped, a tractor dumped and spread the chips throughout the woods. The family worked hard and finished what they started, knowing that in three years they would repeat the process on the other half of their land.

As predicted, the deer returned. This forest had the only apple trees, and the scent of apples, fresh acorns, and new growth lured them back. They roamed, foraged, and eventually decided to bed down and stay. Other animals returned for the same reasons.

In the beginning, the tiny animals loved the cushion of the wood chips and eagerly carried them down into their newly constructed burrows to line the floors of their homes. Ants and other insects took shade under the chips during hot summer days. Returning raccoons watched their young frolic and kick the chips into the air.

Sun-loving flowers grew tall reaching toward the sun. Deer nibbled on their blossoms, unaware that their grazing caused the waiting flower buds to open sooner. It was a win-win situation for everyone.

All of Belle's cubs were grown and on their own. She missed having cubs but relished her independence from motherhood. Her home forest had received advance warning that they were next this spring for select-cutting. Belle decided to leave and search for Max, not knowing he had passed years earlier. Her search brought her to his old forest. She inquired about Max and received the news of his passing. She liked what the forest had to offer and decided to settle there. After discovering a matted area under the birches that still had Max's scent, she decided to make it her new home.

Belle was a likable and social bear who made friends easily. The next spring, she emerged from hibernation with two cubs in tow. She had mated with the new dominant male bear the previous year. He would walk through occasionally but never approached her. She spent the next two years alone, devoted entirely to raising her cubs.

Meanwhile, the trees had rebounded and produced many new offspring. Plants found favorable spots to grow, some loved the sun, but others like the ferns and mosses, preferred the shade. The forest now offered a preferred habitat for everyone.

Little Tree was still the tallest tree and had several smaller oaks nearby, calling him Father. He towered over them, passing down knowledge learned from his parents.

There were new generations of foxes, raccoons, squirrels, and rabbits each found quiet corners to call home. A pileated woodpecker had carved out a home in Little Tree and raised several families there. The crows still annoyed but were tolerated, and the blue jays were back stealing food from the deer.

The forest had also adapted to the presence of humans. They came into the forest often to pick berries, walk the trails they had created, and sometimes hunt. The animals sensed their presence long before they arrived and usually disappeared into the brush.

Occasionally, however, animals and humans met by accident. Animals and humans stopped, surprised to see each other. They would exchange wary glances, and inevitably, the animals always bolted first.

The forest held secrets no human would ever know. It had knowledge of the births and deaths of every living creature in their forest. It saw, listened, and communicated in ways humans would never understand. Like humans, they were a community of plants and animals who lived together, had their times of happiness and merriment, and fear and surviving trauma.

And then there were the butterfly fairies. These little girls, with their iridescent wings, flew virtually unnoticed by humans. Every spring they flew in, blessed the land, and returned to their southern home. They were Mother Nature's gift to the forest and her secret.

Mother Nature moved unseen, slipping in and out of her sphere, as she watched, hovered, and monitored. She determined the change of seasons, the depth of the oceans, and nurtured the health of forests. She was the life-giving force governing nature. In times of catastrophic events, causing extreme sadness and horror, she seemed absent and cruel, but she was always aware and present. The land placed trust in her and waited patiently, for she always had a plan. There was always a plan for renewal.

EPILOGUE

The Follow-up Visit

MOTHER NATURE RETURNED TO look at the eighty-acre forest that was first select cut fifteen years ago and then again five years later. The broccoli canopy today wasn't as thick as it had been on earlier visits, and that made her happy. She steered down closer and knew if she could see through the trees, the sun also streamed in.

When she entered, she had a smile on her face. All was as she had hoped to find it. The owner's planning had paid off, and she knew the forest would be teeming with happy plants and animals. Since the last full logging, trees had again been removed at different intervals to promote healthy plant growth. She was pleased that the owners of this forest had kept to their plan and the forest now held a diverse age of trees, and all looked healthy.

The owner's cabin was in the woods, but she noticed it had been enlarged since her last visit. Several smaller structures also sat next to it. A long driveway extended from the road, crossed the field, and entered the woods. It ran through the trees and stopped at the owner's cabin. A vehicle was parked, and the property owners appeared to be there that day.

The two apple trees looked healthy and happy. Pippen had bounced back nicely, and Finn looked taller and wider than his father. Seeing them reminded her to check on Great Apple. She looked over the field and, yes, there he was still standing and leafing out but with only a few apples. She had watched that tree sprout from a seed. She knew he struggled to settle in this forest almost two hundred years earlier. She was sad knowing that he might not be around on her next visit. A mental note was made to enable a few of Finn's seeds to take root in the area for future generations of apple trees.

She knew her fairies had great fondness for this forest, and many colonies had made return visits there. There had always been a sense of community, with residents helping one another; something she wished more forests would do. She remembered those two cardinals and their egg hatching problem, the moles, the blind rabbit, and, of course, Max. That bear turned out to be the gem of the forest.

Her sphere hovered and waited above the trees. She was about to fly up through the canopy to return to her sphere and depart, when she heard footsteps approaching from behind. She saw the occupants of the cabin taking their morning stroll down their worn path through the woods. She saw them stop and be very quiet. The man held binoculars and was straining to look through the trees at something ahead. He passed them to the woman and she did the same.

Mother Nature knew what they were looking at, as she had witnessed what they were seeing many times. The couple watched quietly for another minute, then, without saying a word, they quickly turned and walked back to their cabin. She sensed that the couple knew something the animals didn't think they knew.

Humans coexisting with wild animals would be a big undertaking. Many years might pass before she saw humans and animals living amicably together. Sometimes, however, it wasn't about animals and humans getting along, but humans getting along with their own species. She hoped that someday that would all resolve itself without her interference. She didn't see that problem happening between the species here.

That day the forest festival had been underway with animals converging from all over the forest to celebrate their life and good fortune. She was glad to see Todd and Grace walking back to their cabin after secretly watching the animals. They had reacted just as she had hoped they would. This made her happy because these two kindred spirits would be helping her with another plan.

Mother Nature took a deep breath and closed her eyes. With outstretched arms, she pretended to pull in each plant and animal for a big motherly hug. Her heart soared as she saw how sunshine streamed in on the forest floor. She felt the love she knew the plants and animals were experiencing. This happy feeling was what her life was all about; this was what she had been put on this Earth to do.

Before departing for her sphere, Mother Nature turned around and saw two chipmunks running up the trail toward the cabin. *Ah, her favorite chipmunks.* She had watched these two siblings grow up in the forest. There was a special something she had in mind for these two, but that would come later. First, she had to fine tune her plan.

The End

Thank you for reading book one, *Under the Broccoli Canopy*. I hope you will check out book two *It's Peanut Time*, coming later in 2026. After that, book three in 2027 will be about the adventures of a little lost masked traveler.

~

If you enjoyed reading *Under the Broccoli Canopy*, I would be grateful if you would consider leaving a review. Reviews help other readers discover the book, and they encourage authors to keep creating new stories. Thank you for reading and for your support.

~

More resources are available for *Under the Broccoli Canopy* by visiting my website: www.barbaralpeterson.com (find under Blog). While there, please sign up for my mailing list to receive future writing updates.

ABOUT THE AUTHOR

Under the Broccoli Canopy is Barbara Peterson's fourth book since she began her writing career in 2024. Before becoming an author, she concentrated on writing short stories, rhymes, and journals strictly for family and friends. Her wish is to write more works of fiction before finally retiring.

Before writing *Under the Broccoli Canopy*, she wrote *The Button Boy trilogy*, which consisted of *The Button Boy* (2024), *Johannes and Berta* (2025), and *Full Circle: The Button Boy's Journey* (2025), all in the genre of literary fiction.

Barbara is originally from Wisconsin Rapids, Wisconsin. After graduating from high school, she moved to Wausau, Wisconsin, and graduated from Wausau's technical college. She worked for many years as an assistant administrator for a family office, in healthcare customer service, and the owner of her own cross stitch design company. Her love for thrifting, antiques, and cross stitch thrust her into the world of online selling, which is one of her favorite pastimes today.

When not writing, you will find her reading, doing needlework, daydreaming, and catching up on sleep. She is married, has two grown sons, and one grandson. Their cat, Mosey, can be a thorn in her side, but she still loves her mischievous ways.